STRAY FEARS

A NOVEL

GREGORY ASHE

H&B

Stray Fears
Copyright © 2020 Gregory Ashe

Published by Hodgkin & Blount
https://www.hodgkinandblount.com/
contact@hodgkinandblount.com

Published 2020
Printed in the United States of America

Version 1.07

Trade Paperback ISBN: 978-1-63621-007-0
eBook ISBN: 978-1-63621-006-3

.

I

There is a certain spirit that lives in marshy places—often along the edges of swamps. It is never seen during the day, only at night, and even then its heart is the only part visible. Its heart appears as a small ball of fire that may be seen moving about, a short distance above the surface of the water.

- "Myths of the Louisiana Choctaw," David I. Bushnell, Jr.

ELIEN (1)

The DuPage-St. Tammany Parish Support Group for Survivors with PTSD—DSTP-PTSD, as it was printed on every email, bulletin, and placard—didn't have donuts. I guess somebody had thought that palindrome was cute. Or funny. That's what we're known for, us *survivors with PTSD*: our sense of humor. But not donuts. That was one of the reasons I kept coming. AA had donuts. NA had donuts. SAA had donuts. GA had donuts. And even though I didn't exactly need to go to any of those meetings—at twenty-two years old, I didn't gamble, all my scrips were legal, and I'd given up Chardonnay when I'd taken up Prozac. As for sex addiction, well, very funny, tell me another. Just knowing about the other support groups was risky. Donuts were a clear and present danger.

I kept coming to DSTP-PTSD for a lot of reasons, I guess. No donuts, obvs. And I kept coming because it was one of those things you were supposed to do. I kept coming because I didn't work, I didn't have any hobbies, and I didn't have any friends. I kept coming because I could only vacuum the living room or organize the pantry or launder dust ruffles so many times before I started thinking very seriously about wading out into the bayou to meet a hungry gator. But really, gun to my head, I kept coming because I knew Richard would leave me if I didn't.

I had a Walkman when I was twelve, and the thing I remember about the Walkman was I could put in my Alanis Morissette CD—*Jagged Little Pill*, not *Supposed Former Infatuation Junkie*, thank you very much—and I could hit Repeat and listen to "All I Really Want" for as long as I wanted, as many times as I wanted. And then one time the Repeat button broke, and I listened to "All I Really Want" for six days straight before I swapped CDs. Coming to group was like that.

Today, Leola was talking about her mom. Her mom had been a junkie—about half the people in the room had moms who were junkies—and her mom had run a dry-cleaning business. The junkie part wasn't what Leola talked about, most of the time. The junkie part was whipped cream, I guess, in comparison. What Leola talked about was the times her mom was sober and mean and vicious. Wire hangers. Chemical burns. Those thin plastic bags wrapped around her face until she lost consciousness.

The basement of Du Page First Methodist had a wall of long, narrow windows that let in the afternoon light. The walls were painted concrete, and the floor had those high-traffic carpet squares that you can replace easily. We met on Tuesdays, after the preschool let out. You could still smell animal crackers, soiled diapers, and rubber cement.

The thing about hearing tragedy, week after week, is you can let it keep hurting you, let the razor blades slice you up every single time, or you can turn off inside. Even if it's your own tragedy. Especially if it's your own tragedy.

When Leola finished, we all looked at Zahra. She had glided into middle age pretty comfortably, although her graying hair was in a severe bun, which made her long face look a little longer. She worked in the same practice as Richard; the support group was her personal project.

"Elien, how about you?"

"Not much to report," I said.

"How did things go last Wednesday?"

"Wednesday?" I said, raising my eyebrows.

"It was your mom's birthday, bitch," Tamika said. "Don't pretend."

"Tamika," Zahra said. "That's not the way we talk to each other in here."

"I guess it wasn't perfect," I said.

Zahra waited. They all waited: Dave, Leola, Kenny, Ray, Mason, Willie, Tamika, Stephanie, Danielle. The whole circle. Waiting.

"I kind of had a meltdown that morning," I said, shrugging.

Willie, on my right, nodded and lowered his head. Kenny ran a hand through his locs and said, "You got this, man."

"I mean, it wasn't really any different than my other meltdowns," I said. "I was folding some of Richard's clothes. I . . . I guess he didn't shut the shower off all the way. I don't know. Maybe it was me. Maybe I didn't, but I don't think I took a shower that morning. I heard the water. Just that, you know, drip. But it's kind of like plonk, the sound, because there's a little bit of water around the drain." I shrugged again and smiled. "I, uh, didn't, you know, punish myself, so that's a big deal, right?"

"Way to go, man," Kenny said. "Fucking way to go."

"I did, however, spend a couple of hours screaming in the closet. So, yeah, not a total win."

Dave burst out laughing. Shrill, escalating laughter. It ended as abruptly as it had started, with Dave staring at the ground, flexing his gloved hands, his lips twitching as though he might start laughing again. The rest of us traded the same looks we always did.

"Oh, Elien," Stephanie said, wiping tears from her dark eyes. "I feel like this is my fault. I can't believe I asked you last week about her birthday. If I'd just kept my mouth shut, you probably would have been fine."

"Bitch," Tamika said, "who the fuck do you think you are? God? One question isn't going to do anything."

"All right, Tamika," Zahra said.

"I didn't mean—" Stephanie's face was crumbling. "Oh, I know you're right."

"Don't you dare fucking cry," Tamika said. "You can't go one day without crying?"

"Tamika," Zahra said.

"You know," I said, "I'm really glad you asked me, Stephanie. Last week, I mean. Nobody knows what to say. Nobody knows what to ask. I'd rather have somebody ask me about it than tiptoe around and pretend nothing's happening."

Stephanie sniffed a few times, wiped her eyes, and tried to smile.

For a moment, Zahra worried at a bandage on her hand, and she looked like she might press the issue with Tamika. But all Zahra said was, "Kenny, what about you?" And we moved on.

I'd finished my obligatory performance; it was very important, in times like these, to keep the cover story straight, to make sure the details were consistent. Lying in group wasn't encouraged, but if I'd told them the truth, they would have kicked me out. I was running through what I'd said, making sure I hadn't messed up. I think that's why it took me a moment to realize Mason was staring at me. Not just staring. Glaring.

Mason was relatively new to the group. A couple of months before, he'd been shot by a kid he was trying to arrest. Mason had almost died. The kid, with the help of mom and dad's money, had pled down to a lesser charge, and was apparently serving jail time in a cushy juvenile facility. Mason talked about that part a lot; that was his word, cushy. Like they were playing badminton all day. He was a cute guy: wavy blond hair, a great nose—a nose can be a make it or break it feature on a guy—and a little gap between his front teeth. Frankly, that little gap was adorable. He had talked about a girlfriend, Mary Ann, a few times, but that didn't keep me from looking.

Right then, though, Mason's very nice nose was wrinkled in a scowl, and he was looking at me like I'd had the bad taste to root for the Falcons during a Saints game. I met his gaze, held it, and turned my hands palm up. Mason didn't react. He just stared until I finally looked away.

I missed most of the rest of group. I kept glancing over at Mason and finding him still staring at me, and then I'd miss what Ray or Danielle was saying. I'd drag my attention back to the meeting, and thirty seconds later I'd be thinking about Mason, about his very cute nose scrunched up, and what I'd done to piss him off. And then, no matter how hard I tried, I'd look, and he'd be staring right back at me, like he'd been waiting.

When the meeting ended, I put away my chair and moved over to the refreshments, where coffee and iced tea were waiting, along with a selection of store-bought cookies. I skipped the cookies and the iced tea—one glass had about a million calories, the way Danielle always sweetened it—and poured myself a cup of coffee, black. I tasted it, the chicory and the dark roast, and then I found a stirrer and stood there, swishing it through the coffee, glancing up now and then.

Mason was still there, hands in his pockets, standing by the door. Watching me.

"Elien," Zahra said in her quiet voice as she joined me.

Coffee slopped onto my fingers, and I swore under my breath and shook off the drops.

"Oh. Hi."

"Are you doing ok today?"

My eyes drifted over Zahra's shoulders to Mason. "Yeah," I said. "Great."

"You seemed distracted in our meeting."

"Processing," I said. Processing was a magic word with people like Zahra and Richard.

"Elien."

Her tone brought my attention back to her face.

"What?" I asked.

"Elien, you know that people who are experiencing post-traumatic stress—"

"Oh boy," I said.

"—often have the mistaken belief that they deserve to suffer. They hold on to the past because they think it gives meaning to the suffering they witnessed."

"I believe I've heard that a time or two."

Mason was still standing there; it was hard to tell from a distance, but I was pretty sure his hands were balled up into fists in his pockets.

"And you know that getting better depends on the individual. Nobody can do this for you."

"I believe I've heard that a time or two as well." Then, because I couldn't help myself, "Maybe you should be reminding Mason of this stuff."

Zahra's dark eyes caught mine. "Mason didn't lie to everyone today."

Slowly, I drew out the coffee stirrer and flicked droplets into the trash.

"You're not going to say anything?"

I shrugged.

"So, we're both going to pretend I didn't run into you and Richard at Café Bartolome Wednesday morning. We're both going to pretend you weren't having a wonderful day."

I shrugged again. "I've got a killer eye cream; keeps them from getting puffy no matter how much I bawl. I can scream and sob and fifteen minutes later, I look like a million bucks again. Well, a thousand bucks, anyway."

"Elien."

It was the same clinical, professional frustration that I'd heard one too many times from Richard. I let my gaze slide away and realized Mason had left.

"Gotta catch my ride," I said, slipping around Zahra.

She caught my arm. "Elien, I'm sorry. That wasn't appropriate; I didn't mean to confront you like that. I just think—you have a way with people here. You help them. You helped Stephanie today, when Tamika was giving her a hard time."

"Put it in my chart," I said. "So you'll have something to gab about with Richard at lunch tomorrow."

Zahra pursed her lips. "May I ask you for a favor?"

"I'm pretty busy," I said. "Tomorrow I have to have a panic attack and slit my wrists."

"I think Ray is really struggling. Could you check in on him this week? Do you have his number?"

"Yeah," I said. I tried to think back to what Ray had said, but it had vanished. Alanis Morissette on repeat. "I'll text him."

"You're kind of a senior member," Zahra said. "I think you could be a leader in the group, Elien. That might be good for you."

"The only thing I'm a leader in," I said, patting my stomach, "is carbs. If you need a general for the cinnamon roll army, give me a call."

Zahra pursed her lips again, but I slipped away before she could say anything else. When I got outside, Muriel was already sitting at the curb in the Subaru. I flashed her an apology wave as I hurried down the steps of DuPage First Methodist. A few cars down, Mason was getting into the passenger seat of a brown Ford sedan. He paused, and then he turned and stared at me, as though somehow he had sensed me looking at him. I broke toward the car, slid in beside Muriel, and said, "Home, Jeeves."

"I do not get paid enough for this," Muriel grumbled as she pulled into traffic.

DAG (2)

Mason continued to look over his shoulder as he got in the car.

"In or out," I said. "It's a million degrees out there."

"Yeah," he said, dropping into the seat and dragging the door shut.

I fiddled with the A/C, which cooled the car to an arctic eighty degrees, and then realized the audio had cut out.

"Hey," I said. "You're sitting on my iPod."

"You are twenty-seven years old," Mason said, digging the brick of black plastic out from under his butt. He fiddled with the wire that ran to the tape deck, where an adapter was—in theory—supposed to be playing whale songs. Somehow Mason got himself tangled in the cord, and after almost a full minute of watching him get more and more wound up, I reached over and started the detangling process.

"You're twenty-seven years old," Mason repeated when he was free, shoving the iPod into my hands. "Twenty-seven. Two. Seven."

"You're twenty-eight."

"You have a job," Mason said, flopping back in the seat, arms across his chest.

"We have the same job," I said.

"You have a savings account."

"Twenty-seven dollars," I said, "before I had to buy you lunch last week."

"You have a checking account."

"Actually, I don't."

Mason stopped, his jaw hanging open, but then he recovered and waved that aside. "And, as a sheriff's deputy, you have a pension."

"We have the same pension."

"You are, by any legal standard, an adult."

"I'm going to repeat the fact that you are one year older than me." I brushed at my temple. "And you've got a little, you know, gray. It's just coming in. You're blond, so it doesn't matter that much. But just so you know."

"Look who's talking," Mason said. "And presumably one day, some nice guy is going to put a baby inside you."

"I think that might be homophobic."

"It's not, because I fully support you one day having a baby inside you."

"I still think—"

"And all of this is my way of saying, why are you not a fucking adult yet? You've got mustard on your face, and you've got an iPod from nineteen-fucking-ninety-seven and a car from nineteen-fucking-nineteen."

"Ah," I said, catching the mustard on the corner of my mouth with a thumb. "Bad day."

I hit Play on the iPod, and whale songs filled the car again as I eased away from the curb.

"No," Mason said.

I turned up the whale songs. Just a little.

"No, do not dismiss this as a bad day."

"A little quieter, please. I'm listening to this."

"Do not ignore what I'm saying just because I had a bad day."

"So you did have a bad day."

Mason rolled down the window, and hot, steamy Louisiana-even-in-October air whipped through the car. It smelled like the lake, like wet vegetation, and diesel exhaust. There was also a little of Mason's cologne, which was probably called something like Bro or Douche, but with an accent mark so it looked French.

"So," I said. "How was the meeting?"

"I don't want to talk about the meeting."

I bumped up the volume of the whale songs.

After we drove another two blocks, Mason punched the radio off.

"I'm an asshole," he announced.

"You have your moments."

"I'm a fucking dick munch."

"You brought me coffee on Friday. That wasn't a dick munch move."

"No, I'm a total dick munch. It's those meetings." Mason scrubbed a hand through his hair. "That's a lie; it's not those meetings. There's this guy. Elien." He said the name with playground-level disgust. "He's such a . . ."

"Dick munch?"

"Yes." Mason threw his head back, and it bounced off the cloth-covered headrest. "He's the absolute worst. You should have seen him today."

Bragg, LA, wasn't exactly hopping even during rush hour; it was a quiet city, the parish seat of a quiet parish. If you wanted small-city excitement, you could drive over to Covington, in St. Tammany Parish. And if you wanted big-city excitement, you could drive across Lake Pontchartrain and head into New Orleans. Although, in that case, you'd have a high chance of having to deal with tourists, which was kind of like saying you'd have a high chance of having to scrape the shit crust out of a toilet, so it was kind of a toss-up. Traffic was starting to pick up, Cadillacs and Mercedes mixed with Chevys and Pontiacs, some of them almost as old as my Ford Escort. When we got to the next light, the smell of butter and Tony Chachere and shrimp came in from the fry shop on the corner.

"What'd he do?"

"It's not so much what he did."

"What'd he say?"

"It wasn't even what he said."

"So, what? The way he said it?"

"Never mind. He's just an asshole, ok? That's my point."

"Got it. Asshole. I'll hate him on sight."

"Please. You'll probably fall in love with him. That's your problem, just so you know. You're way too desperate. All those pretty gay boys can sense it, and that's why you're alone and single and sad."

I let the car drift right as I rolled my eyes.

"Jesus," Mason laughed, grabbing the wheel.

"Sorry," I said. "Stroked out for a minute."

"This is why I need a new partner."

"You can't get a new partner because nobody wants to deal with you."

"Martinez would work with me."

"Martinez would eat you alive before lunch."

"Hey," Mason said. "Martinez and I get along great."

"Uh huh."

"We do."

"That's why you begged me to go to his bachelor party."

"I didn't beg you."

"When the absolute last thing I need is to see lady parts bouncing in my face."

"Lady parts?"

I mimed in front of my chest. "Not interested in any part of that package. Just put it away, girls."

"Seriously, how old are you?"

"Didn't we just do this?"

"I'm just asking because I've never heard a grown man call boobs 'lady parts,' so, you know, I'm naturally curious."

"Speaking of lady parts—"

"No. No segues."

"How's Mary Ann?"

"She's great."

"She's great?"

"She's visiting her sister in Baton Rouge."

"Still?"

Mason frowned and played with the window's handle. "What do you mean?"

"Last week when you needed a ride from your meeting, she was up there."

"No, last week she was visiting her Mom."

"And the week before that," I said, "she couldn't drive you because her car was making a clunking noise."

"Right," Mason said, working the handle back and forth.

"And the week before that," I said.

"Dag," Mason said, his eyes cutting toward me. "Come on."

I raised one hand in surrender.

"Things are fine," Mason mumbled, giving the handle a final whack. "Things with Mary Ann are just great."

ELIEN (3)

The rest of the week passed quickly and quietly, the way all my weeks passed. I watched Ellen in the afternoon. I chopped bell peppers and packaged individual servings in plastic baggies. I had Richard's Sazerac waiting for him every day when he got home from work. I did ferocious amounts of what Richard laughingly called jazzercise—cardio workouts with pseudo-militaristic themes like Boot Camp and Basic Training. I was fighting a losing battle, though; most days, my pants had elastic waistbands.

On Saturday morning, I was lying on the couch, watching Richard read the paper. He had thick gray hair on his arms and the backs of his hands; I could see the little spot where his hair was thinning when he turned the page. I dug my toe into his side, and he grunted. When I did it again, he took my foot and gently moved it aside, but he kept his hand there, his thumb running over my ankle.

"I'm trying to annoy you," I said.

"That sounds like attention-seeking behavior," he said. He had a lovely voice, rich and cultured and commanding. He squeezed my ankle once and then let go so he could turn the page again.

I got my toe back against his ribs again. "I'm seeking attention."

He pushed my foot away. Again. Gently.

Dig. Dig. Dig.

Behind the paper, he sighed. "Elien, I would really like to read my paper."

"I could start a fight."

He turned the page. "That sounds like a lot of work."

"I could do something really drastic. I could do something bad."

He must have found something interesting, because now he was shaking out the fold, trying to follow a line of text.

"Maybe I'll drive into town and buy a dozen donuts and eat all of them."

"That sounds nice."

"A baker's dozen. That's thirteen."

"Mmhmm."

"I'll eat them in the car so you won't know and then I'll pull over and stick a finger down my throat and barf it all up on the shoulder."

From behind the paper came another sigh, and then Richard folded the *Times-Picayune* and set it aside. He had soft brown eyes that always looked like he was about to cry.

The worst part about dating a psychiatrist—well, besides his absolute refusal to write me a scrip, and making me go to Zahra for everything—was that he did very annoying things like Pay Full Attention and Really Listen and Ask Good Questions. He was doing all three of them right then.

"I understand that you are asking for my attention, and now I'm giving it to you. I hear you, and I see you, Elien. What's this about? Do you really want to talk about your diet?"

"I just told you my new diet: it's all donuts."

"I think it's important for you to be able to eat whatever you want in moderation."

"Nope. No moderation."

"Is this about how you feel about your body?"

I rubbed my belly. "I love these curves. I love my new, sexy look. Voluptuous. I think that's the word, right?"

"I don't like it when you make jokes about how you look, Elien. It makes me uncomfortable because I love you and I find you attractive, and it also worries me because you have a history of not taking care of your body."

Another really fucking annoying thing psychiatrist boyfriends do is Say True Things.

"You find me attractive?" I said, tugging up my tank, rubbing my belly again. "You want to go upstairs and prove it?"

"Yes," Richard said. "I would like that. Would you like that?"

He held my gaze, and I broke first, my eyes dropping, my face heating.

"How would you feel if I talked about how old and decrepit I am?" Richard asked. "What if I told you every day how stupid I feel next to you?"

"You're not old."

"I'm almost thirty years older than you."

"Ok, but you're not old."

"Please look at me when we're talking."

I did, but I only lasted a second before my eyes started stinging and I hid my face in my elbow.

"How would you feel?" Richard asked again.

"I wouldn't like it."

"And I don't like it when you make jokes about hurting yourself because you don't like how you look. I understand that you aren't happy with your body, but I also know that you're working on this with Zahra."

My eyes were hot and sticky against the inside of my arm.

"Body dysmorphia is not an easy thing to treat," Richard said softly, his hand light on my ankle again. "And the weight gain is one side effect of the medication. We knew that before you started it. Do you want to go off the medication?"

I shook my head.

"Ok, I support that choice. I don't think it would be the right thing for you either." He squeezed my ankle lightly. "Hey. Forget the paper. Let's go for a drive. Let's get some good food and have a picnic. We'll find somewhere shady. We'll drink iced tea. It'll be perfect."

I rolled off the couch, scrubbed my face once, and said, "I can't. I forgot."

"Elien, this feels like avoidance behavior. You're not running away from me because you're upset, are you?"

Shaking my head, I moved toward the stairs. "No, I just forgot. I told Zahra I'd check in on Ray this week."

"Ok, I can drive you into town. Who's Ray?"

"Just a guy from group. I'll get an Uber." Shoving my bare feet into tennis shoes, I was out the door and into the bayou's heat before Richard could answer.

DAG (4)

"He's smoking hot," my dad said. His voice sounded tinny playing from the phone where it lay on the dash.

Mason pretended to upchuck into his takeout bag.

"Gross," I said.

"No, Dag, you're not listening. He's gorgeous. He's perfect."

My mom's voice came from the background: "He's very handsome."

"Do you hear that?" my dad said. "Your mom says he's very handsome."

"I heard. Thank you. I appreciate your unconditional love and support. Now, I'm officially terminating this conversation."

"I told him I didn't know if you preferred to host."

I wondered if I could melt into my seat. "Dad, you cannot talk to guys about stuff like that for me."

"Is that what it's called when guys come over for sex? Hosting?"

"I think it's called running a train," my mom shouted in the background.

"You are no longer my parents," I said. "Goodbye, strangers. I wish you the best of luck."

"You've got to text him," my dad said. "Promise me you'll text him. I see him every week at Rouses, and I won't be able to look him in the eyes if you don't text him."

"So go to another grocery store."

"You know Rouses has the chicken salad I like."

"Dad—"

"Promise me."

"Fine, I'll text him if it means we never have to talk about this again."

"And you've got to put some effort in when you host, Dagobert," my dad said.

"I really think it's called running a train," my mom said.

"This is the best thing of my life," Mason whispered.

I reached for the phone to take it off speaker, and Mason wrestled me away from it.

"I'm just saying," my dad added, "if you shave, if you pick up the place, if you put on a nice jockstrap, I think you have a chance. This guy's right at the edge of your weight class, but I think you've got a chance."

"Jesus, Dad," I said, giving up and letting Mason force me away from the phone. "Give your only son a little credit."

"Do not take the Lord's name in vain, young man," my mom said.

"I was reading on *Out.com* that jockstraps are highly in demand if you are a bottom," Dad said. "But a lot of the commenters said tops or bottoms look hot in a jock."

"You are a straight, middle-aged Republican in Louisiana. Why are you reading *Out.com*?"

"The world is changing," my mom said.

"This guy, he looks a little bit like that twink you used to bring over. Gloria, what was his name?"

"Jackson," Mom called back.

"Jackson," my dad said. "He looks like Jackson, only hotter." I could picture him sitting back, glowing with self-satisfaction as he added, "How's that for father of the year?"

"Jackson?" Mason whispered. "Jackson Sanders?"

"Shut up," I whispered back. Louder, I said, "Mom, Dad, I've got to go. I'm working."

My mom's voice came on the line now; she must have stopped whatever she was doing. "Sweetheart, you will not believe who called me. Donna Comeaux. Can you believe that? Sobbing. Did you know they are making her boy go back to work?"

"Of course I know. He's my partner."

"He was shot, Dagobert," Mom said like she was announcing the end of the world. "He should be taking care of himself."

"I'm fine, Mrs. LeBlanc," Mason said. "Honestly, I'm fine. Back at work and feeling great."

"Mason, sweetheart? Is that you?"

"Mason," my dad said, "do you remember Jackson?"

"Goodbye," I said, grabbing the phone. "Please find yourself a new son."

As I disconnected the call, I threw a wary look at Mason.

"What?" he finally said.

"I'm just waiting for it."

"You're such a weirdo sometimes." He munched a few fries. Then he said, "Ketchup."

I ran my thumb at the corners of my mouth, but Mason shook his head and gestured higher on his jawline. I tried again, got a good bit of it with the heel of my hand, and then picked up the rest with a napkin.

"Seriously," I said. "Just get it out of your system."

"I have no idea what you're talking about."

I gestured to the dash, where the phone had sat.

"It's nice," he said. "They care about you. They want you to be happy."

"Great. I'm going to be so happy that they'll have to lock me in padded room."

"You know what?" Mason said through a mouthful of fries. He swallowed. "Sometimes, you're a drama queen."

"This is why we're still friends," I said. "This, right here. What would I do without this?"

"That's right," Mason said, throwing a fry like a mini spear. It barely missed my eye.

"I'm going to tell Sarge to put you with Martinez. I'm going to ask if I can work alone."

"Great," Mason said. "I'll do great with Martinez."

Shifting into reverse, I eased the car out of the parking stall behind the Zaxby's, and then we pulled out onto the street.

"Seriously, man," Mason said, squeezing the back of my neck. "I'm fine. I'm ready to be back. It feels good to be back, you know, just normal stuff like this. Doing the job. You know that, right?"

"I know."

He squeezed once more, and then his arm dropped back at his side. "And if this guy looks like Jackson fucking Sanders, we are sure as fuck getting you a diamond-studded jock."

I sighed as I signaled to turn right. "And there it is."

ELIEN (5)

The truly humiliating part was I had to stand on the porch and wait for my Uber. The house was a good twenty minutes northeast of Bragg. I liked to joke that Richard had bought a bipolar house to match all his patients: the front of the house was carefully manicured, with St. Augustine grass trimmed like it had its own barber, as well as magnolia trees, sugar maples, oaks, and pines, all of them draped in Spanish moss. Behind the house, though, we controlled a few hundred feet of land, just as carefully groomed as the front of the house, before everything ended at the Okhlili, a tributary of the Tangipahoa. Beyond the Okhlili was dense Louisiana old growth, which I had absolutely no interest in getting any closer to. Less than a mile north of us, the Okhlili emerged from Bayou Pere Rigaud, where fan boats and alligators drew a cheaper class of tourists out of New Orleans for the 'real Cajun experience.'

I didn't drive anymore, so unless I, too, wanted the 'real Cajun experience,' which in my imagination mostly consisted of falling into a pit of cottonmouths, I was stuck at home. I had to rely on Ubers, Richard, and Muriel, who was technically a nurse but filled some sort of administrative role at DuPage Behavioral. Her job apparently consisted of doing whatever the doctors in the practice needed her to do—including driving me around.

So I stood on the porch. Richard made a few casual passes by the window, holding two glasses of iced tea, but every time he veered away. He was Being Thoughtful again and Giving Me Space. Sometimes I missed fighting, just the really nasty, say-every-hateful-thing kind of fights I used to have. Sometimes, these days, I had so much space I felt like I needed one of those astronaut suits.

When I was five, I had run away from home. I had made it approximately as far as the porch, and on that day, just like today, I'd walked back and forth, ignoring the midges that buzzed in the air. I remembered my parents helicoptering through the front room, keeping an eye on me, and I remembered ignoring them as I tried to figure out, at five years old, my next step in emancipation. I'd done a lot of pacing on the porch until Gard came out with a bag of boiled peanuts. He didn't say anything. He was three years older, so if he'd said anything to me, it would have been scripture. But he didn't say anything. He just sat in one of the rocking chairs, and after a while I sat down too, and then he took some of the boiled peanuts and started working on them, and then I started working on them too, and when the peanuts were gone he said we should go inside, and we did. I don't even remember why I'd wanted to run away.

But Gard was a black hole in my head now. And so were my parents. They weren't triggers or anything like that—they were just gone. I could trace their absence the same way scientists studied black holes: the absences of something that should have been there, the gravitational pull of something I couldn't see. They were dead; I guess it's easy enough to say it that way. They were dead. Now, I ate boiled peanuts when I went to the cemetery.

My Uber finally arrived, a Ford Escape that looked brand new and was one of the nicer trims, leather, the works. My driver was Jerome, young—probably my age, but Christ, on someone else that looked really young—with a skin fade and bleached tips. He liked to talk, make jokes. He had this really deep laugh. Once or twice, I caught him looking at me in the rearview mirror, and I considered it. Richard had insisted on an open relationship, insisted being the key word. Against my objections. Against all my protesting that I didn't care that he was older, didn't care that he was worried I hadn't dated enough. Richard had insisted. So I thought about letting Jerome drive me somewhere else. I thought about what it would feel like to take a drink from his hand, our fingers brushing. I thought about what it would feel like if he was standing behind me, his breath hot on my neck, a hand wandering down my chest. It was a game I played sometimes. I'd run the story all the way out, just to see. I used to be able to feel a flush in the hollow of my neck. I used to hear my heart hammering in my ears. I used to be able to throw a little wood now and then.

"Hey," Jerome said when he pulled up in front of Ray's building. "I don't usually do this, but—"

I slid out of the car, shut the door, and tipped him on the app. For a moment, the Escape idled at the curb, and I thought Jerome might do something really stupid like buzz down a window. After another moment, though, the Escape pulled away. He had one of those LED Uber signs in the back window, and it clicked on as he turned at the next corner.

Ray lived in Moulinbas, which was the older and seedier side of Bragg. In many ways, it could have passed for the rougher sister of New Orleans' French Quarter: narrow streets of Creole townhouses with painted brick, cast-iron balconies, and steeply pitched roofs. The glass was old and thick and wavy where it hadn't been replaced; the October sun glinted off the dormers set high on the townhouses. In many ways, Moulinbas catered to the same general population as the French Quarter. Many of the townhouses had been converted into bars and restaurants; others held shops selling souvenirs, or offering day trips, or spa treatments, or manicures. There were even a few herbal supplement stores that offered a convenient place to get weed, and I thought about buying some just to see how Richard would react. In the end, I decided not to; I was afraid I would get Worried Patience when what I wanted was hissing-cat fury.

Some of the townhouses still had apartments and residences on the upper floors; Ray lived in one of the half-story apartments in the building in front of me. I had visited a few times because Ray was easy to talk to, easy to be quiet around, and an easy escape from that beautiful, bipolar house. I'd always been irritated by the low ceilings in the half-story unit, although the dormer windows offered a beautiful view of Bragg at sunset, the whole city lit up and glowing in pastels, with the light making it impossible to see the chipped brick and broken stucco and the rust trails left by the cast iron. I climbed the stairs to Ray's apartment and knocked. No answer.

I waited, knocked again, a little harder this time. The door slipped out of its frame a quarter inch. The stairwell smelled like dust and the boozy, body-odor funk of Moulinbas, but now something else crept into the mix: shit.

"Ray?"

No answer.

I pressed on the door, and it swung open another quarter inch before the chain caught. Through the opening, I could make out the cramped living space of Ray's apartment: the patched floral wingbacks, the knock-off Tiffany lamp, the plastic skull he'd rescued from the dumpster behind a pop-up Halloween store.

"Ray, are you ok?"

I waited a full minute. Then I got out my phone and called 911. I explained the situation, by which I mean I lied. I told the dispatcher I'd been trying to get in touch with Ray for days, I'd tried the landlord, I'd talked to anybody who might know where he was, and nobody could tell me anything. I asked for a wellness check, and the dispatcher told me to sit tight. When I disconnected, I went downstairs and stepped inside the low-end jewelry boutique that occupied the ground floor. In contrast to the exterior, with its Old-World aesthetic, the interior was gratingly modern: steel and glass and slate. A middle-aged woman, trim, her hair neatly gray, was arranging things in one of the display cases; I barely gave the pieces a glance. Lots of synthetic stones, lots of silver that would probably turn your skin green, maybe a few diamonds that were too yellow to be sold for a premium. My first boyfriend had bought me a bracelet from a place like this, although that had been in New Orleans. It was a pretty piece with a lot of flashy stones that had all fallen out by the time we got home. I asked the woman about Ray, but she couldn't give me any answers; she didn't even know who Ray was, and she talked like a Yankee. She also talked a lot.

By the time I got back outside, a blue-and-white SUV with DuPage Sheriff's Department on the side was pulling up to the curb. The passenger door opened, and Mason got out. I'd never seen him in uniform before; khaki looked good on him. He stared at me for a moment and then looked across the SUV's hood. The driver looked familiar. I was pretty sure he was the guy I'd seen dropping off and picking up Mason at the support group. His hair was buzzed short and almost totally gray, and although he was wearing the same khaki shirt and brown pants as Mason, he somehow managed to look rumpled in them, as though he'd slept in them. His badge was askew, and I wanted to know why Mason hadn't pointed that out.

"Mr. Martel?" the driver said.

"Yeah, yes. That's me."

"What the fuck are you doing here?" Mason said.

"I'm visiting Ray," I said. "Trying to. He's not answering the door."

"Jesus fucking Christ." Mason had his fists on his hips. "Is this some kind of joke?"

"Why would it be a joke? I'm worried. Something's not right, so I just wanted somebody to do a wellness check."

"This is fucking typical," Mason said, rounding on the other deputy. "Let's go. This is a bullshit call."

"Why don't you check the jewelry store?" the other deputy said to Mason. His name tag said LeBlanc. "I'll go upstairs with Mr. Martel, and he can explain what's wrong."

"I already checked with the woman in there," I said.

"Can I talk to you for a minute?" Mason said, dragging LeBlanc to the street side of the SUV. They conversed in low voices. Mason was expressive with his hands as he talked, the movements growing choppier, until finally he yanked on the brim of his campaign cover and said, "The little prick is up to something, ok? That's what I'm trying to get through your thick fucking head."

LeBlanc's eyes shot toward me before cutting back. He said something very quietly, and Mason stomped toward the jewelry store.

"Why don't we go upstairs," LeBlanc said as he came around the SUV, "and we'll see what's going on."

"What's his problem?" I asked as we took the stairs.

"No problem."

"Oh, great. All that shouting and swearing and stomping like he's a toddler getting his toy taken away. I'm really glad that means there's no problem."

The sound of our steps on the treads filled the stairwell.

"Because you could have fooled me," I said. "I could have sworn Mason has a really big fucking problem with me."

"Deputy Comeaux—"

"I know his name is Mason. I know him from our support group, ok? And just because he's got his balls in a twist about me, it doesn't mean I'm making this up."

We had reached the landing at the top of the stairs, and I turned to face LeBlanc. He was about my height but built with a lot more muscle. He had legitimate biceps. Very legitimate. Like, cuff those fucking sleeves, big boy.

"Does he hate fags or something?" I asked.

LeBlanc face was very serious as he looked at me. "No."

"I think that's what it is. He's been acting weird as fuck around me lately, and I think that's what it is."

"Well, I came out to him when we were in high school," LeBlanc said with a shrug. "I thought maybe that would send him running, but he's like a cockroach."

I was suddenly very aware of the clock ticking inside Ray's apartment.

"This is him?" LeBlanc said, nodding at the partially open door.

"Yeah."

"Mr. Ray Field?"

"That's right."

LeBlanc jiggled the handle, although the door was open and the chain was visible. "And how do you know Mr. Field?"

"From the support group. The same one Mason goes to; Mason knows him too."

"Mr. Field?" LeBlanc called. "Are you home? This is Deputy LeBlanc from the DuPage Sheriff's Department."

The clock seemed even louder.

"Mr. Field, we're just checking if you're ok. If you're home, could you please respond?"

I shoved my hands in my pockets; LeBlanc smelled like talcum powder and something else, woodsy, that I couldn't quite put my finger on. I was starting to think I should have taken my chances downstairs with Mason.

"You told the dispatcher that you've been trying to make contact for days?" LeBlanc asked, glancing over his shoulder at me.

"Yeah."

"How long?"

"I don't know. Three or four days."

Very soft brown eyes, the color of sandalwood, stared at me. I wondered if I wasn't as good of a liar as I'd always believed.

"I could cut the chain," LeBlanc finally said.

"Yeah, please. If he's mad, I'll pay for it."

"Right," LeBlanc said, thick eyebrows shooting up as he took in my tank and jersey shorts.

"I can afford to pay for a chain."

"Of course, sir."

I laughed. "And I'm definitely not old enough that you should be calling me sir."

LeBlanc didn't laugh, though. He didn't smile either. "I'll get the cutters."

"I'm twenty-two," I called after him. "In case you're wondering."

"I wasn't," he said without looking back.

When he returned, he had a pair of bolt cutters as long as his arms. He hooked the jaws around the chain, and his big hands compressed the handles. The chain folded and parted like butter.

"Mr. Field?" he called again, giving the door a push. It squeaked as it caught against the floor, and LeBlanc gave it another, stiffer shove that forced it open the rest of the way.

The lights were on throughout the apartment. The clock was ticking. The smell of shit was much, much stronger. LeBlanc stepped inside, and I followed.

"Please stay on the landing, Mr. Martel."

"Sure."

We'd gone two more steps before he turned and said, "Mr. Martel."

"Loud and clear, big boy."

The look of frustration on his face only lasted an instant, and then he turned and advanced into the apartment. Ray's unit wasn't quite a studio, although the living area and the galley kitchen occupied most of the area. In the kitchen, one of the burners was on, the coil orange under a kettle that must have boiled dry. Across from us, the bathroom door was open, and the light was on in there too. A trickle of water ran from the tap; on the sink, a brown prescription bottle stood with the cap next to it. No sign of Ray. The only place left to look was the bedroom, which was separated from the main area by a short wall that gave the illusion of privacy.

LeBlanc must have reached the same conclusion because he put one of those big hands on my chest, stopping me, and he made sure I was staying put before he started walking again. He looked around the dividing wall, grabbed his shoulder radio, and called for an ambulance.

I moved toward the opening; LeBlanc grabbed for me, but he was still talking into the radio, and I dodged. I slid past him, entered the bedroom, and stopped.

Ray lay on the bed. I'd seen dead people before, and I knew Ray was dead the moment I saw him. He was waxy and puffy, his body already past rigor and slack now, bloating in the October heat. In death, people rarely look the way we knew them in life; in Ray's case, this was even truer than usual.

"Shit," I whispered. I dropped down onto the sill of the French window that led out to the balcony. I balled up my hands and covered my eyes.

"Mr. Martel," LeBlanc said, his voice distant, as though he'd already moved back to the door.

"Can you give me a fucking minute, please?"

LeBlanc didn't answer.

I tried taking deep breaths, but that didn't help; I could taste the corruption, the shit, the putrefaction, and I wanted to be sick. I dropped my head between my knees. Episodes like these were cluster bombs: an explosion of sensory input that I couldn't control. The smell of fried catfish. The run of greasy skin against my face. Someone shouting. A hand around my neck, choking me. The unrelenting invasion of my body. Flashbacks, episodes, whatever you wanted to call them—when they happened, it was all happening now. It wasn't the past. It was this moment, right now, and it was going to last forever.

A hand around my neck, choking me.

"Mr. Martel?"

A hand on my arm, grabbing me, twisting my wrist, pulling, pinning.

"Get the fuck off me," I shouted, stumbling up from the window seat, trying to pull free from LeBlanc. Only it wasn't LeBlanc who gripped my wrist.

It was Ray. He had dragged himself across the bed and now lay at an angle, his legs still tangled in the bedding. His eyes were open; blue fire danced in the milky depths. Where he clutched my arm, his bloated fingers had split, oozing black liquid down my arm.

Ray yanked, dragging me towards him; his mouth opened. No, not opened. His jaw dropped, unhinged, like he was going to try to swallow me whole. I stumbled back, screaming, trying to rip free. Ray held on. His grip was iron. My tennis shoes slid along the polished floor, and I couldn't get my footing. He dragged me toward him again, his puffy flesh slipping through the twisted sheets. I was still screaming. The blue in his eyes was brighter: huge, dancing walls of fire that fell in sheets across my vision.

Then two strong hands had my shoulders, and my feet left the ground as I was hauled backwards. My weight must have overbalanced LeBlanc, because both of us tumbled to the ground. I twisted and scratched and clawed, not even sure what I was doing, just trying to get free. LeBlanc had rolled away, got onto his knees, and had out his service weapon.

Ray lay in bed, just the way I'd found him. No blue fire. No twisted, crawling abomination. His eyes were half open and filmed with death. I crabbed back a few more feet until I hit the wall, and then I scrubbed at my arm. No black juice from putrefaction. I could hear my breathing, shrill and hysterical, but I couldn't seem to get it under control. LeBlanc held the gun fixed on Ray, but his hands were shaking.

And then, something blue drifted out of Ray's mouth. A firefly, my mind supplied, although I'd never seen a blue firefly before. It circled lazily once, and then it slid through the French window and drifted away, vanishing against the intense blue of the sky.

DAG (6)

I'd heard about hallucinations people experienced after combat. Psychotic symptoms manifested occasionally in people suffering from PTSD.

I had seen a dead man grappling with Martel, trying to drag the kid forward, trying to . . . to bite him.

No, I had seen a dead man lying in bed. Dead. Motionless, the way dead people are supposed to be.

I had seen something blue.

No, I had seen a sunspot.

The panicked breathing behind me dragged me back, inch by inch, from my own terror. Holstering my Sig, I turned and saw Martel against the wall, knees drawn to his chest, running a hand over his arm.

"Are you ok?" I asked.

He kept turning his arm over, studying it, his breathing shallow and rapid.

"Mr. Martel, are you ok?"

He raked his nails down his arms, leaving faint white tracks. Then he did it again, harder.

Squatting next to him, I said, "Hey, you're ok."

He was really digging in now, his nails furrowing the skin; in a few places, flecks of red showed where he had scraped the flesh raw.

"Ok," I said, taking his wrist. "You're—"

"No," he shouted, twisting away. He scrambled across the floor, not quite getting to his feet, and then he ran into the two-person table. A plate slid off and shattered, and Martel flinched and pulled himself into a ball.

Footsteps on the stairs made me get to my feet. Mason stepped into the apartment a moment later, his face tight. "What the hell is going on?"

"Mr. Field is dead," I said, thumbing at the partitioned bedroom. "Mr. Martel is having a reaction."

Mason's face twisted further in anger. He stood there, worrying the palm of one hand with his thumb, his face getting darker and darker. Then he kicked the chair next to Martel and sent it toppling end over end.

"What the fuck, Elien? You were supposed to make sure he was ok."

"Mason, Jesus Christ."

"You were supposed to be looking out for him," Mason screamed, bending over Martel—Elien—who was trying to make himself smaller and smaller. "Zahra asked you to do one fucking thing and you couldn't even do that."

"That's enough," I said, stepping toward them. "What has gotten into you—"

Bending, Mason grabbed Elien's tank and jerked him upright. Elien came up awkwardly, slapping at Mason's hand, shouting something that didn't even sound like words. Mason was shaking him, shouting back, and then Elien twisted and got in a punch that caught Mason in the eye. Mason dropped the kid, and then he reached for his gun.

"You are fucking kidding me," I shouted, grabbing Mason in a wrist lock and forcing him out to the landing.

"Get the fuck off me," Mason said, trying to twist free.

"What the hell is happening with you?" When he tried to lunge past me, I tightened the lock, and Mason howled. "Jesus, Mase, get a handle on it."

With a growl, Mason dropped back, and I released him. We stared at each other. In the distance, sirens moved closer.

"I cannot believe what I just saw in there," I said.

"Don't be so fucking dramatic," Mason said, massaging his wrist.

"What the hell was that?"

"He knows something he's not telling us. I was just trying to put a scare into him."

Shaking my head, I pointed. "Downstairs."

"Fine."

"I'm taking him outside, and I want you to stay the fuck away from him."

Mason's mouth twisted. "Told you."

"What?"

"You see his whole poor, defenseless gay-boy routine, and you pop a boner so hard you can't even think straight."

I took a deep breath. And then another. And then I said, "Go downstairs before I say something I regret."

Mason was still sneering as he took the first step.

Elien had righted the chair, and now he was on his hands and knees picking up ceramic splinters from the plate.

"Leave that," I said.

"I can't—" He glanced at the wall that blocked Ray from view. "I don't want it like this. His place, I mean. He tried to keep it clean."

"Mr. Martel, please leave it. The coroner is going to have to determine cause of death, and you can't be in here."

He tried to argue, but he kept looking at the wall that divided the kitchen from the bedroom. Every time he looked, his color dropped. Finally, he let me herd him out onto the landing, and then down the stairs and onto the street. The sun was setting in a huge banner of red and orange, but the heat hadn't dipped at all, and the smell of booze and piss in the Moulinbas street was thick enough to choke on. Mason was pacing in front of the jewelry store, so I made Elien walk to the end of the block and sit on the curb.

"Head between your knees," I said.

He rolled his eyes. "Is that an order?"

"It can help you control your breathing, and that can help you deal with feeling panicked or out of control."

"Great," he said, leaning back, every movement exaggerated, and planted his hands on the sidewalk. "Thanks for the medical advice, Dr. LeBlanc."

The sirens were moving closer, but this street was still strangely quiet. Elien was watching me, and I found myself looking up and down the block, adjusting my shoulder radio, running my tongue over my teeth. I looked at Elien a few times; it was hard not to look. He was pretty much perfect: long and lean, probably 0.1% body fat, light brown skin, his thick, straight hair perfectly windswept. In short shorts and a tank, there was a lot to look at.

"You saw it," Elien said.

I just about swallowed my tongue.

"Upstairs," Elien said, his voice low and urgent. "You saw . . . you saw what happened with Ray."

I saw a dead man clutching at him, dragging him forward, jaw hinged unnaturally wide.

"Yes," I said. "I'm sorry he's passed away."

"That's not what I mean. You saw." He laid emphasis on the word, the intensity straining his voice. "You saw him grab me."

Our eyes met. His were hazel, more green than brown, full of tears and a desperate need.

I opened my mouth, thinking of that blue thing that reminded me of a firefly.

The ambulance turned onto the street, sirens blatting.

"I'm very sorry for your loss," I said.

His eyes held mine for another moment, and, very clearly, he said, "You cowardly little fucker." Then he raised his chin and looked away.

ELIEN (7)

Richard came and picked me up. By that time, it was almost night, and the evening breeze off the lake stirred humid heat. Thick clouds massed along the horizon as we drove home, and then we were under the thick canopy of the trees and the darkness was complete, swallowing the sky and the clouds. The whole way home, Richard was Giving Me Space and Offering Unconditional Support, which made me want to open the window, stick my head out, and improvise a reverse guillotine.

When we parked at home, I tried to calculate how much the garage had cost. The house was worth well over a million dollars; Richard hadn't told me that, but I knew how to use Google. The garage had three bays, and it was insulated and climate controlled. A hundred thousand dollars? It had an apartment above the garage, a kind of efficiency unit—my mind flashed back to Ray's half-story apartment, the wallpaper with a cameo silhouette, the ticking clock—so maybe a hundred and fifty thousand? A hundred and fifty thousand dollars for a garage. The house where I'd grown up, on the last Zillow estimate, was worth a hundred and fifty-four thousand dollars. Almost exactly the equivalent, the whole house, of Richard's garage. I wondered if Richard would buy the house if I asked. I wondered what he'd say when I showed up to the closing with a jerry can of gasoline and a book of matches.

"I want you to know," Richard said with Quiet Understanding, "that I'm ready to talk whenever you are."

"How much did the garage cost?" I asked.

His hand closed over mine; I shut my eyes, because I knew if I didn't, I'd end up looking at him.

"Elien, the deputies told me you had an episode. That's ok. You're still processing everything that happened to you. You're still trying to make sense of it. What happened today, finding your friend like that—"

"He wasn't really a friend, though," I said, slipping my hand free from Richard's and getting out of the Lexus. "I just knew him from the support group."

"Elien," Richard said as he got out of the car.

"What?" I asked as I headed into the house. "He's was just some fucked-up loser, and every week, I sat in a circle with him, the whole lot of us just a bunch of fucked-up losers."

Richard followed me into the kitchen. I opened the refrigerator, took out a can of La Croix, and popped the top. I took a sip before I realized it was coconut.

"This is disgusting," I said.

"I know that you're upset," Richard said. "You don't have to talk about it now. You're allowed to feel whatever you need to feel."

"Why did you buy this?"

Richard blinked those ready-to-cry eyes.

"I just don't understand," I said.

"It hurts when someone we care about takes their own life."

"No," I said, shaking my head. "Jesus, you don't listen to me. I just don't understand why you would buy something so fucking disgusting."

Sighing, Richard shook his head. "I understand that you're upset. But it's not fair to take your anger out on me."

"Yeah," I said. "You're right." Then I pitched the can as hard as I could. It hit one of the upper cabinets, shattering the glass door and then smashing the wineglasses stored inside. "You know what? I guess I am upset. I'm upset you bought that fucking suntan-tasting garbage when I told you I don't like it."

"I'll be upstairs, Elien."

Sometimes, he looked like such a pathetic old piece of shit. Sometimes, with his shoulders slumped, with his hair thinning, with those iron-gray curls on his arms and the back of his hands, he looked like a ruin that was about to come tumbling down. His footsteps carried through the house; the stairs creaked under his weight; a door upstairs clicked shut.

Inside the cabinet, the can of La Croix sputtered and fizzed, the carbonated water forcing its way out of a hole in the aluminum. I leaned on the counter for a minute, my face in my hands, breathing. Then I grabbed a towel. Glass crunched under my tennis shoes as I made my way to the ruined cabinet. I picked out the biggest shards from the door and dumped them in the trash. Then I used the towel to retrieve the can from the mess of splintered wineglasses. I let it finish emptying into the sink. I wiped out the cabinet as best I could, transferring towelfuls of glass into the trash and mopping up the La

Croix. Two wineglasses had survived, and I washed them in the sink. When I'd done the best I could with the cabinet, I got online, found a similar style of wineglasses, and ordered replacements. The money wasn't a problem—when Mom and Dad and Gard had died, I'd been the only one left. It wasn't much, but it was enough that I didn't have to get a job right away, especially with Richard footing the big bills. No, money wasn't a problem at all. It's just everything else that was a problem.

I took the kitchen trash, now full of glass, to the outside bin. When I emptied it, it made a tinging, crystalline shimmer. The day had died completely; above me, the sky was a pool of stars that went only to the edge of the property. Then the wall of trees closed off the rest of the world. Mayflies darted around the porch lights; mosquitos hummed in my ears. Behind the house, something big splashed into the Okhlili. A gator, maybe. But it could have been something else.

No fireflies, a part of my brain noted. Not a single one. Not any color. Nothing.

Something deep in the trees startled, its sudden burst of speed snapping branches, and I dropped the lid on the trash bin and hurried back inside. I leaned against the door. I could feel Ray's cold, stiff hand clutching my arm. I could smell rot. Eyes closed, I fumbled for the deadbolt and threw it home, and then I wiped my face and stumbled through the house, drawing the curtains closed. We lived far enough out that we never bothered with the curtains, but tonight was different. I did all the locks too, doors and windows. Better than most people, I knew that safety was illusion. Locks were all well and good, but they couldn't stop real danger. If someone wanted to get into the house, they could pick a lock or break a window or set the house on fire. Even that wasn't what really scared me, though. What scared me was the reality that sometimes, you locked the danger inside with you. In my case, I'd been getting my brains fucked out in my safely locked house while Gard and Mom and Dad died in the next room.

When I went upstairs, the door to Richard's study was open, and the room was dark and empty. I continued down the hall to our bedroom. This door was open too, and the lights were off, the bedcovers pulled back as though Richard had tried to sleep and then given up. Under his bathroom door—we each had our own bathroom, just another nice touch—a line of light showed. I knocked.

"Richard?"

I pressed my ear to the wood.

"Richard, I'm really sorry."

We'd been here before, of course. Even saints like Richard finally ran out of Quiet Understanding and reached Just About Fucking Enough.

"I'll call tomorrow and have someone come out and fix the glass on the cabinet," I said, but my voice was getting smaller and smaller. "I'm ready to talk about what happened today, whenever you are."

A series of soft splashes came from the other side of the door; Richard easing himself into the tub, I guessed. The house settled around us, and crickets called from the lawn, and I set my hand gently on the door and tapped a few times. Finally, stripping out of my clothes, I showered and got ready for bed. When I'd finished, Richard still hadn't emerged from his bathroom. I crawled into bed naked and pushed the sheet below my waist; maybe Richard would ravish me. Maybe I'd sleep through it. I drifted off, wishing I weren't so fucked up.

The dreams were like the flashbacks: explosions of sensory information, there and then vanished, going on and on. The light of the clock radio, neon green. The smell of fried catfish. The hand over my mouth. The hand around my neck. The pressure building in my head. Forever. That was the problem with this kind of nightmare: it was real, it was now, it never faded or got any easier. The dumbass I'd picked up at the club just kept plowing into me, drilling, and I whimpered into his hand as each thrust carried me closer to climax. A little sound. Something soft. A thud. Dripping. The taste of grass in my mouth. All of it happening somewhere else. The light of the clock radio. The smell of fried catfish. The hand over my mouth. The hand around my neck. The light of the clock radio. Drilling into me. My pathetic moaning into his hand. The smell of something foul and corrupted. A hand on my arm, grabbing me, dragging me forward. The light of the clock radio.

The light of the clock radio.

Not green anymore. A soft, firefly blue.

I sat up, gasping for breath, covered in sweat. I was shaking. My legs were tangled in the sheet. For a moment, I had to press a hand over my mouth, rocking back and forth as I sucked air through my nose. And then, bit by bit, the nightmare pulled back. I kicked my way free of the bedding, only now noticing that Richard was still in his bathroom, that less than half an hour had passed since I'd dozed off. I stumbled into my bathroom and splashed water on my face. I grabbed the towel, still wet from my shower, and dried off my sweat. When I was getting back into bed, Richard's door opened. He was an outline against the grayscale darkness behind him.

"How are you?" he asked quietly as he got into bed. "Are you still angry at me?"

I focused on the folds of the sheet, tracing them, trying to disappear into their pattern.

He kissed my shoulder, and I shivered, and then I started to cry.

"Come here," he whispered, pulling me against him, his arms wrapping around me. "It's ok. Things are going to be ok."

DAG (8)

At end of shift, I cornered Mason in the locker room.

"Nelly's," I said.

"Man, I'm beat. I just want to go home and see Mary Ann."

"This isn't optional."

He didn't meet my gaze; he was staring at one of the changing benches. Then he sucked his teeth, shrugged, and said, "Yeah, ok."

Nelly's was a cop bar just off the Quartier, the docks district. Bragg didn't have any major industries that still operated on the lake; by this point, the docks were purely a tourist attraction. Sometime in the 90s, someone had gotten the grand idea to "revive the Quartier" and "stimulate local businesses," which was a fancy way of saying they wanted to sell most of the Quartier to a St. Tammany Parish developer. It happened the way a lot of Louisiana business still happened, and most of the original architecture was bulldozed and replaced with chain restaurants and boutiques, all of it housed in a faux Creole style. Kind of the Disneyland version of Moulinbas or the French Quarter.

Because Nelly's wasn't on a major thoroughfare, it was spared. Inside, it consisted of a chain of smoke-filled rooms, the plaster walls yellow with cigarette tar and nicotine, small tables crammed into every available inch. City cops tended to take the back room; deputies stayed near the front. I attributed this to the fact that the deputies had to handle just about everything on their own; we might as well have an easy exit.

Mason had already gotten a table in the front room, and I sat opposite him. When Amanda patted my shoulder, I asked for Sugarfield on the rocks. Mason had already placed an order, I figured, because he just nodded when she asked if he was ok.

"Look, Mary Ann's waiting—"

"Mary Ann can't be bothered to drive you to your support group," I said. "She can wait a fucking minute while I talk to you."

"What the fuck did you just say?"

"What the hell happened today?"

"Don't ever talk about her like that again, do you hear me?"

"Mason, Jesus, we had a civilian call for a wellness check, and you treated that guy like he was robbing a bank."

"He's fine."

"He was scared. Really scared. And he was worried about his friend, and—"

"Christ, if I have to hear one more person worship Elien fucking Martel, I'm just going to put a fucking bullet in my head."

I sat back in my chair until Amanda got back with the Sugarfield and a draft beer for Mason. Then I rolled the tumbler on the edge of its base, the ice clinking. I took a drink. Then I rolled the glass a little more.

"I'm sorry," Mason said. He was rubbing his thumb on his glass. "I haven't been sleeping, and when I do, I have these fucked-up dreams."

"Are you apologizing for this, right now? Or for earlier, with the civilian?"

"Can you just call him Elien? You're obviously in love with him already, just like everybody is."

I raised an eyebrow.

"Both, I guess," he said with a sigh.

"What's your deal with him? You said he was an asshole."

Mason took a long drink, watching me over the glass.

"Ok, he's kind of got a smart mouth," I said. "But he actually seemed kind of sweet."

"Oh my God."

"Don't do this."

"Oh my God. I was just joking, but you really do like him."

"I responded to a callout, Mason. I didn't show up for a fucking Grindr hookup."

"You think he's cute."

"So what's his deal?

"He's an asshole."

"You keep saying that. What does that even mean?"

For a moment, Mason looked at a loss. Then he took another drink. When he set down the glass, he said, "I don't know. I don't know why I keep saying that. I guess I don't like him. People in the support group practically fall over for him. He's kind of funny, you know, making fun of himself. And he's good looking, fine. He does help people. I know that's not the first time he's checked in with Ray, and he's done that for other people. He even texted me a few times when I first started going. I kind of . . . I kind of didn't respond, and he stopped after a while."

"He said he thinks you don't like him because he's gay."

"I like you."

I sipped the Sugarfield. "That's what I told him."

Mason released his drink, spread his hands on the table, and drummed his fingers. Then he stopped, and the look he shot me was intense and direct. "Don't you think he looks like him?"

"What?"

"Elien. Don't you think he looks like Noah?"

"Noah's white."

"Ok."

"I don't know, maybe a little."

"Not just a little. Elien's close to Noah's age. He's got the same hair—"

"Elien has way more hair than Noah." I mimed over my head. "It's probably takes him an hour to blow it out."

"But it's all windswept and brushed back just like Noah's. And he's got green eyes like Noah."

"Elien has hazel eyes." My face heated, and I took a drink. "I mean, that's what it looked like to me."

"You're pathetic," Mason said.

"So, you're telling me you hate Elien, even though he's sweet and funny and supportive of all the people in group, because he has a vague resemblance to the kid who shot you? I mean, like probably fifty million other guys, he's young and has green eyes and blow dries his hair. That's why?"

"I thought his eyes were hazel."

"God, you are really determined to piss me off tonight."

"I know it doesn't make sense. I just don't like being around him. I look at him, and I start thinking about Noah, and, I don't know, I want to punch him in the face."

I rattled the ice in the tumbler again. "Mason, if you don't like him, that's fine. If you hate his guts, I don't care. If you want to punch him in the middle of your support group, go right ahead, as long as I don't have to bail your ass out. But you cannot lose your mind like you did today. Because at some point, we're going to have to deal with another kid who resembles Noah, and I can't have you going off the rails."

"I'm getting better."

When I couldn't think of anything to say, I sipped the Sugarfield again.

"I am," Mason said, quiet and firm as he met my eyes.

"So show me."

"Easy. Ask pretty boy out, and we'll double."

"Ha ha."

"I'm serious. He's cute. You're into him. Ask him out."

"He's got a boyfriend, dumbass. He picked Elien up."

"Yeah, I know he's got a boyfriend. He's also in an open relationship."

"What?"

"An open relationship. He can date whoever he wants."

I shook my head.

"So ask him out," Mason said.

"I still don't think that's a good idea. I managed to piss him off pretty good."

"You did? What happened?"

I thought of the blue light like a firefly. I thought of Elien's mouth twisting as he said, *You cowardly little fucker.*

"Who knows? Just didn't make a good impression, I guess."

Mason finished his beer, slapped a ten on the table, and stood. As he passed me, he put a hand on my shoulder.

"Buddy, we've got to get you laid. Fast. Fuck, maybe I need to get laid too. These dreams I've been having, dreams about burning blue eyes and shit. Is that fucked up? Jesus." He laughed, but it sounded off. "Just don't answer that."

ELIEN (9)

Zahra had her hands neatly folded in her lap. It was Tuesday again; I was back in the basement of DuPage First Methodist. The preschool kids must have been trying to level up their Halloween game. On the wall, they had hung masks made out of construction paper. Black cats, robots, soldiers, astronauts. One mask, off to the side, low on the wall where most people might have missed it, was just a black circle with two pale blue eyes. I dragged my gaze back to Zahra, feeling choked by the smell of rubber cement.

"As I'm sure many of you already know," Zahra said, "we lost one of our friends this week."

"He wasn't my friend," Tamika said.

"Cowardly son of a bitch," Willie said.

Zahra waited a moment. Willie had the good grace to blush, sinking lower in his seat, but Tamika just stared off into space, thrusting her chin out.

"Ray died by suicide—" Zahra began.

David's shrill laughter cut her off. He bent forward in his seat, wringing his hands. He was still wearing those heavy winter gloves, even though it was the hottest October on record. The laughter dragged on.

"What the fuck is wrong with you?" Tamika shouted.

"Tamika," Zahra said, "we're here to support each other, and David—"

"He's laughing like a fucking lunatic and Ray's dead. How the fuck is that supporting each other?"

"Ok," I said, "it's just a reaction. He can't help it."

But David was still laughing, and the hairs on the back of my neck were standing up.

"E, shut up," Kenny said. "Keep your skinny gay ass quiet."

"You like my gay ass," I told Kenny with a smile. I stood, touched David's arm, and nodded toward the hall. David was laughing so hard he was crying now. He got out of the seat, and I nudged him away from the group.

"Here he goes," Mason said to no one in particular. "Elien, just sit down and let Zahra handle things."

"No," Zahra said, "I appreciate how you're showing support to David, Elien. Thank you."

Mason slouched lower in his chair. He was staring at me, and he was obviously furious.

We made our way to the bathroom, and David waved me off when he stepped inside. It was a single-user facility, and I heard the bolt slide home after he shut the door. Water ran. I heard splashing. David was still laughing like he was on acid and had heard the best fucking joke in the world. I shivered in spite of myself.

David had been in the restroom for maybe five minutes, the laughter dying down and bubbling back up from time to time, when Mason stepped into the hall. He shut the door behind him, looked at me once, and then stepped past me and rattled the handle on the bathroom door.

"I need to pee."

"Get in line."

"Jesus, get off your fucking high horse." Mason hammered on the door. "David, get the fuck out. I need to pee."

"Hey," I said, planting a hand on Mason's chest. "Leave him alone."

"Fuck off," Mason said.

"Go back in to the group," I said. "When David's feeling better, we'll join you. Then you can pee."

Mason's lip curled. He knocked my arm away and rattled the handle again.

"Get out of here," I said, sliding between Mason and the door.

Grabbing me by the throat, Mason swung me around and slammed me against the wall. Like the rest of the basement, it was poured concrete with a thin layer of paint; my head rebounded and, I felt my legs go loose.

Mason took shallow, frantic breaths. We were close enough that I could feel his exhalations on my cheek, see the flare of his nostrils, sense the tremors in his body.

"This is it, huh?" I asked. "You get tired of having to be around a queer?"

For another long moment, Mason clutched me. He was shaking harder now.

"Why's it such a big deal, Mase?" I smirked. "You've been looking at me a lot. Maybe you're getting a little interested—is that it? Maybe you've been thinking dirty thoughts." I nudged his knee with mine. "Get down right now, ask nice, and maybe I'll let you suck me off in the bathroom when David's out of there."

"Fuck you," Mason mumbled.

"One-time offer."

"Fuck you," he said more forcefully, and then he slammed my head against the wall again. The world went slippery. His fingers tightened, and for an instant, I couldn't breathe.

Then the door opened, and Tamika stepped out into the hall.

"What the fuck is going on?" she asked.

Mason's fingers loosened, and he stepped back.

"Hey Tamika," I said, leaning against the wall like it had been my idea all along. "Mase and I were just having a special moment."

Mason was taking huge gulps of air; sweat glistened on his forehead, fat drops of it, and he looked sick.

"Isn't that right, Mase? He asked me on a date. Isn't that cute?"

Tamika looked at him.

Rocking from side to side, Mason looked like he might puke or fall over. Then he wiped his face and pushed past Tamika, mumbling something as he headed back into the room.

"What the fuck was that?" Tamika asked me.

"My next hookup."

"Bullshit."

I just grinned, and then David came out of the bathroom, still wringing his gloved hands. We went back into the room together.

But when we sat down, when Zahra went through her spiel about Ray, when we moved into our regular material, when I gave my update—something off the cuff, a few details about throwing the can of La Croix and cleaning up the broken glass, just enough truth that the lies weren't visible—through all of it, Mason stared at me, his mouth working soundlessly, his eyes fixed and glassy, a tic in his cheek flashing on and off, his body jerking from time to time as though he were starting awake from a nightmare.

Something was really, really off about him. He'd been weird the last few weeks at group. He'd been weird when he and his partner had shown up at Ray's. But today, he was acting crazy. At first, I tried to meet his gaze. He just stared through me, and every time, I looked away first. After that, I kept my gaze on the floor. I had one hand on my phone. Who were you supposed to call when a cop went psycho on your ass?

As soon as Zahra ended the meeting, I shot out of my seat and went for the door, praying Muriel would already be waiting at the curb.

Rapid footsteps followed, and I glanced back to see Mason jogging after me.

"Hey," he called. "Hold on!"

When I got outside, the sunlight blinded me for a moment. I staggered down the steps, clutching the rail, hoping I wouldn't fall. The door flew open behind me, crashing against the stop, and Mason tumbled out.

"You fucking son of a bitch," he shouted. "Stop right there."

I glanced back.

He had a gun.

DAG (10)

Mary Ann had bailed again, so I was sitting at the curb outside DuPage First Methodist, waiting to pick up Mason. I didn't feel like pretending with the Escort's A/C, so I had the windows down; the October day was warm, with just a hint of a breeze off the lake. A really nice orca track had just started when I heard shouting. I looked in the rearview mirror.

Elien was racing down the steps. Behind him, Mason was waving a gun and shouting.

Throwing open the door, I jumped out of the car and sprinted to the sidewalk. The big, red-brick bulk of DuPage First Methodist framed Mason. He was still shouting, still waving the gun. I understood the words he was saying, repeated variations of "stop" "hold it" "freeze," but the way he was saying them was off, like he was reading them from a page without any idea what they meant. His eyes were wide and rolling; a tic pulled at his cheek. Even in the church's shadow, Mason's blue eyes seemed to catch the light. I thought of a dead man in a Moulinbas apartment.

"Mason," I called. "Hey, buddy, what's going on?"

Mason swung the pistol to aim at Elien; when Elien glanced back the next time, he stumbled. His knee caught the brass support of the handrail, and he cried out and fell, rolling four steps until he came up against the next support. I kept my gaze fixed on Mason, only peripherally aware of Elien wiping a hand across his face, of something that might have been blood.

"Hey, Mason. Hey!" I jogged at a diagonal up the stairs. "What's going on? Put the gun down."

The muzzle dipped an inch.

"Yeah, good. Talk to me. What's wrong?"

Mason pivoted. The pistol snapped up and toward me, and I froze, hands open and out. I had on a Tulane t-shirt and shorts. I might as well have been naked. Behind Mason, a black woman with short, buzzed hair emerged from the church door. Her mouth opened, but she didn't make any noise. She slipped back inside the church. The blue in Mason's eyes was brighter, like June sunlight on glass. Blue, blue, blue.

"Hi," I said. "Hey. It's Dag. You know me, right?"

"Yeah." The word was sullen and distant.

"Good, great. Because I was worried for a minute. I was kind of freaking out. You've got that gun, and you're pointing it right at me, and I thought maybe you didn't know who I was."

"I know."

"Mason, why don't you put that down?"

"He's going to do it again. He's going to shoot me. He's been planning it. I'm not going to let him do that."

"He's not going to do anything. That's not Noah, ok? That's Elien. He's not planning anything. He's not going to hurt you. He can't hurt you. Look, he fell down. He's on the ground. He can't do anything to you."

Mason's hand wavered; the gun dropped a few inches.

"Come on," I said. "I'm your friend. I'm your best friend, right? And we got through all that stuff with Noah together. You're ok. Look how much better you are today. Just put the gun down, and we'll talk about this. We'll figure it out."

The gun slipped down a few more inches.

"Yep, that's right. Just let it go. Just drop it. Drop it, Mason. Drop it."

He said something I couldn't hear over the roar of blood in my ears and the traffic whipping along the cross street. It was just a word. By the shape of his mouth, I thought maybe he said *can't.*

Then he spun toward Elien, who was lying motionless, and he screamed, "Don't move, don't move, don't move."

I charged. Sprinting up the stairs, I bulled into Mason as he tried to pivot back toward me. He was too slow. I caught him just below the solar plexus with my shoulder, and the force of the charge carried both of us forward. He slammed into the church door; breath exploded from his lungs. I grabbed one arm, dragging him down, trying to force him onto his stomach. His other hand came around, and the butt of the pistol connected with the side of my head. The world got hazy; my grip on Mason's wrist slipped.

He tried to shove me off, but I grabbed him again, and we both went down. I landed on my back. Mason landed on top of me. I got both his wrists this time, forcing the hand with the gun off to one side. He squeezed off a shot. The clap deafened me, but I could feel my voice in my chest, could feel myself shouting at him to stop.

Mason kneed me in the side, and I lost my hold. He brought the gun up, swinging in Elien's direction. I didn't know what had happened to Elien, didn't know if he'd managed to find cover. I just saw the gun slicing through the air above me, moving toward the spot I had last seen the dark-haired kid. I grabbed Mason, and we rolled together. He came down beneath me, his head cracking against the stone. The shadow of DuPage First Methodist covered us, but his eyes were firefly bright. He brought the gun toward me now.

I grabbed him again. I was using both hands, trying to force him to drop the pistol. He was bucking like a crazy man, stronger than I could believe, the gun inching closer and closer to me. Sweat made my grip slick—slick against his fingers, slick against the composite frame of the pistol. Mason was screaming at me, but I could barely hear him after the gunshot. The gun slipped closer. I grunted, one hand wrapped around Mason's, the other twisting the barrel, forcing away.

I still don't know if Mason pulled the trigger, or if I somehow did it while I was trying to pull the gun loose.

His body jerked once, and then he went still.

A high-pitched whining filled my ears; something drifted in the air. Sunspots, I told myself. But the sun was behind DuPage First Methodist, and sunspots weren't blue. I squeezed my eyes shut for a moment; my center of gravity was off, like I was falling.

When I opened them again, the sunspots were gone. I pulled off my t-shirt and wadded it up against the hole in Mason's chest. Red stained the cotton, ran under my nails, slid between my fingers. Hot; cold, where it thinned and the air wicked away the heat.

After that, his eyes were empty and dark.

II

And while the hunter is thus prostrated on the ground, it approaches and sticks a small thorn into his hand or foot, and by so doing bewitches the hunter and transmits to him the power of doing evil to others.

- "Myths of the Louisiana Choctaw," David I. Bushnell, Jr.

ELIEN (1)

In the week that followed, I ate, I watched TV with Richard, I made Sazeracs and chopped bell peppers and bagged them for Richard to take as a snack. Day-to-day stuff. Sure, little things were different. Richard asked me more often if I was all right. Richard insisted on doing the dishes. One night, Richard and I were watching *Shark Tank,* and I started hyperventilating and had to run outside to stand with the St. Augustine grass needling my bare feet. I met with Zahra—once in person, at her office in DuPage Behavioral, and then once over Skype, the night I ran out into the darkness. But mostly, day to day, it was normal in spite of everything that had happened.

When I slept, though, I dreamed. Every night, the same dream: the hand around my neck, the hand over my mouth, the smell of fried catfish, the taste of grass, the dumbass whose name I'd forgotten, the dumbass from the club, deep inside me, pounding, pounding, pounding, until the world came apart. I was whimpering into his hand as I came down from the orgasm. He was still thrusting. The taste of grass in my mouth was stronger now. A soft thud punctuated his grunts as he came and went still, his chin against my back, his stubble rough against sensitive skin.

And then, bathed in the light of the clock radio—firefly blue, when a part of my brain stubbornly insisted it should have been green—I lay still, the dumbass's weight on top of me, and listened to a steady drip, drip, drip.

In the dream, I already knew what was going to happen. In the dream, I already knew what I was going to find. I wanted to scream, but the dumbass still had a hand around my throat.

Dreams never had the same logic of sequence and event, cause and effect. In real life, I had elbowed the dumbass in the ribs, and he'd pulled out and stripped off the condom. He'd tied it, swung it back and forth, and landed it in the trash can. In real life, the dumbass had been proud of his little post-coital display of hand-eye coordination.

He'd wanted to tickle me. He'd run his hands over my collar bone. He'd asked about my neck, and I'd said I needed water; did he want a glass?

In the dream, though, all of that got edited out. One moment I was lying under him, tasting grass in my mouth, smelling the fried catfish on his hand. The next moment I was already out of the room, stepping lightly through my parents' living room, picking my way over the boards I knew squeaked.

In real life, I had been worried about waking them.

The drip drip drip came from the kitchen. That night, I had imagined a leaky pipe; I thought maybe Gard hadn't turned off the tap all the way. In the dream, though, I knew.

I found my mom first. She had fallen halfway out of a chair at the kitchen table. Blood pooled on the wooden seat of the chair, beaded at the lip, and dripped steadily onto the floor. The graying fringe of her hair touched the pool of blood on the boards. It reminded me of the bristles of a paintbrush.

In real life, I had tried to help her. I had found her nightgown stained with a red oval. I had found the gunshot wound to her chest.

In the dream, I drifted on.

I found my dad next. That part was flat-out untrue; in real life, he had died in his bed, shot in the head while he was still asleep. I had found him last. But now, in the dream, he was in the kitchen too, lying spread eagle on the floor, his head blown open, brain and bone and blood like grayscale confetti on the boards.

The door to the porte cochere was open; it was December, and even in New Orleans, December was cold. The frigid air came in like waves that hit me at the knee; in real life, everything had smelled like shit and piss and body cavities blown open, but now I tasted grass, tasted mud, tasted catfish, tasted the cool, wet gravel of the drive under the porte cochere. That night, I had thought the killer had escaped through the door. I went after him. I had some idea—I must have believed—that I could catch him.

And I had caught him, in a way, I guess. Gard was sitting in a webbed lawn chair, where he and Dad liked to drink on hot nights under the porte cochere. One hand was wrapped around the aluminum arm rest; the other held the .38, which had slipped out of his mouth and had snagged on the pearl-snap shirt he thought made him look like a cowboy. On the ground was the pillow he had used to improvise a silencer—why I'd heard thumps instead of gunshots, why I hadn't interrupted my fuck. Gard's back was to me, his head hanging over the lawn chair, facing me upside down. His eyes were blue, a bioluminescent glow.

He raised the .38. Some of the soft tissue from his palate clung to the barrel, a black clump that broke the gun's clean lines. He traced a circle in the air.

Every night, I woke screaming.

Tonight was Sunday, almost a week since Mason had tried to shoot me on the steps of DuPage First Methodist. I sat in bed, hunched over, sobbing into my knees.

Richard's breathing changed when he woke. His hand found my back, ran up my spine, squeezed my shoulder.

"I'm sorry," I whispered.

He pulled me down to lie next to him, hugging me against him while I cried, his chin resting on my shoulder. After a while, he started shifting around, trying to pull his hips back. I sniffled into the pillow, wiped my face, and scooted back until I made contact again. Richard pulled his hips back again. I slid with him, grinding into his erection.

"Elien," he said, his breathing uneven. "I'm sorry, it's just a reaction to . . . to what I feel for you. I know it's inappropriate, and I—"

I pressed back harder, and then I took his wrist, and slid his hand down between my legs. I never got hard anymore. Never. Weight gain, emotional numbness, and sexual dysfunction—including the inability to orgasm. The holy trinity of side effects from antidepressants, and I had enough antidepressants in me to pep up a clown college. But I kept Richard's hand in place. We'd done this before, and he knew what I wanted. He touched me for a while through my briefs. Then he rocked into me, slowly at first, then with more insistence. I wasn't going to bone up, but it was still nice to be appreciated.

"Make love to me," I whispered into the pillow.

He kissed my neck. "Another night, when you're feeling better."

Kicking my way free of the briefs, I wrapped his hand around me, still limp, and said, "Fuck me."

"I don't think—"

I rolled over, kissed him, and forced him onto his back. I worked his boxers down, took him in my mouth, and gave him some attention. First-class attention. I knew when he was close because he got mouthy, started saying dirty things he'd never normally let slip, and that's when I pulled off.

"Fuck me," I said, wiping the back of my hand across my mouth.

Richard pressed me into the mattress, got my leg over his shoulder, and worked a lubed finger into me. Then another.

"Just fuck me," I said.

"You get what I give you," he said. This was the side that came out during sex. His fingers twisted, punching the breath out of me. "Who owns this ass?"

"You do," I whispered.

"Who decides what you get?"

"You do," I said, a little louder.

He played with me for a while, and then he fucked me. At first, the pace was steady. Then it grew ragged, harder. I kept my eyes open, staring up at the ceiling. Not feeling anything, I had discovered, wasn't the same as feeling nothing. It was kind of the opposite actually. It was intense. An intense inversion. A hunger to feel something. Anything. I hooked my free leg, trying to pull Richard into me. I put my arm over my eyes and started to cry.

Richard's hips bucked. He had one hand on my chest like he was trying to stop a train. "Elien—Elien—"

"Just fuck me," I said through the tears.

He jerked his way through the orgasm, and then he fell on top of me. The first few times, I had thought maybe he'd had a heart attack. Then, for a while, it had been endearing. Now I lay there, pinned by his weight, by sweaty, sagging skin, his mouth hot against my neck.

I visualized the farthest point in space I could imagine, the farthest distance a particle could travel away from anything else—no stars, no planets, no comets, not even a black hole. That distant place. Just a particle, floating by itself. I kept telling myself I felt nothing, felt absolutely nothing, felt absolutely nothing at all. I was distantly aware that I was sobbing so hard I was shaking, even with Richard's weight on top of me.

After a while, he got up, favoring one knee, and made his way to the locked bag where he kept the good stuff. He fumbled with something. A hypodermic needle flashed in the light of the clock radio. He tapped the syringe, tested the plunger.

"Ok," he whispered as he sat next to me, stroking my hair. "Give me an arm." The cold wetness of a sterilizing wipe ran over my bicep, and then the sting of the needle followed.

I cried for a while, my head in Richard's lap, and then I wasn't me anymore. I was a thousand drops of something better, suspended in ether. I was blue. I was a swarm of fireflies.

In my last moments of clarity, I remembered Mason's eyes as he tried to kill me, the glint of blue fire. I had to know. I had to know. I had to know.

And then the wind blew, and I was nothing.

DAG (2)

I was slumped over the kitchen table, listening to a really nice beluga track, when Mom sat down next to me. She took out one of my earbuds and said, "Dagobert, your father and I would like to talk to you."

I took the earbud and put it back in.

It had been a week.

A week since I had looked in my rearview mirror and seen Mason on the steps of DuPage First Methodist.

A week since I had watched my best friend from high school pull a gun on an innocent man.

A week since I had grappled with him.

A week since the gun had bucked in my hand, and a blue firefly had floated out of Mason's mouth, and the world had stopped making sense.

"Dagobert. Dagobert!"

I thumbed up the volume on the iPod, and after a while, my mom went away.

The kitchen smelled like chili powder and garlic, like sage and oregano, like trout done in Mom's cast iron skillet. The table was smooth and cool under my cheek. From where I sat, I could see out the back door, across the little stretch of grass, all the way to the Montgomery's shed on the lot behind us. I might as well have been looking across an ocean.

A hand came to rest on my back; even through my shirt, I could tell it was my dad's: the calluses, the size, the way he nudged the same vertebra with his thumb every time. He sat down in the seat Mom had vacated. He took the iPod from me, mashed it—the poor guy had no idea what he was doing—and eventually swore and gave up.

"This is pathetic," I said, plucking out the earbuds.

"Oh," he said. "You should see me with the VCR. I'm a whiz with the VCR."

"You still own a VCR?"

"Some of your mom's favorite movies are on videocassette. *Black Beauty, The Buttercream Gang*, that one about the dumplings. *The Dumpling Gang*. Is that it?"

"Lot of movies about gangs."

"I'm not sure." He called over my head. "Sweetheart, what was the dumpling movie?"

Mom's footsteps moved behind me. "*The Buttercream Gang*."

"No, the one about dumplings."

"I don't know what you're talking about with dumplings, Hubert, I really don't."

"Mom, sit down," I said. "Let's get this over with so you can both go back to feeling incredibly self-satisfied about how good you are as parents."

"Ouch," Mom said as she took a seat at the table.

"That's not very fair," Dad said.

"It's true. You were so proud when I came out. You were so proud when I decided to be a cop. You were so proud when I got a participation trophy in soccer in third grade."

"You kicked a goal," Dad said.

"Against my own team," I said, and then I had to pinch the corners of my eyes and breathe slowly. "Guess Mason just got to experience the adult version of that."

"Dagobert LeBlanc," Dad said. "You might be twenty-seven years old, but I will beat your ass red with my belt if you ever say anything like that again."

"You don't even own a belt," I said. "You got suspenders because you said your last belt gave you a hernia."

Mom's fingers ran over my head, tickling the short, buzzed hairs. "Your father was right. That belt was a menace."

"He was my best friend," I said. "And I killed him."

"The preliminary findings said it was self-inflicted," Dad said.

I turned into the table.

"Dag, sweetheart," Mom said. "It was not your fault."

"He would have shot that boy," Dad said. "You said so yourself."

The image that came on me was so sudden and so shocking that I had to tense against it: knocking over the table, beating the shit out of them, hitting them over and over again until they wouldn't talk anymore, wouldn't say anything anymore. It was hard to breathe through the intensity of the thought. My fists were too tight, my back was too tight, my chest was too tight.

"Yeah," I finally whispered. "I know."

"Your father and I think you should see someone," Mom said. "This is killing you, Dagobert."

When I closed my eyes, I could feel the gun between our hands. I remembered the force of it, driving into my palm when it fired. I groped blindly across the table until I found the earbuds, and then I jammed them back into place and disappeared under the sea.

I couldn't hear the disappointed sighs. I couldn't see the disappointed glances. After a while, they left.

The problem, though, was that they'd stirred up all the shit that had been sinking so nicely to the bottom of my brain. The problem was that I knew they were partially right: this was killing me. I knew that what I'd seen was impossible: there was no such thing as blue fireflies that came out of someone's mouth, no such thing as blue fire that burned in someone's eyes. But I also knew that I'd seen it. I'd seen it at Ray Field's house. I'd seen it again with Mason.

I wondered if this was how Mason had felt: this creeping uncertainty, the feeling that he couldn't trust his own senses, couldn't put himself back together because somebody had mixed in pieces from the wrong puzzle. He'd said those bizarre things about Elien. He'd been trying to tell me, I realized now, that he needed help. And I hadn't listened. I'd been too irritated with him. I'd been sick of shouldering all the slack that Mary Ann had sloughed. I'd wanted him to lay off of Elien. I'd missed the warning signs. I'd missed Mason's cry for help. I'd been so focused on Elien that—

My head shot up from the table. I blinked. I'd been so focused on Elien being cute and funny and maybe a little sweet that somehow I'd missed the strangest link in the last few days: Elien had been at both of those inexplicable occurrences. As a deputy, I'd come across a few deceased people—usually elderly people, while I was responding to a callout for a wellness check, the way I had for Ray. But I'd never seen the blue fireflies until Elien was there. The same thing had happened when Mason had died: another blue light.

Except it all sounded batshit crazy.

And that was the choice it came down to: either I was crazy, or I wasn't. Deciding I was crazy wouldn't get me any answers about Mason's death. If I wasn't crazy, though, then something seriously weird was happening, and Elien Martel was involved in it. I wanted to know what it was.

For the first time in days, my stomach grumbled. I got up from the table, dug around in the refrigerator until I came up with the leftover trout, the slaw, and a crock of baked beans. I was making myself a plate when Dad walked into the kitchen.

His eyes went immediately to the food. "Oh," was all he said.

"I'm on paid leave for at least two weeks," I said, hearing the disjointed remark, not fully able to explain why it mattered.

Dad just nodded.

"I'm not dead."

"No, son." He shoved his hands in his pockets, brought them out, shoved them in again. "Are you thinking about hurting yourself?"

"No, I'm thinking about that chocolate silk pie Mom made." I added another portion of the trout and then, just to be safe, some more beans. "For dessert."

Dad looked more confused than ever, but he just nodded.

Carrying the plate back to my room, I placed a call to Brennan Kade, a buddy who did investigative work on the side. I told him what I needed, and then I found my tablet and pulled up a browser. I was going to find out what had happened to Mason. What had really happened. And I was going to start by figuring out who the fuck Elien Martel really was.

ELIEN (3)

The next morning, while Richard was in the shower, I went down to the kitchen. I poured myself orange juice and stood at the island. I was sore from the night before. Sex with Richard had never been that frequent, and it had become less so as the pills took effect. Sipping my orange juice, I opened my pill organizer and dumped the vitamins and supplements and prescriptions into my hand. Blues and yellows and whites. I had almost died a week before, and those moments of visceral fear had been the closest thing to feeling alive since Gard had killed my parents and then himself.

I went back upstairs to Richard's bathroom. The water wasn't running, but when I touched the handle, the door was locked. I knocked softly.

No answer.

I knocked a little harder.

Nothing.

It wasn't hard to imagine why; Richard hated giving me ketamine, hated when I got so out of control. He didn't want to deal with me yet. Fine. Fair. He didn't have to. I had a question for him, a pretty important one. It was also a pretty straightforward one.

Why the fuck was I still alive if I couldn't feel anything?

I went back down to the kitchen and fed the pills into the garbage disposal.

When Richard came downstairs, I was sitting at the island, sipping my orange juice. He kissed my temple and ran a hand down my back.

"Do you need another shot?"

I shook my head.

"Elien."

"No. I'm fine."

"No ideations?"

"Not a single one."

"You're not thinking about harming yourself?"

I met his eyes and smiled. "I'm thinking about going to the library."

"That's a change."

"I can read."

"I know you can read, sweetheart." He poured coffee; when he held it out to me, I shook my head. "I don't think you've ever gone to the library while we've been dating. What's going on?"

"Do you keep track of where I go?"

"I just meant you've never talked about going to the library."

Smiling over the orange juice, I said, "You didn't answer my question."

"No, I don't keep track of your movements, Elien. You know that."

"You could."

"I don't."

"I'd put an app on my phone if you wanted me to."

Richard sighed, spooned sugar into his coffee, and stirred.

"You could watch me on your phone, follow me as I drive into the city, find one of those cosmetic surgery places where the only limit is money." I squeezed the flab hanging over my waistband. "How much to have them lipo me, do you think?"

"Are you upset with me?" Richard asked.

"No."

"Is this about last night?"

"I got exactly what I wanted last night. Did you like last night?"

"Yes, I enjoyed it very much. I love you, and I love making love to you." Richard tried to catch my gaze. "Are you saying these things to hurt yourself? Body dysphoria—"

"Please don't talk to me about body dysphoria or dysmorphia or any of that stuff today."

Richard's spoon chimed against the mug as he ran it in circles through the coffee.

"I'd like a ride to the library, please. Or I can take an Uber."

"I have to be in New Orleans today. Muriel can take you."

"Muriel needs to go to work. I'll Uber."

"She drives right by the house. She can take you. Do you want to stay in Bragg all day?"

"I don't know," I said. "I'll take an Uber back." I smiled over the rim of my glass again. "You can keep track of me with your little app."

"I don't know why you're upset with me," Richard said, taking out his phone to place the call, "but I wish you'd tell me."

"I'm not upset," I said. "I'm having a great day. Maybe if you watch your little app, you'll see me pay a visit to a special friend."

"Morning, Muriel," Richard said. "Do you think you could pick up Elien on your way in? Perfect. Thank you."

When Richard disconnected, I said, "He's a fireman."

"Have you seen my briefcase?"

"I put it in your study. He's very strong. Just a few years older than me. He lets me wear his helmet."

"Elien, we've talked about this. I'm perfectly happy for you to have other consensual relationships; in fact, at your age, I expect it."

"What does that mean?"

"It means this is why I insisted we agree on an open relationship."

I carried my half-drunk juice to the sink. "Richard?"

"Yes, dear?"

I hesitated, and then I dumped out the juice. "Never mind."

When he came back down with his briefcase, he kissed me. Pulling back, he added, "Elien, sweetheart, I think you should talk to Zahra about this."

"About what?" I asked as I loaded the few dishes from breakfast.

"This defensiveness after intimacy."

"Oh, I thought you meant my nymphomania."

My back was to him, and he didn't quite sigh, but I could feel his weariness. "Have a nice day."

"Or maybe my anorexia."

His steps clicked toward the front door.

"I'm wasting away, Richard."

I waited until I couldn't hear the Lexus anymore, and then I went out to the porch. It was a bright October day, cooler than usual, and the sun outlined the bald cedars and the tupelo trees on the far side of the Okhlili. Something moved along the bank, disturbing the brush; the morning painted the vegetation gold. A swamp rabbit, maybe. Or a cottonmouth. Farther north, where the river fanned out to form Bayou Pere Rigaud, alligators swam under curtains of Spanish moss. Tourists often sighted black bears along the Tangipahoa. I wondered if any of those wild beasts were as vicious as me.

Muriel arrived in her Subaru. When I hopped into the passenger seat, she was applying eyeliner.

"Want me to do that?" I asked.

"Good gravy, you'd probably do better than I am." She touched up a corner and then checked herself in the mirror. Muriel was probably in her fifties, wanted to look like she was in her forties, and acted like she was in her sixties. I guessed she'd always been mothering and clucking, probably ever since she was old enough to walk. In a cartoon, she'd have worn a long white apron that she fanned herself with. "Child, you are skin and bones."

"Richard's been talking behind my back."

She pinched my wrist. "I'm getting you a beignet and a coffee."

"Hey, ow."

"I could fit your heinie in a pencil box."

"That sounds awful."

"And you're grumpy today, too." She turned her full attention on me, one hand reaching out. "Why are you grumpy when you're just so cute?"

"If you pinch my cheek, I'm going to bite off those fake nails."

"Lord, Elien. You are on a tear, aren't you?"

"To the library, Jeeves."

"I am a highly educated professional," she said, pointing a tube of lipstick at me before returning her attention to the mirror.

"Noted."

"I have a B.S.N. from Tulane."

"The Harvard of the Bayou."

"I have an M.S.N. from Louisiana State."

"I've heard the stories. Stonewall Jackson was at the commencement, right?"

"I am a PMHNP-BC. Do you know what that means?"

"It sounds like a mouthful."

"Why are you being so awful?"

"Because I feel awful."

"Well," she said, stuffing the tube of lipstick away and focusing on me again, "do what any decent person does: bottle it up, smile, and tell your priest."

"I will remember that."

"And just so we're clear, young man, I am not your chauffeur."

"Yet here we are." I clapped. "Library, Jeeves."

Sighing, she shifted into drive, and we headed toward Bragg.

Muriel dropped me at the Bragg branch of the DuPage Parish Library; when she asked about picking me up, I told her to keep the car running at the end of the block, at which point she rolled her eyes and drove off.

The library was from the 70s, built of brick, with skinny, floor-to-ceiling windows breaking the walls at regular intervals. I went inside, passed through the RFID gates, and found myself in one of those spaces that was desperately bleak in spite of everyone's best efforts. Clearly, the library staff had tried to gussy up the place with banners and posters and colorful displays of books and puzzles and DVDs. But nothing could fix what was really wrong with the space: the low ceilings, the fluorescent lighting, the industrial carpet, the smell of cabbage.

I hadn't been in a library since high school. College hadn't interested me, although Richard still brought it up from time to time, and even in high school, my visits to the library had been strictly functional and as short as possible. Now, staring around me, I remembered why. I saw the retirees, the housewives, the kids. Newspapers on sticks. An ancient man paying a fine with pennies. A bulletin board with a flyer advertising WARHAMMER GAME NIGHT BRING YOUR OWN ARMY SLAY A CHAOS LORD. I wished somebody would slay—slew?—me.

"Good morning," a young woman said. She was black, her hair in tight braids, and she was beautiful in a bright yellow dress. "May I help you?"

"Do I look that out of place?"

"Just a little lost."

Pointing at the sign, I said, "Slay or slew?"

"Slew is the past tense. Why? Did you slay a chaos lord?"

"Just ten or so."

She smiled. "That's very impressive."

"I try to keep my hand in."

"All right," she said, "If you need anything—"

"Actually, I'm doing some research on monsters."

"Monsters?"

"Yeah. Can you point me to the books?"

With a grin, she waved a hand around us.

"Very funny. The monster books."

"Well, you'll have to tell me a little more. Stories about monsters? There's this really great gay vampire series. Something like that?"

"No, not—wait. Maybe. Just, you know, for research."

"Of course."

"But really I'm looking for, I don't know. Legends, I guess. Or history. Something like that."

"Cultural anthropology, folklore, that kind of thing?"

I shrugged. "Sorry. When you're this pretty, you don't have to learn big words like that."

"Oh Lord. All right, I think we can find some stuff. What monster?"

"Don't you just have a—I don't know. Like a Wikipedia on them. But in book form."

Her eyebrows went up. "Like, an encyclopedia?"

"Sure, that's a thing."

"Uh huh. Well. We actually might have a monster encyclopedia. Or something similar. And that's a good starting place, I guess. Let's see what we can find."

"First, you have to tell me your name."

"Kennedy."

"All right, Miss Kennedy: to the books."

"Uh huh," Kennedy said to herself as she led me to a computer.

A few minutes later, after roving the shelves, Kennedy sat me at a table and laid down three books. *A Beginner's Guide to Monsters*, *Monsters A-Z*, and what was clearly an illustrated book for children called *Sneaky, Scary, Bump in the Night*.

I tapped the cover.

"I was worried," Kennedy said. "These others have some pretty big words."

"Miss Kennedy."

Shrugging, she opened *A Beginner's Guide to Monsters* to the table of contents. "What were you looking for in particular?"

"It's like a blue fire that floats around. Maybe it comes out of someone's mouth. Maybe it's in their eyes."

"Uh huh," Kennedy said again, so quietly this time that I barely heard her. "Is this something you saw?"

"Oh no. I mean, just on TV. I don't know what it's called."

"What show?"

"I don't even remember."

"Well—"

"Oh, maybe it's like a firefly. Is there a firefly monster?"

Kennedy paused, and then she flipped pages. "There's something called a will o' the wisp. Have you heard of that?"

I shook my head.

"It might look like a firefly." She found the entry in the table of contents and turned to the entry. The illustration was a pretty lame glowing blue ball. "People thought they would lead you astray, maybe even lead you to your death if you followed them. It was probably swamp gas or bioluminescence."

I scanned the entry. "It doesn't say anything about possession. Or bringing people back to life."

Kennedy was staring at me now.

"It was in the TV show," I added.

"Well, let's try the index in this one," she said, grabbing *Monsters A-Z*. She ran her finger down the page. "Possession. Ghosts, vampires. Ok, what about reanimation. Blech. It's just got zombies."

"What if I told you it was local?"

Kennedy closed the book slowly. "The TV show?"

"Right, the TV show. Would it make a difference if the TV show were set in Louisiana?"

"Maybe," Kennedy said. "If it were relying on regional folklore."

"Let's go with that."

A few minute later, Kennedy came back with a massive book that looked at least a hundred years old. The leather binding was flaking in places, and the lettering looked like genuine gold leaf. When she set it down, dust floated up from the cover. *New Orleans and La Louisiane: Chorography, Ethnology, and the Native Episteme.*

"Uh."

"Lots of big words in this one."

"Yeah, I can see that."

"Better take this one too," she said, laying *Sneaky, Scary, Bump in the Night* on top. "Just in case you need reference material."

"That seems like a good idea."

"Great. Let's check these out. Do you have your library card?"

"Uh."

"Ok," she said. "We'll do that too."

"Thanks, Miss Kennedy."

"Uh huh."

"Oh, um, Miss Kennedy?"

"Yes?"

"You did say something about a gay vampire book."

DAG (4)

I got to Mills Diner on time for my meeting with Kade, snagged a booth, and considered calling the whole thing off. Asking Kade to look into Mason's life was one thing; Mason was dead, and it couldn't hurt him. Asking Kade to investigate Elien was something else entirely. Instead of leaving, though, I put my earbuds in and listened to a nice *Whales of the South Pacific* track. I ran my hands along the table's chrome banding. My fingers left smears in the greasy skim on top of the Masonite. Every breath brought in the smell of cheap coffee and a well-seasoned griddle.

The diner wasn't exactly busy at this hour, but Mills never really quieted down until ten or eleven. It had the usual diner décor: vinyl banquettes, smudged chrome, a jukebox that only played Elvis. On the walls, framed newspapers provided a brief cultural history of Bragg for the uninitiated and the nostalgic. Up there, you could see the day Mary Balomer won Miss Louisiana 1978, as well as Hank Chuck Lagard's six-foot gator, football jerseys from the Braxton Bragg Memorial High team that took 2nd place in state, and, of course, an autographed photo of Huey Long, with the Kingfish shaking hands with Bragg's mayor at the time, Emile Crawford.

I was trying to think of a clever way to combine the Kingfish and the Crawfish, and it seemed just within reach, when someone slapped a file down on the table.

"Thought that was you," Kade muttered.

Brennan Kade was tall and built, although some of that build was getting a little . . . softer since he'd left the force. Like Mason, Kade had gotten shot on duty; unlike Mason, it had been a career-ending injury, and Kade's exit from the sheriff's department hadn't been easy on him—or on anyone who liked him, which usually included me. He rubbed a hand over his shaved head, fixed me with a hazel gaze, and waited.

Pulling out my earbuds, I twined the cord around one finger. From the seat next to me, I lifted a second folder and slid it across the table. Deals with Kade weren't about money, at least, not for me; he did PI work, and that meant sometimes he needed access to Sheriff's Department records, so normally, we worked out some kind of trade.

"Please tell me you're going to eat," I said. "I'm starving." I massaged my forehead. "Christ, is that fucked up? I've still got to eat, right?"

"I could eat," Kade said. "A burger sounds good right about now."

Flipping open the folder, I scanned the pages for a moment; some of the pictures slid out, Mason and Mary Ann and Mason's house, and I glanced at them before stuffing them back in. I slapped the folder shut again, dropped it on the table, and put my head in my hands. "Do they serve beer here? Tell me they have beer."

That hazel gaze didn't waver; all Kade said was, "It's a diner. What do you think?"

"This is bad." I tapped the folder. "This is really bad, isn't it? I can see it. You've got no poker face. Strip poker? Please, you'd be naked in five seconds." I sat back, crossed my arms, and said, "Just tell me if it's really bad. That's all I'm asking. I need it to be bad, but fuck me, I just need you to tell me before I read it."

Resting his arms on the table, Kade said, "For starters, it's a good thing we aren't playing strip poker because you don't want to see this naked. But also, it's not good. Mason Comeaux's falling apart. The photographs in that folder will tell you everything you need to know. While his house is in shambles, his homelife isn't any better. Mary Ann moved out a few weeks ago, and he seems to have given up. It looks like he doesn't even know how to start a lawn mower anymore, for fuck's sake."

For a moment, I just sat there, biting my lip. Then I shrugged and said, "Guess he doesn't have to worry about that anymore." I unfolded one of the thin napkins, pinning it to the table between my hands, the paper stretched so tight that it split along one edge. "Mason's . . . he's dead. And fuck, you are going to hear all of it one way or another. He went crazy or something. I had to . . . Jesus, I had to stop him, and then it just happened. He was going to kill this kid." I stopped, staring at the white square between my hands, and then I balled it up and batted it toward the floor. "Paid leave until they figure this out, but there's no possible way of figuring it out, so I guess I'm saying, that," I nodded at the folder I'd brought for Kade, "is the last thing I'm going to be able to get you for a while."

Kade tapped the folder again. "Then who emptied his bank account?"

"Huh?"

Tap. Tap. Tap. "It's all in the folder. I included the bank transaction. His account was emptied less than a week ago."

"Jesus." I stared at the folder and said again, "Jesus." Then, wiping my face, I said, "Yeah, ok. Thank you. I guess . . . maybe drugs? I mean, how do you explain something like this? His mom plays tennis with my mom. What's the fucking warmup? Take a few swings, limber up that tennis elbow. Hey, sorry again my boy killed your boy."

Kade shrugged and grabbed the file I'd given him. "You're asking the wrong guy. All I can tell you is good luck." He flipped the folder open to stare at the papers. "Tell me about Cassandra Mayfield and Cyprus Manor."

"Right." I sat up a little straighter, retrieved my phone, and tapped through several screens. Kade's request this time had been a little odd, and I checked my notes to make sure I had it right. "Twenty-three years old. White. Female. It looks like the investigation started pretty hot. The family filed a missing person report, and the DuPage Sheriff's Department took it seriously. Nothing gets the buzzards flapping like a rich white girl vanishing, and the sheriff wanted Cassandra back home before the AP could send it out. The deputies he put on it are solid guys, Castanera and Fletcher. They had a line on a 'person of interest,'" I drew the quotes with one hand, "who was, of course, a black man who had the bad luck of taking odd jobs in the Mayfields' neighborhood. The guy was new to the area, he'd been in Leakesville for a possession charge, and he immediately moved up to number one on their list." I sat back and shrugged. "You can guess how far they got with him."

Kade leaned back in the booth, the vinyl crackling under him. "I'm assuming they found nothing to hold the guy. Especially with no hard evidence to pin it on him."

I shook my head. "They didn't even get that far. Dante Coleman slipped and accidentally put his head through a noose. They found him a few days later. Castanera and Fletcher are pretty sure the Mayfields weren't involved, at least, not directly, but some good old boys decided to take matters into their own hands. Castanera and Fletcher kept digging. The more they dug, the less they found. Dante Coleman hadn't done jack shit since getting out of Leakesville—just a guy trying to make a living."

"Fuck," Kade said with a sigh. "Anything else I need to know? About the area or her case?"

I shuffled the flatware that had been wrapped in the napkin. Then my hands stopped, and I opened the folder in front of Kade. I started laying out the photographs I'd printed out for him. Some of them looked like they were from college yearbooks. Some of them, with dangerous-looking shoulder pads, looked like they were 80s glamor shots. Some of them were in black and white, women with their hair marcelled and looking like they'd hung out with Douglas Fairbanks on the weekends.

"Eliza Powell," I said, tapping what looked like the earliest photograph. "1927. Lessie Lynne, 1933. Theresa Cannette, 1936. Then it's quiet for a while—or people are being made to be quiet. Cissy Taranto, 1988. Miranda Blanch, 1991. Janice Faulkner, no relation, 2000. Clair Cannette, 2008. That one is a relation, by the way. She's a great niece or something of the one from 36. And, of course, Cassandra Mayfield. All of these girls were reported missing and were never found. All of them lived within a twenty-mile radius of Cyprus Manor. And want to hear the freaky part?"

Kade's eyes moved from picture to picture, following my finger. A waitress wearing a Mills Diner t-shirt stopped at the booth, an order pad in hand, and he glanced up at her.

"Are you two ready to order?" she asked.

"I'll have a double-bacon cheeseburger with a side of fries and a soda," Kade told her before glancing toward me.

"Same."

Her pen flew over the pad, and she left without another word.

"Ok," Kade said. "What's the freaky part?"

"Twenty-three years old." I tapped the first picture. "Twenty-three." I tapped the next. "Twenty-three. Twenty-three. Twenty-three. All of them twenty-three years old." A little grin twisted one side of my mouth. "I thought Theresa Cannette was an outlier because the report said her age was twenty-four. After all the shit with . . . with Mason, I couldn't sleep. I found the 1930 census. I did the math. She was fucking twenty-three years old, Kade. They just got it wrong on the report."

Kade let out a groan. "Why would someone want to kidnap and possibly kill twenty-three-year-old women?"

I shook my head. "Hey, where's the stuff on Elien?"

Kade was off someplace else.

"Kade, hey. The stuff on Elien Martel?"

"There isn't any stuff on Elien Martel."

I shook my head again. "He's twenty-two, maybe twenty-three, lives in DuPage Parish. Boyfriend's name is Richard. He drives a Lexus."

"You want to know how many Elien Martel's I found in the state of Louisiana?"

"I know there's at least one."

"Three. One of them is ninety years old in a nursing home in Baton Rouge. One of them is forty-six and is currently fighting the good fight to get his workman's comp claim processed in Lake Charles. The other is sixty-three, gayer than Cher, and operates the Purple Love Rhino Personal Pleasure Palace in a suburb of Alexandria."

"That's probably him," I said.

Kade rolled his eyes.

"I need that stuff on him, Kade."

"Ok, well, he doesn't exist. Get me another name, and I'll dig up whatever I can."

"Yeah," I said, slumping down in the vinyl banquette. "Ok."

"Sorry, man."

"No problem," I said. "I guess you'll just have to get the check."

ELIEN (5)

New Orleans and La Louisiane: Chorography, Ethnology, and the Native Episteme was not the page turner that its title promised it would be. After my fourth attempt to get through a chapter on a myth about a great flood that sounded real shades-of-Noah's-Ark, I switched over to *Sneaky, Scary, Bump in the Night*, which had cool illustrations and a kickass chapter on mummies and canopic jars, but didn't give me any clues about a blue firefly monster native to Louisiana.

When I finished *Sneaky, Scary, Bump in the Night*, I looked around for Kennedy. She'd gotten me this far—maybe I could hire her as a research assistant or something, with assistant being my very loose term for the person who did all the work and then gave me a nice, one-paragraph summary. But Kennedy was reading to a group of preschoolers, and when I tried to catch her attention by holding *New Orleans and La Louisiane: Chorography, Ethnology, and the Native Episteme* over my head, she gave me a dismissive wave and went back to reading.

I picked up the gay vampire book—vampires were already kind of gay, but this one was uber gay—and read for a while. My brain kept going back to the monster. A part of my brain registered the way that sounded and pointed out, kindly, that there was no such thing as monsters and, even more kindly, I probably just needed Zahra to write me another scrip. But part of me wasn't ready to let go. I had seen that blue light in Mason's eyes. I had seen it drift out of his mouth after he had died. I had seen it in Ray's apartment, and I had seen it in Ray's eyes too. I had dreamed it in Gard's eyes, and now I wondered if the dream was more than a dream. So much of what I remembered from that night was fractured. Classic symptom of PTSD: the inability to integrate sensory input, especially from the traumatic event. I remembered the creak of the boards. I remembered the smell of fried catfish. I remembered the cold air against my legs.

But blue fire in Gard's dead eyes? Christ, I didn't know. It was in the dream, wasn't it?

What I needed was a specialist. Like somebody who specialized in monsters, the way some scientists specialized in bugs or birds or whatever the hell else you could imagine. Even better, I needed someone who could get rid of this damn thing. Kind of like the ghostbusters. Combined with a pest exterminator.

Actually, that wasn't a bad idea.

Setting aside the gay vampire book—the lucky bloodsucker was currently getting *ferociously mounted* by his vampire sire, along with getting a few *languid poundings* and *masterly invasions*, which might have been the title of a sci-fi special on TV—I pulled out my phone and searched for *monster hunters*. I mostly got books and a few cuckoo websites. Then I searched again for *monster hunters real*. That didn't turn up much except for a few blogs praising a company called Critter Catchers. I found their website, and they actually looked legit. They sounded great, in fact, except that they were located in Parson's Hollow, Pennsylvania.

Ok. Maybe not my best idea.

Except I did kind of feel like I was on the right track. Kennedy had looked at me kind of crazy when I'd asked about local monsters, but the more I thought about it, the more it made sense. Encyclopedias and generic web searches were going to give me very general answers. What I needed was something specific. If this . . . thing had been in the area for a while, then someone, at some point, must have written something down.

I did another search, this time for Louisiana folklore, and carried my books to a bench outside the library. Then I started making calls. The woman at the Louisiana Folklore Society hung up on me. The man at the Bayou Culture Collaborative treated me to every English swear word in the book, and quite a few French ones that I had to guess on. I worked my way down the list, hitting every historical and cultural-anthropological society (Kennedy would have been proud of my new vocabulary) I could find. The good news was that historical-cultural-anthropological societies didn't exactly have their phones ringing off the hooks, so it was pretty easy to get through. The bad news was that one gentleman taught me the expression, *I'll fuck your face off and then shit down your mouth hole if you call here again.* Which, it seemed to me, was an extreme response to a question about magic blue fireflies that came out of people's mouths and sometimes made them commit murder.

When I got through to a woman at New Orleans Ghost Tours and Beignets and Real Sweet Tea, I learned why.

"It's the voodoo, honey."

"No, this is about a firefly thing. Wait. Are you telling me this is voodoo?"

"No." She blew out a breath. "Honey, nothing is voodoo, not really. I'm saying you wouldn't believe how many people call trying to figure out how to make a doll so they can stick a pin in their girlfriend's hoohaw and that kind of thing. It's just crazy. Doesn't matter if you have the patience of a saint—you work in a Louisiana, anything to do with history, even a place like this one, and you'll have crazies calling you until you're ready to pull your hair out."

"But this is a legitimate call. I'm doing research."

"About a firefly thing."

"A blue firefly thing."

"That can make people chop each other up."

"Well, I don't know. That's the whole point of doing research. I'm trying to find out."

"Can't help you, honey. My auntie had a touch of the sight, but all I can do is tell if water is fizzy or not."

"Can't everyone do that?"

"I mean before I drink it."

"Yeah, but you can see the bubbles."

"Is that all?" she asked.

"I guess."

She disconnected before I finished both words.

The October day had warmed up considerably; grabbing my books, I moved down a few benches into the shade of a black oak that still had its leaves. The DuPage Parish Library was in a neighborhood known as Fogmile: stolidly middle class, clapboard-sided shotguns with neat lawns and ten-year-old sedans and plenty of minivans. A young couple pushed a stroller on the sidewalk opposite; it wasn't until they got closer that I saw the teacup Yorkie where a baby should have been. I snapped a picture and sent it to Richard.

He sent back a laughing emoji and, *Glad you're feeling better.*

Sorry about this morning. I love you.

Thank you for saying that. I love you too. What do you want for dinner tonight?

I grinned in spite of myself. That was Richard. *Shrimp boil?*

Anything for you and then a kissy emoji..

I sent a kiss back.

My next search was for psychics. I limited myself to DuPage and St. Tammany. I didn't want to drive into New Orleans, in the first place, and in the second, I didn't want to have to deal with the fakes who catered to tourists. I caught the sound of that thought and recognized, again, how far I'd shifted in a few days; just a week before, I would have told anyone who asked that all psychics were fake. Now I was just worried about quality control.

Like historical societies and people selling timeshares, most psychics didn't seem to be overwhelmed with phone calls. The reactions I got to my question, though, were interesting.

The first three—all of them using horrifying faux-Romani accents—promised they could tell me everything I wanted to know about blue fireflies if I gave them my credit card number, for only sixty-six cents per minute plus ten dollars for the connection fee. I wasn't sure if the connection fee was imposed by the phone company or by the astral plane, but I declined.

The fourth psychic hung up.

I tried number five, six, and seven, and I got more offers from them to part the veil and probe the inner darkness, which sounded a lot like the treatment my gay vampire was getting.

I went back to number four. Her name was Suzette Davis, which didn't sound particularly psychic, and her psychic parlor was located half a mile away, just off the Quartier. I guessed a psychic parlor was probably pretty similar to a regular parlor but with more crystals and polyester, but I kept thinking about how she had hung up: no hesitation, no fumbling. Solid and definitive. I called again, and the phone rang until it went to a pre-recorded voicemail.

So I walked half a mile, carrying my books.

Suzette's store was located on the second story of a strip mall that dated back to the 70s and had survived the Quartier's purge and redevelopment. She was located above a Chinese take-out place, and the smell of eggrolls filled the staircase as I went up. From the landing at the top of the stairs came the sound of keys jingling and then hurried footsteps. A woman came into view, barreling toward me.

"Hey," I said. "Hi."

She froze.

Suzette—if that's who she was—had coppery ringlets, the color obviously out of a box, and hard eyes. She was wearing a track suit that had slipped a few inches, exposing the lacy waistband of her underwear. For a moment, she studied me, and then she slipped a vape pen out of her pocket and hit it twice. Some of the vapor slipped out of the corner of her mouth.

"Well?" she said.

"I called."

"Sorry, I'm closed." She took a few steps, obviously trying to sidle past me.

I moved into her path. "I just wanted to ask you a few questions about those firefly things. I'll pay."

"Kid, you're very pretty, but I've got pepper gel on my keyring, and I've got a knife. I will fuck you up if you don't get out of my way."

"Ok, ok," I said, moving down a few steps. Holding up my hands, I said, "You're the only person who acted like they knew what I was talking about. Everybody else just wants to charge me sixty-six cents a minute to channel the Prince of Darkness."

"You're serious? You're really asking about this? It's not some messed-up prank?"

"I saw one come out of a guy's mouth. He was dead, and he grabbed me. Another guy tried to shoot me. I saw one of these things with him, too."

"You want psychic advice? Here's psychic advice: get on a fucking plane, or you're dead."

She charged down the steps.

"Please," I said, getting into her path again, already preparing myself for the pepper spray. "Please, I think . . . I think this thing killed my parents, too." I bit my lip, trying to hold back a crazy laugh, because hearing it out loud was ten times worse than skirting the edges of it in my brain. "Please."

Hitting the vape again, Suzette eyed me. When she pulled the pen away, she said, "Hands."

"What?"

"Show me your hands."

I held them out.

"Left one."

I offered it.

She took it; her touch was dry, and she was shaking slightly as she ran a finger across my palm in one direction, then ran it again at a diagonal. When she released me, she let out a breath like she'd been running.

"What's going on?"

"If I tell you, will you get out of my way?"

"Yeah, whatever you want."

She held up three fingers. Her nail polish was chipped. "One: this thing, what you're talking about. Here, it used to be called a *hashok,* the thing in the grass, but you can call it a vampire or *tiyanak* or a *bantu* or goddamn *chupacabra*. Pretty much every culture has a name for it, and even though the details might be a little different, it's the same damn thing. Two: it feeds on human lives, especially on pain, and it's always hungry. Three: if you've seen it, it wants you. So I'm going to stay with my sister, God help me, and I'm going to spend the next few weeks listening to holy rollers try to save my soul until this shitstorm clears. And if you're smart, you'll do exactly what I said. You get on a plane today, and you don't come back. Now move your skinny ass."

She charged past me, and the sound of her steps on the asphalt faded.

Hashok, the thing in the grass.

I caught an Uber home. The afternoon was sunny; heat radiated up from the drive, and I tasted gravel dust as my ride left. The house looked the way it always did: the fresh white paint, the picture windows, the rocking chairs on the porch. Home. This was home, and it was real, and I laughed because here, with just the sound of the Okhlili murmuring in my ears, the dreams and the craziness, Ray and Mason and Suzette in the stairwell, it all seemed like I'd been half-asleep and was finally waking up.

When the breeze shifted, I smelled shit and rot.

Something had died nearby. Animals came out of the bayou all the time, some of them injured, some of them old. They crossed the Okhlili and died on the lawn. It would upset Richard, so I opened the garage and left my books on the workbench and grabbed a shovel. I followed the stench, hoping it would be small. A swamp rabbit I could just toss back across the river. A fox. A squirrel.

As I came around the house, something burst into motion. I barely caught a glimpse of it, white and thin and tall, crashing into the tree line and disappearing into the brush. A flock of crows startled up from the branches. And then I saw, on Richard's manicured lawn, what was causing the smell. Entrails. Intestines. Yards of it. It took me a moment to recognize what it was because it had been stretched out in a strange pattern.

And then I realized it wasn't a pattern, at least, not the way I'd been thinking. It was my name. Elien. Spelled out in guts across the grass.

DAG (6)

In my bedroom, I spent hours going over the folder that Kade had given me. Nothing on Elien, unfortunately, but plenty of stuff on Mason—all of it bad. Kade had been telling the truth about the bank accounts. Mason hadn't been rolling in money; neither of us was, which was one of the perks of being a public servant. Unlike me, however, Mason had managed his paychecks pretty well. He'd had a small house, a decent car, and eight thousand dollars in a savings account. Up until last week, that was. Then he'd withdrawn it all in cash. Somehow, Kade had even gotten a video of the transaction from the bank's security camera, and sure as hell, it was Mason standing at the teller's window.

I wanted to know where that money was.

Another thing that bothered me was Mary Ann. Where was she in all of this? The pictures in the file Kade had given me had obviously been pulled from social media, and Kade had dated them and sorted them. The most recent one was from months ago, right after Mason had been shot. It showed them in the hospital, Mason still in a gown and propped up in bed, Mary Ann with her arm around his shoulders. Before Mason had been shot, they had lots of pictures together. Mary Ann, who had red hair and freckles, looked happy in all them. After the shooting, though, there was just the one. I thought of all the times Mason had told me Mary Ann had gone out of town to visit a relative. I thought of all the times I had to give a last-minute ride. I felt like an idiot for not figuring it out earlier.

The pictures of the house surprised me too. Kade had obviously swung by the house as part of his investigation, and many of the photographs showed the interior. I didn't want to know how Kade had gotten inside. I'd been to Mason's house, of course. I'd been plenty of times, even after the shooting. I'd give him rides, and sometimes I'd go inside for a beer or to watch a game. But now I was realizing I'd only seen the stuff Mason wanted me to see. I'd noticed the front lawn got a little shaggy sometimes. I'd noticed that sometimes the dishes piled up in the sink, and sometimes he'd have some clothes lying around in the living room. I'd attributed all of that to a straight guy living by himself; I'd known Mason for a long time, and he'd never been a clean freak.

But I hadn't been in the backyard in months, and it looked like a disaster. Beer cans littered the ground below the deck. Weeds and grass grew knee high. The back rooms of the house, to judge by the photographs, were just as bad. Mason's bedroom looked like a tornado had gone through it. The room he used as an office and guest room had huge holes in the walls and a long brown streak of something across the floor. It didn't make any sense, and I couldn't believe I had missed so many red flags.

A practical part of my brain told me that Mason had wanted me to miss them; he'd been careful to cut the grass in front before it got too bad, careful to keep the front rooms relatively clean in case I stepped inside. He'd perfected this mask of looking normal and talking normal and seeming normal, while the reality was that his life was spiraling out of control. That's what happened with some people suffering from depression. Sometimes, nobody had a clue because they were just so good at hiding things.

That same part of my brain told me that all the pieces were there: Mason had been struggling with severe mental illness, and in spite of seeing a therapist and attending a support group, he clearly hadn't received the help he needed. People died all the time from mental illness. In my line of work, I was the first one to find a lot of them.

But I had seen those weird blue lights. I knew, in my gut, that there was something else going on here.

From what I could tell, that something else had to do with Elien Martel, or whatever his real name was.

Dark had fallen outside. I packed up the file, grabbed my keys and then, after a moment, my Sig. I headed out through the kitchen. Mom was searing a chicken breast, and the smell of garlic was a powerful lure.

"Dinner's in five," she said.

"Save some?"

"Dagobert."

"I'll be back later, Mom."

I was out of the house before she could stop me. I drove to the DuPage Parish Sheriff's Department offices, which consisted of four buildings of brown brick in a neat cluster on the north side of Bragg. Paid leave meant a lot of things, but fortunately, it hadn't meant surrendering my keys. I let myself in through the side door, passed the locker rooms, and grabbed an empty workstation. DuPage was a quiet parish, and most of the deputies were either off duty now or out on patrol. For the moment, I had the room to myself.

Logging on, I was relieved to see my username and password still worked. I navigated to the incident reports, found the one that I'd filled out for the wellness check on Ray Fields, and copied Elien Martel's name and address into my phone. It was entirely possible Elien had lied about where he lived. It was more than possible, actually; if he were involved in this, as I thought he was, then the odds were high that he had lied. But it was my only starting place. If I hit a dead end, I'd go to the support group Tuesday and try to find him that way.

I had just logged out of the workstation when a hand came down on my shoulder.

Amrey Kimmons, chief deputy, smiled down at me, but his hand was tight. He was an older black man, with neatly clipped gray hair, and he never shouted and never blustered. He didn't need to.

"Deputy LeBlanc," Kimmons said. "What's got you in here so late?"

"Just needed to use the computer, sir."

"You remember that you're on paid leave, correct?"

"Yes, sir. Sorry. I was trying to check something with my bank, and I couldn't do it on my phone."

Kimmons studied me. "Well," he said, "in case it wasn't clear, paid leave means you aren't to be in the office for any reason."

"I'm sorry, sir."

"No need to be sorry, Deputy." Kimmons's grip eased. "How are you handling things?"

"Well enough, I guess."

"Are you seeing someone?"

"Just my, uh, psych eval, sir. You know."

Kimmons's smile broadened. "I meant personally, Deputy. I'm not trying to pry into your personal life, but I want to know if you have someone helping you through this."

"Oh. No, not seeing anyone. But I'm with my parents still, so I'm not home alone, if that's what you mean."

"They're lucky to have you," Kimmons said. He released me, patted my shoulder, and said, "I'll see you when it's time for you to come back, Deputy."

"Yes, sir."

"Let me walk you out."

He followed me to the front door. Mize, a deputy who'd only been with us for a year, was on the desk, and I knew from the look on her face that she wanted to kick my ass for sneaking past her.

Outside, I breathed in the cool October air, jogged back to the Ford, and followed my phone's directions to Elien Martel's address.

I was surprised when the phone took me outside of Bragg; Elien didn't look like the country type. I was more surprised when the GPS sent me cutting east on a tiny state road that tunneled through the old growth of trees on this side of the parish. Branches grew so close together that they formed a web overhead, and the air from the Ford's passage made them shiver. When I rolled down the window, the sound of bark clicking against bark reached me over the engine's grumbling. The air smelled wet, like leaf mold, and the headlights carved a bubble out of the darkness.

When I turned onto a gravel drive, the trees seemed even thicker. Where the hell was my phone taking me? I pictured barns on the verge of falling over, saltbox houses with tarpaper roofs, guys who wouldn't think twice about opening up with a shotgun if a stranger drove onto their property.

I followed the gravel around the next corner, and a wall of light met me. The house in front of me was spectacular. Multi-million-dollar spectacular. It was a modern take on a farmhouse style, updated with elegant lighting and bright white paint and walls of glass. I killed the headlights, pulled off the drive, and examined the scene in front of me. Perfectly tended lawn. Artful landscaping around the house itself. Behind the house, at the edge of the ring of light, I could see where the wilderness began again. With the engine quiet now, the ripple of flowing water filled the stillness. This was very much the kind of place I could imagine Elien living.

Rolling up the window, I grabbed my flashlight. Then I let myself out of the car and moved toward the house. I wanted to talk to Elien, but not yet. First, I wanted to take a look around. I knew what Mason would tell me, if Mason were there: he'd tell me I was being a major fucking dumbass, he'd tell me I was cutting corners and threatening the integrity of the investigation. He'd be right. But the fact was that nobody would believe me if I told a story about blue lights and a dead man who grabbed Elien's arm. Nobody thought Mason's death was anything besides a tragedy. There wasn't an investigation to jeopardize, and at this rate, there never would be.

My first stop was the garage. The roll up door was down and didn't open when I messed with it. I went around to the side and saw a half-lite door. This one was locked too. When I flashed a light through the glass, I saw a nice three-bay with a Lexus sedan in the bay closest to the house. The garage was finished and, I judged by the weather stripping, climate controlled. Lots of money to burn, it seemed.

Following a cement walk to the back of the house, I caught a whiff of jessamine and sweet olive and shit. The mixture brought me to a stop. Exterior lights on the house flooded the backyard all the way to a rocky bank and running water, the currents throwing back crescents of light. Maybe a big stream. Maybe a small river. Hard to tell in the dark. On the far bank, a branch snapped, and then several more in succession. Something big was moving over there. Something big moving fast. A black bear, maybe. Still a good number of black bears in DuPage Parish. I was trying to remember how many calls we got a year on black bears, but all I could think about was those branches snapping like firecrackers.

A soft noise came from my left, slick and vaguely metallic. And then again. And again. Rhythmic. On my next breath, I could smell something rotting.

I took a step off the cement walk. My hand rested on the Sig as I moved toward the sound. Shick. Shick. I eased the Sig loose. The sound was coming from somewhere ahead of me. A magnolia tree marked the edge of the lawn; the thick, glossy leaves curtained off everything beyond it. I ducked under the lowest branches, picking a path over the roots, concentrating on slow, even breaths. The soft shick-shick continued. I could see something now, a faint white spot between the oaks and pines. A pinecone crunched under foot, and I froze, but the shick-shick continued. I was more careful after that, watching the ground with every step, picking clear patches where the fallen needles were green and thick.

Then I realized the noise had stopped.

Someone screamed, and the white spot shot out of the darkness toward me.

I brought up the flashlight and the Sig, recognized Elien, and stumbled to one side. The shovel whistled through the air, barely missing my head.

"On the ground, on the ground," I shouted.

"Get on the ground your fucking self," he shouted back. "I'll take your fucking head off!"

I shone the light in his face; he was holding the shovel like a baseball bat.

"Drop it," I shouted. "Police! Drop the weapon!"

The shovel came down a few inches; he shielded his eyes with one hand.

"Officer LeBlanc?" he asked. "What the fuck are you doing?"

"Jesus," I said, lowering the Sig. "What were you—are you ok?"

"Am I ok? I almost smashed your face in. Are you ok?"

"Will you put the shovel down, please?"

"Will you stop shining the light in my face?"

I lowered the beam, and I heard the shovel's blade bite into the soil. "What are you doing out here?" I asked.

"I live here. Why are you sneaking around on my property?"

"I . . ."

Elien stared at me. Shadows hid his expression, but my face heated anyway.

"I wanted to make sure you were ok."

"Oh, yeah, I'm great. Or, I was, until this asshole sneaked up behind me and tried to shoot me in the back."

Holstering the Sig, I said, "I'm sorry. I was going to knock, but I heard a strange sound. I wanted to see what it was."

"You didn't hear me from the front door," Elien said, "which means you'd already come around the side of the house, which means you were sneaking. Why were you sneaking around?"

"I was worried," I said; I could hear how lame it was as soon as it was out of my mouth.

After a moment, Elien sighed. "Since you're here, I guess I owe you something for saving my life. Let me finish up and we can go inside."

I followed him farther into the trees; Elien was carrying a flashlight too, and he turned it on now, shining it across the ground until he found what he was looking for. I saw a hole about three feet deep. Next to it was a pile of something that looked like rope.

"Are those intestines?"

"Yes," Elien said.

"Do you want to explain that?"

"Not really." He used the shovel to slide the pile of viscera into the hole, and then he began filling in the dirt. With every shovelful, he grunted and swore, and after a minute, he paused and turned the flashlight on, inspecting his hand. Blisters had already split across Elien's palm and fingers.

"Give me that," I said, and I swapped the flashlight for the shovel before Elien could object.

"I can do it."

"I know."

"I do not need you to do that."

"I know."

"I didn't ask you to do it."

"Consider this a mission of mercy. You've got nice hands; no point ruining them."

For a while, I just worked. After days of moping around the house, it felt good to do something. The burn in my muscles. The prickle of sweat across my chest and back. And, of course, the knowledge that Elien was looking at me.

When I finished, I looked at Elien: the perfectly windswept hair; a long, loose white tee that the night breeze pulled tight, translucent where sweat dampened it; the lean musculature underneath.

"Let's take care of your hands," I said.

"I have enough people taking care of me," Elien said. "If I have any more men in my life taking care of me, I'm going to put a bullet through the roof of my mouth."

"That sounds nice," I said.

Elien looked like he was about to say something nasty, but then his face froze. His gaze was fixed on something over my shoulder.

"What?" I said.

Elien's mouth moved, but no sound came out.

I thought back to the snapping branches like a string of firecrackers. A black bear. But bears didn't move like that, not that I'd ever heard. Shifting my grip on the shovel, I turned around slowly.

For a moment, I thought it was some strange fruit: pale and white and long, hanging in the trees. Then the parts came together into a face that was too long to be human

It rushed towards us.

ELIEN (7)

Branches and dead pine needles crackled as the pale thing—the monster—shot toward us. Grabbing Dag, I stumbled between a pair of sugar maples. The monster streaked past us in blur of white, and Dag swore. He slipped, his back connecting with my chest, and we both stumbled. As he caught his footing, he thrust the shovel into my hands and pulled out his pistol. He turned slowly.

I set my back to his and brought up the shovel. We rotated in place, both of us scanning for any sign of the creature. The hashok. The thing in the grass. The thick growth of the forest made it hard to see anything beyond a few yards. Veils of Spanish moss fluttered when the night breeze picked up; the broken limb of a pine sagged in the wind, bending, exposing a white tongue. Dag's back was hot and solid against my own; he was about my height, and for some reason that was ridiculously comforting at the moment.

Something scuffed to my right. I jerked to face it.

"Slow," Dag whispered, setting himself against me again. "It's going to try to trick us."

I took short, shallow breaths, sliding my hand along the composite handle of the shovel. The blisters stung, but the sensation was so real and grounded that it was almost pleasant compared to the panic crawling up my throat.

"Just call out its position," Dag said, still whispering. "Don't stumble around, or it'll separate us."

My breathing sounded like a steam whistle.

"Elien?"

"Yes. Ok. Call it out."

More of that scuffing came from my left, like something being dragged through the fallen pine needles.

"My left," I said.

"I hear it."

Twigs snapped.

"Right," I said.

"I hear it."

Dag released a slow, controlled breath. "It's going to come from your right."

"What? How do you—"

"When I tell you, I want you to run for the house."

"No way, I'm not—"

"One," he whispered.

An owl cried off in the darkness, and my hand jumped along the shovel.

"Two," he whispered. "You can do this."

The breeze picked up again. For a moment, the canopy parted overhead, and I saw stars, and the October air was cool on my superheated skin.

"Three," Dag shouted, and he spun, grabbed my shoulder, and shoved me toward the house.

The creature shot out of the woods from the right, like Dag had predicted. It was just a blur of white at the corner of my vision, moving faster than any animal I'd ever seen. Maybe a cheetah ran that fast. Maybe a grizzly at full speed. Then it was past my field of vision, and I lost track of it.

Dag fired. In the forest's stillness, the sound was so loud that I felt it hit me physically, like it would bowl me over. I stumbled, caught myself on the bole of a pine, kept going. The next shot came. Then two more came.

Dag was fighting this fucking monster for me. By himself.

"Oh fuck," I screamed, and I veered around the broad trunk of a magnolia and sprinted back toward Dag.

He was running toward me; there was something funny about how he moved, and I realized he was cradling one arm against his chest.

"What the hell are you doing?" he roared. "Go, go, go!"

The hashok appeared on the other side of a line of brambles, just a ghostly flicker of movement that ran parallel with Dag, keeping up.

"The bushes," I shouted.

Dag kept running and fired wildly into the brambles: one, two, three. He screamed through each shot. It was a wild noise, a berserker cry. I started screaming too.

And then Dag's foot caught on a root, and he went down.

The noise of pain when he hit the ground was terrible, but even worse was the dull shape of the pistol flying from his hand. I grabbed the flashlight I'd been carrying, turned it on, and ran it back and forth across ground. Nothing. Nothing. Dirt and pinecones and more fucking dirt. Roots. Dag was groaning, rolling onto his back, and then he clutched at his arm and started swearing. I swept the beam of my light faster.

Something white moved at the edge of my vision.

I didn't let myself focus on it. If I focused on it, I'd be lost. Frozen. I stumbled a few yards one way. Then the other. I kept that white spot right at the edge of my sight. It was coming closer, but slowly now. It knew we were helpless. The hashok was enjoying this game.

It feeds on human lives, Suzette had told me, *and it's always hungry.*

The flashlight's beam hit the compact frame of the pistol, and I threw myself at it. I landed on a root, and I felt the breath knocked out of my lungs, but my fingers closed around the gun's butt. I came up on my knees, gasping, the world blurry as tears filled my eyes. Something white. And now that it was close enough, I saw the blue flames of its eyes.

I fired. Once, twice, a third time. Then the trigger clicked, and the slide locked back. Dropping the gun, I scrambled to my feet. I was still trying to pull air into my lungs as I fumbled for the shovel.

My ears rang from the shots, and when I got my first lungful of air, I coughed on the gun smoke. But the hashok was gone. I spun in a circle, the shovel over my shoulder.

Gone.

I moved toward Dag, still making those little circles, waiting for the thing to show itself again. When I reached down, Dag took my hand; he was a big guy, and I probably wasn't much help, but we got him onto his feet. Blood stained his shirt along the chest and sleeve.

"Let's get the fuck out of here," I said.

"My gun," he said.

"Fuck. It's here somewhere. Just keep your eyes open."

"That thing is gone."

"We don't know that."

"I'm pretty sure it's gone. You shot it twice in the chest." With his good hand, Dag mimed two shots. "Center mass. Great job."

"My dad," I said, fighting a giggle. "My dad would be—" A laugh, really a cackle, slipped free. "My dad would be so fucking proud." Another of those awful laughs escaped me, and I had to gasp for air again. "Oh my God, I think I'm having a breakdown."

"Let me find my gun," Dag said, "and then you can have your breakdown."

This time, of course, it was easy to find the gun. Dag grunted as he bent to pick it up, and we started for the house. He was limping pretty badly, so I got an arm around his waist. He smelled like pine sap and sweat and Gain.

Emerging from the woods was like stepping into another world: the bright exterior lights painted everything gold and silver, and the house glowed like something out of one of those cozy domestic magazines where everyone uses white towels and linen place settings.

"Inside," I said.

"Just get me to my car," Dag said. "I can drive."

"You can't even walk," I said. "Richard's a doctor. He can decide if we need to get you to an emergency room."

When the wind picked up again, flattening the blades of St. Augustine grass, it smelled like the Okhlili and stone and cypress. Branches clattered behind us, and we spun together, Dag swearing under his breath.

Nothing moved in the forest.

"Inside," I muttered.

This time, Dag didn't argue.

DAG (8)

My chest and arm were on fire, and I'd done something to my ankle when I fell. I had to lean on Elien more than I liked as he helped me through the French doors at the back of the house.

"Sit," he said, pressing me down onto a leather couch. "I'm going to get Richard."

"I'm bleeding."

"I saw that."

"I'm going to ruin this couch."

"It'll make a great conversation piece."

He darted upstairs before I could answer, and after a moment of struggling, I gave up and sank back into the cushions. The leather was buttery, which was a term I'd heard used to describe leather before and which hadn't made any sense until right now. But God damn, this leather was buttery. And it smelled like leather too. I was pretty sure I was currently bleeding on a piece of furniture that had cost more than my car.

The rest of the living room looked equally expensive and tasteful: a few abstract sculptures in dark metals, driftwood art pieces on the walls, a single, monochromatic painting in blue that accented the rest of the room. I'd already known Elien had money when I'd seen the house from the outside, but now I was starting to understand from the inside. I was starting to understand why he always dressed movie-star casual when I saw him: joggers and t-shirts that draped his lean frame elegantly, tennis shoes that probably cost a few hundred dollars.

The soft, padded sounds of his steps made me look back toward the stairs. Elien appeared first. An older man in a t-shirt and pajama bottoms came after him, coiling a pair of earbuds around one finger.

"—listening to Tchaikovsky," he was saying, "but I still can't believe I didn't hear—" He stopped and drew a sharp breath. "Elien, you didn't say he was bleeding. What in the world happened?"

"I said he got hurt." Elien was lugging a black bag. "What did you think I meant?"

"I'm ok," I said.

The older man—Richard, I assumed—gestured for the bag, and Elien set it on the coffee table.

"I'm really ok." I held out a hand. "No offense, but I'd rather go to an urgent care."

"I'm a trained physician. Let me at least take a look. Elien, call the police. Was this an animal attack? What did you—"

"I'm fine," I said. Ok, I shouted. More calmly, I repeated, "I'm fine. I'm going to leave, and I'm going to—" I had reached the end of rational thought, so I repeated, "I'm going to leave."

Richard glanced at Elien, and Elien shrugged.

"Great," I said. "Now that we've got that settled—"

"Let me talk to him for a minute," Elien said.

Frowning, Richard said, "The police—"

"Go upstairs." Elien nudged Richard. "I'll handle this."

"He really needs attention, Elien."

"I know. I'll call up to you if I can get him to change his mind."

With another frown, Richard trudged back upstairs, putting in his earbuds again as he went.

In his absence, I was suddenly very aware of Elien, the perfect brown lines of his arms, the way he pulled on his shirt with one hand, drawing it tight against his chest. The silence rang in my ears.

"Richard's your boyfriend," I said.

"It's like you've been trained," Elien said. "It's like you're professionally suited for putting clues together to unravel impossible riddles."

"Mostly I unravel domestic disputes."

"I'm going to cut your shirt off and see how bad those cuts are," Elien said, dropping to sit on the coffee table. "And if you tell me one more time that you're fine, I'm going to scream."

He looked serious, so I said, "Ok. But I don't think you have to— Jesus Christ!" I had tried to peel off the shirt, but the blood was already gumming, and it pulled on the wounds on my shoulder and chest.

Elien held up the scissors.

"Yeah," I said. "That's a great idea."

"You're going to want to practice saying that," Elien said. "I like being right."

He snipped away the shirt in pieces, using warm water and a clean cloth to loosen the fabric and work it away. His movements were slow and sure and steady. This wasn't the worried kid pacing outside

Ray Field's apartment. This wasn't the kid who had fallen down the stairs outside DuPage First Methodist. This wasn't the kid who had been hyperventilating in the woods.

This was the guy who had come back for me.

"You're staring," Elien said.

"Sorry."

A tiny smile pulled at the corner of his mouth; he was still intently working a piece of my shirt loose. "Do you still think I have nice hands?"

I swallowed. "Yes. Ow."

"Don't be a baby," he said gently. "That was the last one."

For the first time, I risked a glance. It was worse than I'd thought: four deep cuts that ran from my sternum across my chest, curving around my shoulder and upper arm. They were still bleeding.

"These need stitches," Elien said. "And you probably need antibiotics. I don't know what that thing was, but I don't think it was clean."

"Do you have gauze and tape?"

"Of course."

"Just tape me up, please."

"You didn't hear me: these need stitches. Richard can—"

"No."

Frustration twisted his features. "Then I'll get Richard to drive us to an urgent care."

"Yeah, well," I said, squirming to the edge of the couch, biting back a gasp at how much it hurt. "I can't afford an urgent care."

Elien put a hand on my belly and forced me back down. What happened next wasn't my fault: I still had adrenaline pumping through me, and a hot guy had just cut my shirt off and had his hands all over me. Now the twinkie was manhandling me.

He noticed, of course. I waited for the smile, the jab, the dismissal.

Instead, he slid off the coffee table and straddled me. It sent a wave of pain through me, but a wave of something else too.

"What are you—"

He kissed me.

When he broke for air, he brought my hand to his crotch. He was hard under the denim. He rocked slowly into my touch. He made a low noise in his throat and thrust harder.

"Am I hurting you?" he whispered.

"I can . . ." I gulped. "I can handle it."

"Yeah?"

"God, yes. Yeah."

"I want you to fuck me," he whispered. "Please fuck me. I could come like this, I'm about to come just like this, but I want it to be more than that. Please?"

"Elien, stop. Hey. Stop!"

It was hard to pull my hand away, but I managed to slide my grip up to his hips and force him off my lap. For a moment, he stood there, his face twisted with anger. And then he walked out of the room.

He wasn't the only one who'd been right at the brink. I thought about the Saints. I thought about pass-completion percentages. But then I started thinking about Elien in nothing but football pads.

"It's just a fuck," Elien said, marching back into the room. "What the fuck is wrong with you?"

"Excuse me?"

"It's just a fuck. I think you're hot. I want you to fuck me. I'm hard for the first time in a fucking year, and I want you to drill me, and we both practically died out there. It's a fucking biological reaction, ok? It's a survival-mode fuck. So get off your high horse and let's go upstairs and you can fuck me."

I managed to get out of the buttery—there it was again, that word—couch's embrace. I gave Elien a smile and one-sided shrug.

"Sorry. It's not personal."

"It definitely is personal."

"I really appreciate the interest, but I think I should pass."

"Am I not being clear? Am I not speaking loudly enough? Go upstairs. We are going to fuck."

"Probably a bad time to ask," I said, "but do you think you could help me to my car?"

Elien screamed.

"Ok," I said. "I'll make it on my own."

"No," he said, moving into my path. "Absolutely not. Give me one good reason. I know you're attracted to me. Is it because you're in too much pain? Is it because you're all sliced up and you need stitches?"

"It's definitely not helping."

"Are you worried I'm crazy and I'll get clingy?"

"Well, I am now. Just a little bit."

"I have a boyfriend."

"Yeah, that was one of the big hang-ups for me."

Crossing his arms, Elien said, "It's an open relationship. I can fuck whoever I want. There, now that your conscience has been soothed—"

He reached for my arm, and I angled my body away.

"What the actual fuck?" he asked, his eyes wide.

"You seem like a very nice guy—"

"No, I don't. Don't give me that. I don't seem like a nice guy right now. I'm an asshole, I know I'm an asshole. I know I'm being a total shit to you, and you're hurt, and you saved my life, and I just want—" Elien took a breath. "Let's start over. You sit back down. I'll make you a drink. We'll just talk for a little bit."

"Elien, it's ok. We all strike out every once in a while. And don't worry, I won't tell anyone. I think you're a really good guy, I promise."

"This is crazy. You're crazy. You hit your head when you fell, and you have a concussion."

The house creaked around us.

The poor guy looked so confused I couldn't stop myself from smiling.

"So," I said, "I'm still bleeding and only have half a shirt. I think I'm going to go."

"No."

"Elien."

"No, just—" He seemed like he couldn't quite connect the words. "Just sit down and I'll bandage you."

"That's probably not a good—"

He pointed a finger at me.

"Ok," I said, raising my good arm in surrender. "I can sit down."

The gauze rasped between his hands as he unrolled it. His fingers were soft and cool against my chest.

"You've got a thing for older guys," Elien said quietly.

"Not really."

"It's bears. You're only into bears."

I laughed and then winced.

"Well, come on," Elien said, and his face softened as he grinned suddenly. His gaze stayed on the tape and gauze. "I just humiliated myself. You can at least tell me why."

"Really?"

"Really."

"It'll make you feel better?"

"Just don't tell me it's because I'm fat. I know I've gotten tubby; I don't need any more reminders."

"Uh, is that a joke?"

"No. Trust me: I did not used to be disgusting like this."

I tried to think about how to answer that, but his hand kept brushing the trail of hair low on my belly, and it was like someone playing with the switch on a live wire. The words escaped before I could stop them.

"I think you're the most beautiful person I've ever seen."

"Oh." His hands stopped. "Um. Thanks."

"Number one is because you've got a boyfriend."

"I told you—"

"I know, but it's still a big deal for me. I'm not into that."

Elien nodded as he pressed more tape into place.

"Number two is—hey, watch it."

His hand skimmed the inside of my thigh, slid over my dick, squeezed.

"Sorry," Elien said, eyes coming up dark and innocent. "Slipped."

"Number two is I've done this before, ok? You're a ten. I'm a six. Six and a half if I'm not on carbs. And there's some reason, like you're both wasted, or the guy who's a ten is a closet case, or you just got chased through the woods by a monster, and it seems like hot, frantic, immediate sex is the obvious choice."

"I like where this is going."

"Well, I guess I'm too old to keep embarrassing myself like that," I said. "It just hurts too much."

"That's it?" Elien said. "Two reasons?"

"That's not enough?"

"Not even close. The second one is bullshit anyway. You're not a six."

I laughed again. "Number three is that every gay guy who's found out I'm a cop has wanted to play badge buck, and I just . . . I just get tired of it."

"So, what's your game plan?" Elien said, sitting back to examine his handiwork.

"My game plan?"

His eyes came up again. "Long term?"

"What do you mean?"

"Are you going to have a secret identity or something? You can't automatically dismiss every guy who's interested in you just because you're a cop. Yeah, the job gets fetishized. Yeah, that's not cool for you—not if you want to be treated like a human being. But I mean, at some point, you're going to have to tell a guy, right?"

I guess I don't have a very good poker face, because Elien frowned.

"I'm sorry," he said. "That's not any of my business."

"No, it's . . . it's why I'm twenty-seven and have never had a boyfriend last more than six months, so I mean, it's not like I haven't thought about it."

Leaning back, Elien ran a hand through that long, windswept hair. The white tee had ridden up to expose the light brown skin of his belly.

"I'd like you to call Guinness," he said. "I think I just got the world record for worst seduction ever."

"I'll let them know," I said.

"I guess we need to talk about what happened out there."

Shaking my head, I managed to get to my feet. "Nope. No way."

"What?"

"No way. Not tonight."

"What?"

"I need a drink. I need to sleep on this. I need to feel like I'm not totally batshit insane. End of discussion. Sorry."

"But I need to talk to someone about what's been going on."

"And I feel like I went through a meat slicer. Goodnight, Elien. Thanks, you know. For the bandages. And for trying to seduce me. It really made me feel better about myself."

"Oh my God," Elien said, covering his face. "I think I just figured out why you're single."

"No, it did. It was really endearing how you kept yammering and throwing yourself at me."

"I'm feeling the urge to do some more yammering right now."

With a small sigh, I said, "Pen? Paper?"

He grabbed them from the kitchen.

"My phone number," I said, scribbling. "And my address."

"Why do I need your address?"

"Do you want your boyfriend to be part of this conversation tomorrow?"

"No, I guess not. Wait, tomorrow?"

I nodded.

"Just hold on before you go."

He sprinted upstairs and was back again in a minute. As he walked me to the door, he held out a wad of cash.

"I'm not a gigolo," I said.

Grinning, he said, "Trust me, this wouldn't even start to cover all the things I want to do to you. This is for stitches. You drive straight to an urgent care, and you get them to clean you up and get you on antibiotics."

"I'm not taking your money."

"Sure you are," Elien said. "Or I'm going to call the DuPage Sheriff's Department and explain that a crazy deputy was here firing his gun outside my house."

I stared at him. "That's blackmail."

"So simple," Elien said to himself. "You're lucky you're cute." Then he waved the money.

After a moment, I snatched it.

"Goodnight," he said.

"Thanks," I said. "For blackmailing me, I guess."

Laughing, he shut the door.

I drove to an urgent care on the outside of Bragg, and while I filled out paperwork, I tried to figure out how being chased by a monster and almost killed had been one of the best, most romantic evenings of the last five years.

When I heard that thought, I decided to get back on Grindr.

ELIEN (9)

The next day, Muriel drove me to Dag's house on her way to work.

"I really don't see," she paused to touch up her lipstick at a red light, "why you have an open relationship."

"Oh my God," I said. "I'm not having this conversation with the president of the Lady Baptists' Temperance Union."

"You know perfectly well that it's called the Bragg Baptist Church Ladies of Love."

"That's even worse."

"We're having a cake walk on Sunday."

"It sounds like a sex workers' guild."

"Elien Martel, since when have sex workers ever had a cake walk?"

"They can have a cake walk. Anybody can have a cake walk."

"Richard is a wonderful man."

Groaning, I mashed my face against the window.

"You don't know how lucky you are."

"In the first place," I said, "I am not talking to you about my relationship with Richard. Second, I am not going to a hookup at seven forty-five in the morning. Third, I am not the one who insisted on having an open relationship. And fourth, I am not talking to you about my relationship with Richard."

"Well," she said, "I just don't understand why it has to be an open relationship."

I gritted my teeth so I wouldn't scream.

Dag's parents owned a small house in Fogmile, probably half a mile from the library where I had spent much of the day before. That half mile made a difference: this part of the neighborhood was on the bottom rung of the middle class, with sagging fences and weed-choked lawns. The houses needed touching up with paint; old but well-maintained was about the best you could say for it. Muriel stopped parallel with the ancient Ford Escort that I'd seen Dag use to pick up Mason from the support group.

"Could you wait and make sure they don't shoot me or something, please?"

Muriel was powdering her nose. "Why would your illicit homosexual lover shoot you?"

"He's not my—why does it matter that—Muriel, please."

"Well. I don't know. I really don't feel appreciated."

"I appreciate you."

"You think I'm Richard's secretary.

"No, I don't. I'm very grateful that you're willing to help me."

"You think of me as your personal driver. That's why you call me Jeeves."

"No, no. You are an intelligent, educated professional. You have a nursing degree from the Abraham Lincoln Civil War Museum or something."

She shut the compact with a click.

"Ok," I said. "You're a highly trained psychiatric nurse practitioner and you've got a million impressive letters after your name." I hesitated. "LMNOP?"

She tucked the compact into a tidy purse. "I think if you were really serious about Richard," she began.

"No," I moaned.

"You would tell him that you didn't want an open relationship."

"Yes," I said. "Ok. I will tell him that. Those exact words. Now, will you please wait and make sure they don't shoot me?"

She sniffed.

"You're a saint," I said, and then I kissed her cheek, grabbed my bag, and hopped out of the car.

When I knocked on the door, a woman answered. She had to be in her sixties, and she had iron-gray hair, which I guessed was where Dag had gotten his from. Her face was guarded, and she didn't open the screen door.

"May I help you?"

"I'm here to see Dag."

"Excuse me?"

"I'm here to see Dag. Is he home?" I glanced over my shoulder at Muriel and then back at the woman in the doorway. "Is this the right house?"

"Just a minute," she said.

Quiet voices came through the screen door. A man said, "I heard you, Gloria, but I'm asking is he hot?" More quiet voices. "Well, I think it does matter if he's coming to see Dagobert this early in the morning."

The October morning was cool, but sweat prickled under my arm.

A man's face floated into view, and I saw him just long enough that I noticed the beard and that he was probably the same age as the woman; Dag's father, I guessed. He disappeared almost immediately.

Footsteps came toward the door, and I heard Dag's dad say something like, "He's very handsome."

"Jesus, Dad," Dag said.

"He might even be better looking than Jackson."

"Go away," Dag said. "Please. Can't you do what decent parents do and just be ashamed of me and my abnormal life choices?"

"I think he's a twink," the dad said.

"Oh my God," Dag said in a tone of absolute despair.

When he came to the door, he was wearing pajamas: old man pajamas, a top and a bottom in matching, hunter-green plaid. He rubbed his head. Then he rubbed his eyes. Then he said, "What are you doing here?"

"Good morning," I said.

Muriel honked, and I waved over my shoulder as she drove off.

"Sorry it's early. I don't drive, and my only ride was coming into town right now."

"And you couldn't have texted?"

"Ok," I said. "Sorry. I'll just head over to the library for a few hours. You can text me when you're ready to talk."

"I have work today."

"Oh shit."

Dag rolled his eyes. "Ok, I don't. But what if I did?"

"Point taken. I'm an entitled asshole."

He pushed open the screen door and smiled. "A privileged, entitled asshole."

When I stepped inside, Dag's mom and dad were waiting.

"This is my dad, Hubert," Dag said, and Hubert and I shook. "He's currently rating you on a ten-point scale."

"I think my main competition is someone called Jackson," I said.

Dag groaned. "And this is my mom, Gloria. She thinks I should run a train on you."

I choked on my spit.

"Come on," Dag said, grabbing my arm and steering me down a hallway. "Before they start talking."

"It's very nice to meet you," Gloria called after us.

"Remember to close your door, son," Hubert said, "if you boys are going to pleasure each other."

"Are they for real?" I asked.

"No, my mom doesn't know what running a train means. She keeps using it like she thinks she does, though."

"No, I mean, um. Pleasure each other?"

"Oh, yeah. Rule of the house: door closed." Dag rolled his eyes. "They think they're hippies or something."

"Were they hippies?"

"God, no. They were barely alive for that. They just wish they had been." Dag shut the door behind us. Then he frowned. "Don't get any ideas."

I smirked and looked around. My first impression of his bedroom was that it was dirty: clothes stacked on the dresser, books on the floor, a tangle of charging cords on top of the nightstand. But after a moment, I realized the room wasn't dirty; it was just . . . cluttered. The floor had recently been vacuumed. The furniture was dust free. The books on the floor were in neat stacks, and they'd obviously been placed on the floor because the two bookshelves were already full. A small LED was directed at the wall, projecting a rippling blue light that gave the room an underwater atmosphere, and on the back of the door, he'd hung a poster for the 2008 Braxton Bragg Memorial High School basketball team. A teenage Mason stood in the middle row.

"Sorry," Dag said, grabbing a stack of boxers and shoving them into a drawer that was already bursting. "I didn't know you were—I mean, I don't know what I mean. They gave me something at the urgent care last night, and it knocked me out when I got home."

"So you did go?"

"Yeah, of course. I said I would." A desk and a chair took up one corner of the crowded room, and he pulled out the chair. "You can sit here if you want. I'll sit on the bed."

Instead, I moved to the bookshelf and began running my finger along the spines. A lot of books about whales. Books about marine life. Books about ocean exploration. Books about ships and sailing. Books about tide patterns. Books about silt and river deltas.

"What's your real name?" Dag asked as he sat on the bed.

"Elien."

"No, it's not. I checked you out. You have a few social media accounts, but there's not much on them. And I hired a private investigator to look into you, and he couldn't find anything."

"Why didn't you look me up in the police databases?"

"I'm on paid leave."

"Oh. Sorry."

"I wouldn't have done it anyway. It's not right. This isn't an official investigation; it would be an abuse of power."

"Why do you have so many books about whales?"

Dag blew out a breath. "Fine. If you don't want to tell me your real name, I guess it doesn't matter. We should probably talk about last night."

"I'll tell you my name. But I also want a little information. It's like a trade. Why do you have so many books about whales?"

"I asked first."

"Eli."

"Martel?"

"Martins."

"Why'd you change it?"

"That's a new question," I said.

"I just think they're interesting."

I raised my eyebrows.

A faint blush dusted his cheeks. "Ok, I think they're really interesting," he said. "They're complicated animals. They're smart and social and some of them can be incredibly dangerous. Why'd you change your name?"

"Because Eli Martins sounds like I invented the cotton gin."

"Seriously."

"I am serious. I don't know. Eli Martins is so basic."

"It's a nice name."

"Where's all the rest of it?" I asked.

"Rest of what?"

"You know: action movie posters and your gun collection and your football jersey."

He furrowed his forehead. "Huh?"

"Come on. This is cute." I tapped the spine of a whale book. "But where's the rest of it?"

"This is it. There isn't anything else." He frowned. "What happened between you and Mason?"

"Oh, we're getting serious," I said, sprawling in the chair he'd pulled out for me. "Nothing happened. He didn't like me. He never liked me. One day he tried to shoot me." I worked to clear my throat. "Thank you, again, by the way. I guess I can't say that enough." Then I said, "Why do you hate being a cop?"

"I don't hate it."

I studied him until he dropped his gaze to the floor.

"I just . . . don't think it's a good fit." For a moment, it looked like he might not say anything else. Then he burst out, "It's just not what I thought it'd be. You know what most of my callouts are? Domestics. I hate domestics. You get there, and these people are hurting each other the worst ways they know how. And they used to love each other. I don't know. Or it's kids smoking weed. Or it's vandalism. Or . . . or it's a wellness check."

"What'd you think it would be like?"

Dag smiled and rubbed his head as he looked up. "Well, I'm famously not good about thinking ahead, so I don't really have an answer for that. I just thought I'd be helping people."

"It sounds like you are."

He shrugged. "It doesn't feel like it."

"You're good at your job. You handled me pretty well at Ray's. And you handled that thing last night like a pro."

Dag shrugged again, and now he laid back on the bed, stretching out with one arm behind his head. "You know the first time I had a domestic, it was actually not that bad. I mean, we got there. The wife had barricaded herself in the bedroom. The husband was drunk and breaking things. They were screaming awful things at each other through the door. I was eighteen. Brand new deputy. I bet my eyes were the size of dinner plates. I'd never seen anybody fight like that. We took the husband in, mostly so he could sober up and cool down. Once we got him in the drunk tank, I went in the men's room and cried." His eyes were half closed. "Tell me again I'm good at my job."

"I think you're being hard on yourself."

He probed at his shoulder where he'd been injured.

"I think you're upset because of what happened with Mason, and your whole world got thrown off-kilter last night, and you're struggling right now."

"Sure," Dag said, still testing the wound. "I'm just dog paddling."

"Does it hurt?"

"What? Oh. A little. I think I need to change the bandages."

"Sit up."

"No, it's fine. My mom'll help me."

"Dag, sit up, please. Or I'll start moaning and pounding on the door and I'll give your parents a show."

"Oh my God, they'd be thrilled."

"I'm very believable," I said.

"I'm fine."

"Uhh," I groaned. "Oh, Dag, your hands."

He sat up, his face bright red. "Ok, ok."

When I grinned, I was surprised that he grinned back.

"Where's the stuff?" I said.

"Bathroom down the hall."

I found the bag of supplies, scrubbed my hands, and pulled on a pair of disposable gloves. When I got back to the room, Dag had removed the pajama top, and I decided he was most definitely not a six. He had a chiseled body and abs like you wouldn't believe, but he wasn't waifish, like a lot of guys. He was just muscle packed on top of muscle packed on top of muscle.

"Were you a body builder in a past life?" I asked as I sat next to him.

He just blushed and said, "I'll take off the old bandages."

And he did. He did it the way he seemed to do everything: at his own pace, fully focused, as though he'd totally forgotten I was there.

When he'd finished removing the bandages, I said, "Jesus."

"They just look worse today. They're fine."

I applied the bandages and taped them in place. My fingers lingered. His skin was warm, his chest smooth where they had shaved him at the urgent care and covered by a thick layer of curly dark hair everywhere else. I watched as his skin pebbled under my touch. His breathing was slow and deep, and for some reason, I felt like he'd been taking care of me, instead of the other way around.

"Richard is a psychiatrist," I said, running the tip of my gloved index finger along the edge of the tape, riding it to his clavicle. "He helps people. He helps me. He came into my life when things were really bad, and I honestly don't know what I would have done without him."

"I think you're very lucky, then," Dag said.

"Yes," I said.

"Are you a nurse? Or a med student? You seem to know your way around this stuff pretty well."

I heard the question, but I just kept studying his clavicle, the little freckles on the skin there, the way the tape hugged the line of his shoulder.

"And I know," I said, "I know Richard is helping people. But sometimes I wonder if helping people is the same as caring about people. With me, I mean, sometimes I think he likes things this way. Prefers it, I guess." I stopped and shook my head. "Did you know doctors are high on the list of sociopaths?"

Dag frowned, and his hand closed around mine, stilling my touch. "Is he hurting you?"

"No," I said, and I thought of the shots when things got too wild, ketamine when I was out of control, Special K for what ails you. "I don't know what I'm saying."

"Elien—"

"That thing last night." I forced myself to say, "The monster. What do you know about it?"

"I'm a little worried. What are you trying to say about Richard?"

"I think the monster is called a hashok. Someone called it that. She said it was 'the thing in the grass.'"

Dag hesitated. Then, he released my hand and stood. "I'm going to throw these away and wash up. You should too."

So he washed his hands, and I ditched the gloves and washed my hands, Dag's mom asked if we wanted almond croissants and chicory coffee. I said no. Repeatedly. And somehow, I ended up back in Dag's room with an almond croissant the size of my head and a huge mug of chicory coffee.

"It was a bear," Dag said.

"What?"

"Last night. I thought about it. It was some kind of albino bear."

"No, it wasn't."

"Sure it was. It probably had some kind of disease. Maybe rabies. That's why it attacked."

"Look me in the eyes," I said, "and tell me it was a bear."

Dag picked at his croissant. "It's the only logical—"

"You saw the blue lights. You saw them. I know you did. You saw a dead man grab me. You saw Mason try to kill me, and you know Mason wasn't . . . wasn't himself when he did that. You saw that thing last night, and you know it wasn't a bear. It looked like a man. But thinner. And the shape of the head was wrong. But it wasn't a bear."

"We were both scared—"

"Don't do that," I said. "The first time you pretended you hadn't seen anything, I thought you were a coward. I know you're not a coward, though. Last night, that was the bravest thing I've ever seen anyone do."

"I didn't do anything," Dag said, "except get slashed up."

"I know you're not a coward, so why are you pretending?"

"I don't know." Dag took two huge bites and demolished his croissant. Then he licked crumbs from his fingers. "The other day, I had it all straight in my head. I had convinced myself something weird was happening. I thought maybe it was drugs. Or maybe . . . maybe something else. I thought you were connected to it. But last night— yeah, I am a coward. I am terrified, Elien. That thing could have killed us, and if it wasn't a bear, then I have no idea what it was, and I don't know what to do, and I don't know how to stop it, and I don't know how to keep you safe."

"I told you: I've already got enough people in my life trying to take care of me. I don't need you to take care of me. I need you to help me."

Dag wiped his hands on his pajama bottoms.

"Here," I said, passing him my croissant. "You look like you could use this."

"No," he said. "You're skin and bones."

"Ha ha."

He cocked his head like he didn't get the joke.

"Half," he finally said.

So I split it.

Dag worked a flake of the croissant loose and balanced it on one finger. "If it is this thing, the grass thing, what does that mean?"

"I don't know. I asked this woman who seemed to know about it, and she said it feeds on human lives, on pain and suffering. She said it would try to kill anyone that had seen it, which includes both of us. We saw it at Ray's. We saw it with Mason. And we saw it last night. I don't think leaving it alone is an option, Dag. I think we have to find a way to get rid of it." I touched the bag at my feet. "I found a book that might tell us more, but, um, I need help. I'm not a very good reader. It looks like you are."

"If it's about whales," Dag said, licking almond filling from the side of his hand, "I'm aces."

"Aces? Oh God, what kind of nerd am I teaming up with?"

Dag just had another of those shy smiles as an answer.

"Maybe we could work on it together?" I said.

"Yeah. And the faster, the better."

I rolled my eyes. "I'm not going to force myself on you again."

He must have inhaled some pastry because he coughed and turned bright red. When he'd cleared his throat, he said, "No, I mean, because it's looking for us. It's going to eliminate us."

My phone began to buzz. I pulled it out and saw Kenny's name on the screen.

"Hold on," I said. "I need to take this."

"I wonder what it's feeding cycle is like," Dag said, breaking the croissant into smaller pieces. "Does it need to feed every day? Every week? Every full moon?"

"Kenny? Hey, what's up?"

"If Ray and Mason were meals," Dag said, still talking to himself, "how soon will it need to feed again?"

"It's Tamika," Kenny said, his voice ragged. "She killed herself."

DAG (10)

We drove across town in the Escort, and the whole drive, Elien was pale and restless.

"I'm so sorry," I said for what felt like the hundredth time.

"Tamika wouldn't kill herself."

I nodded.

"This is that . . . that thing again. The hashok."

Ahead of us, Fogmile transitioned into Moulinbas; Creole townhouses replaced the shotgun-style clapboard homes. The October day was mellow, and with the windows down, I could smell beignets frying and, now that I was paying attention, Elien: anise and something peppery, a licoricey kind of heat that curled up in my lungs. I wondered why I hadn't noticed it in my bedroom. Or the night before, when he'd sat on my lap. I was definitely noticing now.

"Well, say something," Elien snapped.

"You smell nice."

His hand came up to his blowout hair, and he said, "I'm trying to pick a fight, Jesus Christ."

"Why do you want to pick a fight?"

"You think I'm wrong. You think Tamika killed herself."

"I don't think anything. I don't even know her."

"You are no fucking help."

"I don't know what you want me to do."

"I don't know, Dag. Any fucking thing would be great right about now."

Pumping the brakes, I pulled the Escort to the curb. We were parked in front of Madeleine's Kiddie Kurls and Kuts; on the other side of the plate glass, a woman, probably Madeleine, was settling a cape over a little boy in a salon chair.

"What the fuck are you doing?"

I flexed my fingers, palms balanced on the wheel. "I don't like people talking to me like that."

"Oh for fuck's sake. Will you drive the fucking car?"

"Elien, stop."

"Jesus Christ. Are you being serious right now? A woman just died, and you're going to stop the car because your feelings are hurt? This is fucking bullshit. Drive the car."

"Don't—"

"Drive the fucking car."

This time, I blew out a breath. Then I turned off the car, took the keys, and got out. Down the block, a Texaco had a spinning sign, and I started walking.

"What the fuck is wrong with you?" Elien screamed.

When a truck blew past me, the air from its passing threw up a flattened foam cup, and it smacked my shoe and fluttered away.

Inside the Texaco's convenience store, I bought two Cokes and a bag of Sun Chips. The girl behind the counter smiled as she gave me my change, and I smiled back. Then I went back outside and sat on the curb. The sun was warm. The breeze, when it picked up, was nice. I'd never told anyone, but I'd always liked the smell of gasoline, although it didn't go with the Sun Chips very well.

Behind me, the convenience store door opened, and the girl poked her head out.

"You need to use the phone?"

"No, thanks."

"You need a ride?"

"No."

"Are you sure, sweetie?"

"Yes, thanks."

Back at the Escort, Elien was getting out of the car. He slammed the door. He had a really prissy angry walk, but he moved a mile a minute.

"What the fuck is wrong with you?" he said when he reached me.

"I don't like conflict." I fished another chip out of the bag. "You're making me uncomfortable."

He ran his hands through his hair again. He paced back and forth. Finally, he came to a stop in front of me.

"I shouldn't have acted that way," he said. "I'm still dealing with a lot of stuff from my own life. Things like this, they trigger me, and I don't think rationally."

I crunched a chip.

"Can we go now, please?"

I held up a Coke.

"Do you have any idea how many calories are in that? Can we please just go?"

"I do not like people talking to me like that," I said. "The way you did in the car."

"I told you, I'm dealing with—"

"Elien, everybody's dealing with something, ok? I just watched my best friend die. I might have killed him. I don't sleep most nights because I think I did. But I don't cuss you out and call you every bad name in the dictionary."

"It's not my fault," he said stiffly. "I'm not responsible when I'm panicking like that."

"Did Richard tell you that?"

"Richard understands me. Richard is patient with me."

"Oh, sure. I bet you treat him just like dog shit sometimes. And he lets you get away with it."

Elien's mouth dropped open, and for another minute, he paced back and forth. Then he pointed a finger at me. "I thought you were sweet. I thought you were this nice, sweet guy."

"I'm pretty nice. I don't know about sweet, but my mom thinks I am, so I guess that's something."

"What the hell is going on?" Elien said.

"Do you want this Coke or not?"

"No. I don't know." And then he took it and spun off the cap. Dropping onto the curb next to me, he took a long drink. He wiped his mouth and said, "Honest to God, I don't know when the last time was I had this much processed sugar. First the croissant, now this."

I poked his arm. "You could use a little more meat on you."

Color ran under his light brown skin. "If I'm not allowed to talk to you like that, then you're not allowed to make jokes about my weight."

"What jokes?"

"I know how I look, Dag. I don't need you making fun of me."

"I wasn't trying to make fun, but I hear you: no more comments about your weight."

An eighteen-wheeler blew past the Texaco, the hot wave of exhaust battering us.

"I'm sorry," Elien said, studying the cap from the Coke.

"It's ok."

He shook his head and took another drink.

"Elien?"

"Yeah?"

"If anybody ever tells you it's not your fault or you're not responsible, and I'm just talking about what you do, that kind of thing, well, I don't think they're helping you."

"Will you please drive me to Tamika's apartment?" he asked.

I nodded, stood, and gave him a hand.

The apartment building was only another mile or so down the road. We parked halfway up the next block; a fire truck, an ambulance, and a pair of Bragg police cruisers sat out front. Elien took the lead, and I followed. On the sidewalk outside the building, a skinny black man with locs was talking into a phone. When he saw Elien, he disconnected and turned toward us.

"Shit," he said, and then he started to cry. Elien pulled him into a hug, and for a long time they just stood there, holding each other.

I jogged down to the cruisers; a guy about my age was leaning against one of the cars, and he was wearing the Bragg uniform.

"Dag LeBlanc," I said. "Deputy with the county. Any chance you can tell me what's going on?"

"Suicide," the guy said. "Blew her head off."

"You're sure?"

"That's what the tranny says."

I glanced back at Kenny, who was wiping his face and listening to Elien. I remembered Mason calling him St. Elien. It was hard to match what I was seeing here, the way Kenny poured out his grief to Elien, the way Elien took that grief and gave back something better for Kenny to hold on to, with the selfish asshole who'd been riding shotgun just ten minutes earlier.

"Say that word again," I said, "and I'll have every newspaper in the country printing your name and badge number. It's the twenty-first fucking century."

"Who the fuck do you think you are?"

I headed back to Elien and Kenny.

"—can handle this, Kenny," Elien was saying, his hand on Kenny's shoulder. "You know you can. You've been through worse, and you came out the other side."

"I know, man, but I was right there. I was right there, and I couldn't do anything."

Elien glanced at me as I approached, and Kenny followed his gaze.

"This is Mason's friend," Elien said.

"I remember you," Kenny said, shaking my hand. Then he went back to wiping away tears. "I'm sorry about Mason, man. Nobody . . . nobody can believe what happened. And now Tamika. Aw, fuck, man. This is so fucked up."

"I'm sorry for your loss," I said, "but I need to ask you a few questions."

Kenny glanced at Elien, and Elien nodded.

"Questions about what? About Tamika?"

"You were with her before she died?"

Sniffling, Kenny nodded.

"Did you see anything strange?"

"She blew her fucking head off, man. I was standing right there. How strange can it get?"

"Kenny," Elien said. "This is important. Did she look different? Act different? Say anything that didn't make sense?"

Kenny shook his head. But when he spoke, his words were slow. "We'd been . . . we'd been seeing each other, you know. Outside the group. We understood each other. I thought we did. We'd started, you know, staying over. Things like that. I didn't even know she had a gun. She'd been acting kind of nasty since Tuesday. I thought she was just having a bad week, with Mason, and Ray just before. Today, though. Today she was just being cruel. Slapped me a few times." Kenny touched his cheek. "Called me some bad shit. She was on something, I think, because her eyes were different. Shiny. Sometimes she'd move her head too fast and I'd swear they were blue. I told her I wasn't going to stick around for her to treat me like that. She grabbed the gun, put it right here," he touched his temple, "and said, 'Please stop me, please stop me, please Kenny, oh Christ, please stop me.' And then she did it, man." Kenny started to cry again. "And I didn't stop her, man. I couldn't even move."

"Did you notice—" I began.

Elien jerked his head at me, folding Kenny into an embrace.

"I think I need to stay with Kenny," Elien said quietly. "Thanks for driving me over."

"I'll stay."

"You don't have to do that."

"Elien, I'll stay."

I gave them space, and after a while they sat together, their backs to the painted brick of the apartment building, holding hands. I went back to the Escort and got my Coke and perched on the trunk. The late morning smelled like cigarette smoke and garbage heating in the sun.

Part of my brain was turning this over and over. Kenny hadn't said anything about blue lights. What he'd described could have been an ordinary suicide—if any suicide could be ordinary. It was a tragedy, yes, but it didn't match what Elien and I had seen.

But I didn't believe it was ordinary. First Ray. Then Mason. Elien had been attacked in the woods outside his house. And now Tamika. Four people who were part of the same support group. That wasn't a coincidence.

It feeds on human lives, especially on pain.

Well, for a creature that fed on pain, a PTSD support group would be a banquet.

Two thoughts came to me. First, this thing, the hashok, was going through its . . . cattle, for lack of a better word, fast. Too fast, it seemed to me. Which meant that either its feeding wasn't on the kind of regular schedule I had imagined—perhaps it had active and inactive periods, or something like hibernation—or something was wrong.

My second thought came because of the cigarette smoke. The smell of something burning made me look at the fire truck slanted across the street, and the fire truck made me think of arsonists. The thing about arsonists, a lot of them anyway, was that they got picked up pretty easily because they hung around the scene of the crime, or they came back, or they kept coming back. They liked to see their handiwork.

Could the hashok be like that? It had lingered after Ray's death. Did it stay to watch the fallout from its feeding?

A crowd had gathered, and I searched the faces, snapping pictures with my phone to try to record all of them. I watched one man in particular: he wore winter gloves, and he walked up and down the sidewalk opposite Tamika's building, laughing.

ELIEN (11)

The helplessness was almost as bad as the grief itself. Outside Tamika's building, I hugged Kenny, I talked to the cops, I called Zahra and let her know what had happened. But I couldn't really do anything—not anything that mattered. Kenny still blamed himself, no matter what I said. The cops wouldn't tell me anything because I wasn't family. And Zahra told me to take care of myself.

"Richard and I have a conference tonight," she said, "and I don't want you to be alone."

"I'll be fine."

"Frankly, Elien, I don't think any of us are going to be fine for quite a while. You've heard of suicide clusters? Well, we're right in the middle of one, and if we don't take care of ourselves, it's going to get worse." On the phone, she sounded flat, almost distracted, as though she were finishing up dinner and couldn't manage to get me off the phone. "I'm telling you as your doctor, I don't want you to be alone tonight. Who can you call? Go to a friend's house. Go out and have dinner, see a movie, do something until Richard's on his way home. I'll tell him to call you. I think you and I should meet as soon as we can. How about Monday?"

"What's the conference?" I said.

"The Louisiana Mental Health Professionals Network. I'm serious about having a session together, Elien. You missed the support group this week."

"Well, funny story: someone tried to shoot me last week."

"Elien."

"I'd really hate for Richard to have to miss his fucking conference."

I disconnected and glanced up the block. Dag was still sitting on the trunk of his piece of shit car, and he gave me a wave. He'd been there for hours now; it was early afternoon, and the coroner's office had already come and taken Tamika. Kenny was gone, and the firetruck had left a while before. The cops were packing up too.

When I got to the Ford, Dag hopped off the trunk. "How are you?"

"I want to pick a fight."

"I'd rather not."

"I want to break some of Richard's expensive shit."

"I don't think that's a good idea."

"I want to scream."

"You can scream. Screaming is allowed."

I cocked my head, studying him.

He gave back an uncertain grin.

"One time," he said, "I stepped on a canebrake rattlesnake. It was just a baby, and it zipped off as fast as it could. I screamed so loud I hurt my throat."

"No," I finally said. "It's no fun if it doesn't bother you."

"Can I give you a ride somewhere?"

"Home, I guess. Please."

So we got in the car, and thankfully the windows were down, because on the drive over I was sure I had smelled a Big Mac lurking in the back seat. Dag pulled away from the curb, and we looped north and then east, following the edge of Moulinbas toward the state highway.

Then Dag pulled into a small parking lot; the building ahead of us looked like the rest of Moulinbas, a Creole townhouse with ancient panes of glass, the wrought-iron balcony pulling away from the brick in places. A sign proclaimed this place Taverne Grise.

"They've got good po'boys," Dag said.

"I'm not hungry."

"You had half a croissant and some coffee."

"And about a million calories of Coke."

"Nobody thinks clearly on an empty stomach. You'll feel better too."

"Oh, really? I'll feel better about my friend blowing her brains out if I eat a po'boy? Jesus fucking Christ, where were you last week? Or the week before that? I really could have used some great fucking advice like this."

Dag sighed and got out of the car.

"You can't just leave me out here," I screamed after him.

"The windows are down."

"I'm not a fucking dog."

He muttered something that sounded like, "Yeah, I like dogs."

I stalled for five minutes after he went into the restaurant, getting angrier and angrier, revving myself up. Then I headed into Taverne

Grise. It consisted of a single, large dining room, with one wall painted lilac, picture windows looking out onto the street, and a bar. Dag was sitting at the bar, a drink, maybe whisky, in front of him while he did something with his phone.

Sliding onto the stool next to him, I said, "Where the fuck do you get off?"

"I told you: I don't like being talked to that way."

"I'll talk to you however I—"

"Please don't talk to me like that."

It was the tone, more than the words, that stopped me: he sounded like a kid. I forgot what I'd been about to say. His dark eyes flitted over my face, and then he looked back at his phone.

I squirmed on the stool, pressed hands to my flushed cheeks, and took a few breaths.

"Maybe some food would help," I said.

He swiped at something on his phone.

"I guess I got out of control again," I said.

He swiped again. I tried to look over his shoulder, but he angled the phone away. I wondered if he was on Grindr.

"I shouldn't have talked to you like that."

Dag held up two fingers.

"I know, I know. It was the second time. Strike two."

"No, Elien." He swiped at his phone again. "Jesus. Two words. You've got to say two words."

"Two words?"

"Two magic words."

"Oh, right. Those two magic words." The bartender, a pretty young woman with a mountain of brown curls, came toward us. "Rum and Coke," I said to her. "Bacardi. And what kind of salads—"

"I already ordered you a po'boy," Dag said.

"No, that's too much bread."

Looking up from his phone, Dag caught the bartender's eye and said, "He's still having the po'boy."

She smirked. She was still smirking when she brought back my rum and Coke.

"Two words," I said. "Two magic words."

Dag waved two fingers again, his attention still on his phone.

"Fuck me," I said.

A slight shake of his head.

"Do me."

Another.

"Bone me."

"This is boring, Elien."

"Doggy style."

I thought I detected the first signs of a grin.

"Bend over," I said.

He actually looked away from the phone that time and met my gaze.

"Spread 'em," I said.

He rolled his eyes.

"Blow job."

"You have a one-track mind," Dag said, already turning back to his phone.

"I'm sorry," I said.

"It's ok," he said, pocketing the phone, and giving me a smile. "Thank you for saying that."

And the worst part was that he sounded like he meant it.

When the bartender came back, she had two po'boys plated with French fries. I stared at the concoction in front of me: fried shrimp, lettuce, tomato, pickles, and mayo, all of it on what was basically the equivalent of a loaf of bread. My stomach growled.

"So," I said, picking out a fried shrimp and eating. "You don't ever get in fights? Not with anybody?"

"I mean, I guess I do."

"When was the last time you were in a fight?"

"I don't know. Mason liked to give me shit. I probably got mad at him for something." Dag picked up his sandwich and took a huge bite. Around a mouthful of food, he said, "Probably about a boy."

"Mason liked guys too?"

Dag swallowed, took a drink, and shook his head. "No, but he liked to give me shit about them, and I can get sensitive."

"You?"

He shrugged and took another bite.

"I can't even get you to tell me to shut up."

"Try your sandwich," he said.

"You just politely disengage and leave me screaming mad."

Wiping his mouth with a napkin, he smiled again and said, "I think you'll like the sandwich."

"Oh my Christ, what is it with you and this po'boy?" I grabbed it, took a bite, and groaned. I chewed as fast as I could and said, "That's good."

"Uh huh."

I had three more bites before I put it down. "That's really good," I said.

Dag was halfway through his, and he was staring at me, at the po'boy on my plate.

I said, "Yeah, I'm not really hungry."

"Oh," he said and took another huge bite.

I shrugged. "Honestly."

"Ok."

"Actually, I am hungry," I said.

His chewing slowed, and he watched me.

"I want to eat this whole thing because it's delicious, and I never have bread, and fried shrimp is one of my top five favorite foods, and I haven't really eaten anything today. But I know if I do eat it, I'll feel terrible in five minutes, and I'll end up in the bathroom with my finger down my throat. I don't even know if I really have an eating disorder or if I just do it to piss Richard off. So, there. I guess that's the real answer."

After some more chewing, Dag ran the back of his hand across his mouth, picking up some extra mayonnaise.

"Kind of more than you wanted to hear, right?"

"Nope," he said. "I like learning about you."

"Yeah, well, you just cracked the lid on a barrel of really fucked-up stuff."

"I don't think you're fucked up. A little rude sometimes. Definitely spoiled. But you're actually really sweet. I don't think anybody else could have talked to Kenny the way you did. He was right on the edge, and somehow you helped him come back down. It's one of the coolest things I've ever seen. I wish I knew how to do that. Every day, I talk to people, and I try to get them to come down like that. You did it without even trying. That's some powerful stuff."

Taking a drink of my rum and Coke, I looked away, staring at the bottles at the back of the bar. When I pulled the glass away, I ran my thumb along its base and studied the ice, the wedge of lime, the glint of light under my fingers.

"Spoiled," I said.

"Oh yeah, definitely. Let me guess: only child."

I shook my head.

"Youngest."

"Yep," I said.

"How many siblings do you have?"

"Have? Zero. My brother is dead."

"Oh damn. I'm sorry."

"Here we go," I said, "just to get it all out of the way: he killed my parents and then himself."

I kept my gaze on the glass. It blurred and doubled and the light on the rim turned into a white crescent when I tilted it at the right angle.

"Elien, I am so sorry." Dag touched my shoulder, and I realized he was pulling me into a hug. For a moment, I pulled back, not sure what was happening. Then my face was against his neck, and I smelled his deodorant and his hair and the detergent on his shirt, and he squeezed me tight, and I started crying.

"It's the rum," I said, pulling away and wiping my eyes. "Jesus, it was over a year ago, and I don't cry about it anymore, but I haven't had a drink in a long time. It's hitting me pretty hard right now."

"You can cry about it," Dag said. "Come here, I want to hug you again."

And he did. This time, he squeezed so hard I grunted and had to tap out.

"Ok," I croaked, and I drew in a huge breath. "Ok, so, now I realize you are a murderously compassionate teddy bear. Any more sympathy hugs and I'm going to have punctured lungs."

Then I started crying again, but not as hard, and I finished the rum and Coke and started eating my sandwich so I wouldn't have to talk. I had another drink, and even though Dag objected, I had a third, and I finished my sandwich and all my fries.

Dag had to help me out to the car. He got me stretched out in the backseat. The sun felt good on me, and the breeze when he drove, and I smelled clover and sorghum and the cool, damp places under trees, dead leaves and the shadowy greenness of Spanish moss. I wasn't sure if I slept, but when my head was clearer, I sat up and realized the car had stopped moving.

"I have to pee," I said.

"Pick a tree," Dag said.

I staggered out of the car, put a few of the old oaks between me and the car, and peed. I took in my surroundings and guessed we were in a state park: lots of oaks, a few magnolia trees along the gravel road, Spanish moss and ferns and a thick layer of wet leaves that was spongy when I walked on it. Water glistened to my right, and I guessed that was Lake Pontchartrain.

When I got back to the car, Dag had hand sanitizer and a bottle of water.

"You're a regular mother hen," I said.

He just smiled.

"I'm sorry," I said.

"You're going to be sorrier if you don't drink all that water. You said you haven't had a drink lately, but you put those rum and Cokes back pretty fast."

So I drank the bottle of water, and we leaned against the car, the heat of his body brighter than the sunlight.

"This is a nice place," I said.

"My dad used to take me camping here."

"Do you have siblings?"

"No, just me and my parents."

"And they're insane about you."

"They're definitely insane," he said with a smile.

I set the cap on the empty bottle and spun it closed, open, closed. "My parents loved me, I guess. But they were just kind of . . . quiet about it. I don't know. They freaked out when I told them I was gay, and then they tried to be nice about it, but it was like this huge gap that never really closed. It's not like they kicked me out or anything. I just couldn't talk to them. Gard, that's my brother, he and I were really close when we were young, but it got harder and harder. I mean, now I know he was really ill. But at the time, I just thought he was strange. He spent more and more time in his room. He wouldn't talk to my parents, then he wouldn't even talk to me, and I thought maybe he had really good friends online."

Dag put his arm over my shoulders and pulled me against him.

"I know it's not my fault," I said. "I know, I know, I know."

He made a noise low in his chest.

"I was in the other room getting fucked, if you want the whole picture," I said. "My first time. I'd done other stuff, you know, but that was my first time getting fucked. You think I'm fucked up? There's one more piece of the puzzle."

"I don't think you're fucked up."

"You're not the first person I've told this. I don't even know why I'm telling you this. I told Zahra; she's my shrink. I told Richard."

"Thanks for telling me," he said. "Thanks for trusting me."

"I wasn't always such a brat, by the way. It's just . . . I don't know. Richard puts up with it. And I know I can get away with it. That's a bad reason. But I didn't . . . I didn't used to act like this."

"Nobody's perfect," Dag said.

I let my head rest on his shoulder.

"The longest I ever had a boyfriend was close to six months," Dag said. "I'm just telling you to make a point. And when he left, he just left. He stopped answering my calls. Cut me off completely without a word. And I am not, um, very good with money. So it was two more months before I realized he had stolen my debit card, and my rent checks had been bouncing, my tuition check bounced, and he'd emptied my savings, and I was so embarrassed because I'm a deputy that I didn't even file charges. I moved back in with my parents when I got evicted, and then I just stayed, I guess. I couldn't figure out why I should move out again."

"What was his name?"

"Why?"

"Because I will go cut that bitch."

Dag laughed. His hand slid to the back of my neck, and he ran his thumb over two vertebrae before turning so he could look at me.

"Can I ask you something serious?"

"My story about my dead brother and parents wasn't serious enough?"

"Do you know who this guy is?"

He displayed his phone. On the screen was a picture of David, pacing the sidewalk opposite Tamika's building. He was wearing his winter gloves, the way he always did. The picture had obviously been taken today: I recognized the fire truck parked across the street and the police cruisers.

"Why'd you take this?"

And then Dag explained his thoughts about cattle and feeding, an irregular cycle of hibernation or maybe something had gone wrong, and the idea that the hashok might like to see the results of its work.

"You think David is the hashok?"

"Well, he was there, which was weird, and he was laughing, which was weird, and—"

"David could have been there for a lot of reasons. It could have been coincidence. And the laughing is weird, but it's not . . . I mean, he's always done it."

But I remembered Suzette telling me, *It feeds on human lives, especially on pain,* and I remembered David laughing at the strangest times, laughing at the worst, most painful parts of people's stories. Nerves, I had always said. Or just not processing emotions properly. But something twisted in my gut as I looked at the picture on Dag's phone.

"Well, it's actually the gloves that make me worried." Dag reached into the car and pulled out the book from the library. Raising *New Orleans and La Louisiane: Chorography, Ethnography, and the Native Episteme,* he said, "Have you read the part about the hashok in here?"

I shook my head.

"It's not called that. It's called—here it is, 'A Native Vampirum of Lake Pontchartrain,' and a lot of the article is this ethnographer talking about how he interviewed an old Choctaw woman who lived in a log house right by the lake, and he goes on and on about how she gathered wood and how she built a fire and how she made her tea and the different uses she had for moss. I mean, kind of your typical ethnography."

"Right," I said. "Just your typical ethnography."

"But when he gets into the folklore, it's like . . . uncanny. She tells him about the hashok, although he keeps calling it a vampirum. She talks about people hurting themselves, about people killing themselves." Dag took a breath. "People killing their loved ones."

I remembered the dream, and the blue fire in Gard's dead eyes.

"It's like this chain reaction," Dag said. "Somehow, it gets into a population, and it just goes wild. One person does something terrible, and then someone else is affected by it, and they do something terrible, and they affect two people, maybe, or three, and they do something terrible."

"And more and more people suffer," I said. "And the hashok has more and more to eat."

"Yes. Up to a point. And then it stops. It reaches critical mass, or its sated, or it hibernates. Or something. Until it starts all over again." Dag paged through the book. "She talks about blue fire; she's says the hashok can be invisible except for its heart, which is like a firefly. Glowing, I guess. The ethnographer guy takes it as an opportunity to give a whole lecture on cultural similarities to the English will o' the wisp, and it does kind of sound similar."

"Leads people astray, right? That's what a will o' the wisp does. Leads them off the path. Leads them to their death."

"That's what this ethnographer goes on and on about," Dag said. "But that's not what the woman says. She says it leads them in circles. I think she's talking about these . . . these cycles, I guess. People getting caught in these horrible tragedies."

"That's a pretty common metaphor for PTSD," I said. "Stuck in a loop. Repeating the same thing over and over again."

Dag nodded.

"Suzette said other cultures had the same thing. She said another word for it was vampire, and that it feeds on human lives, on pain."

"Vampire," Dag said. "A kind of vampire, I guess. It's definitely feeding on people. The pain and suffering are part of it, but these people are dead, physically dead. Feeding on human lives sounds literal to me."

"So," I said, "it's feeding on the support group. And there are these ripples, so Ray dies, and it affects Mason, and Mason affects Tamika. Is that it?"

"Maybe. I think . . . I think it might go deeper than that."

"What do you mean?"

"Well, if it is a vampire, or like a vampire, there's a lot of folklore about them. They can pass for human in some circumstances. They can change shape—bats and wolves, but in some stories they can become fog or mist. You know, kind of like how this thing becomes a firefly. They're fast and strong, like this thing. They're hard to kill, like this thing. They can raise the dead, I guess, when they make them into their vampire servants."

"Ok. Vampires. Spooky, scary, lots of abilities. So why are you focused on David's gloves?"

"Oh, right. So this Choctaw woman, she tells him that the hashok puts a thorn in the hand of sleeping hunters. Hand or foot, actually. And it makes them capable of evil. So the ethnographer goes off on this long tangent about the aetiology of evil—"

"Right, everybody knows about the aetiology of evil."

"—and takes it as another piece of folklore. But we know the blue fire is real. We know the hashok is real. We saw it. Why wouldn't the thorn be real? In lots of stories, vampires have the ability to dominate the will of other creatures, even humans. They turn some of them into servants, like Renfield in the Dracula stories. And sometimes this ability is linked to physical wounds that the vampire gives—bite marks, right? But here, it's a thorn in the hand."

"How do you know so much about vampires?"

"I don't only read about whales."

"Oh my God, have I got a book for you. In chapter eight this guy asks his dark lord to give him an infernal breeding—"

"Anyway," Dag said, a flush in his cheeks, "I think David might be, you know, like a Renfield."

I blinked. "Wait, you think David is like an evil servant to this thing?"

"He's wearing gloves, right? That's a good way to hide a wound. He shows up at the scene of a tragedy that we think is connected to the hashok. He's in the support group. And we know the hashok is feeding off the support group."

"It could be a suicide cluster," I said. "Statistically—"

"We've got to decide, both of us, right now," Dag said. "Either we believe this is real, or we don't. I know I'm not the right person to say that; I've been a chickenshit about it. But we've got to decide. We can't keep going back and forth."

The lake lapped against the shore; an egret broke from a clump of brush, wings flapping hard to bear him up over the water. A jolt went through me, and I blew out a sharp breath.

"Yes, ok. I guess I believe it. I'm crazy otherwise, because I know what I saw. So I guess I believe it."

"Me too," Dag said.

"So what now?" I said.

"Now, we start investigating your friend David."

DAG (12)

We went back to my parents' house, and the smell of garlic and bacon met us at the door. Dad was in the living room, kicked back in an easy chair; Mom was moving around in the kitchen.

"Oh my God," Elien said. "That smells so good."

"Hi, boys," my dad said. He was flipping channels and settled on golf. "Dag, that nice young man at Rouses asked me why you stopped texting him."

I herded Elien toward the hall.

"What nice young man?" Elien called over my shoulder.

"Oh, Elien," my dad said, twisting in the chair to talk to him. "He's got these great eyes. Aquamarine, right, Gloria?"

"Turquoise," she screamed from the kitchen.

"Turquoise," my dad said.

"Nobody has turquoise eyes," I said.

Elien was being surprisingly hard to manhandle into my bedroom.

"What about his body?" Elien said.

"Well, he's very muscular," my dad said.

"He's not a bear," my mom shouted from the kitchen.

"No, he's not a bear," my dad said. "More of a twunk."

"Please stop," I said—to Elien, my dad, the universe.

"Dag, he's a twunk," Elien said. "Is that Dag's type?"

"Oh," my dad said. "I mean, Jackson wasn't quite as muscular. But Robbie had really strong thighs."

"What about body hair?" Elien said.

"That's it," I said, and I got him over my good shoulder and carried him into my room.

"I think he manscapes," my mom called after us. "He'd look very nice in a thong, I think."

Elien giggled into my neck until we got to the room, and then I tossed him on the bed and pointed a finger at him. "You are still drunk."

"A little. Your parents are cute."

"Please don't encourage them."

He sprawled on the bed, dragging his arms and legs across the bedding. "This is comfy."

"Great. I'm glad you like it. You can rent it out from my parents when I leave, and they'll set you up with Chad from Rouses."

"Oh my God, you actually texted him?"

"My dad made me promise."

"And?"

"And what?"

"And what happened?"

I rolled my eyes. "Let's work on finding David."

"In a minute. You texted him. What did you say?"

"Normal things."

Rolling onto his side, Elien propped his head in his hand and said, "I'm really good at dating. And flirting."

"Ok."

"Let me help you."

"That's not really the focus here."

"Hey," Elien said, his hazel eyes still soft from the rum. "It'll take five minutes. You deserve to be happy. This guy sounds super hot."

"Yeah, well, I told you about my awesome track history with guys."

"Don't do that."

I dropped into the desk chair. "What?"

"Don't shut everything down because one asshole got inside your life and messed things up."

"It's not just—"

"I know, I know. Badge bucks. That's just an excuse, though."

"No, it's—"

"Read me your texts to Chad."

"No."

With a grin creeping across his face, Elien began to bounce on the bed. "Oh, Dag, yes, give it to me!"

"Stop it," I hissed. "Fine, please, I will read you the texts."

As Elien bounced to a stop, he made a go-ahead gesture.

"Hi, Chad," I read. "This is Dag. My dad said he met you at the grocery store. Super weird, sorry about that."

"I mean, it's not great," Elien said.

"I do not need a running commentary."

"Ok, ok. What'd he say?"

"'Hahaha, no prob, your dad is really cool.' And then I said, 'No, my parents are the worst. Just murder me and you can pretend this never happened.' And then he said, 'Your dad said you were a deputy. I think murdering a deputy might be frowned on.' And then I said, 'Well, it's justified if you get approached creepily while you're doing your job.' Elien, please, do I have to do this?"

"It's cute. You guys are kind of bantering. He sounds smarter than I expected. A muscly twunk who works at Rouses and has a brain? You might be set for life."

I stared at him.

Laughing, he said, "Ok, just tell me how you guys left it."

"I said, 'Maybe we could get a drink sometime,' and he said, 'Yeah, I'd like that.'"

"And?"

"And what?"

"Oh my God. What did he say when you gave him a date and a time?"

"I, um, didn't want to annoy him."

Elien gave me a look.

"And he brought up the deputy thing. It feels like more of the same badge buck shit."

"He knows, like, two facts about you, and he learned them from having your dad proxy hit on him in a grocery store, while he was working. Maybe you can cut him a little slack."

"Ok, we talked about this, so now let's figure out where David—"

"No, no, no. We're going to get you on a date, and we are going to get you boned within an inch of your life."

"I don't really want to be boned within an inch of my life. It sounds uncomfortable, and—"

Elien surged off the bed and grabbed the phone out of my hands.

"Hey," I said, scrambling after him. "Give that back."

I caught up to him in the kitchen.

"Hi, Mrs. L," Elien said, smiling at my mom like he was just some beautiful, innocent waif who had wandered into our kitchen, when really he was a sexual dervish, the stuff of which nightmares are made.

"Well, hello, Elien," she said. She was kneading dough; in the cast iron skillet, bacon and garlic had finished cooking together and now sat at the back of the range.

"Just going to borrow a few things, Mrs. L," Elien said as he opened the fridge.

"Of course, sweetheart. But you really have to call me Gloria."

While Elien rummaged in the fridge, my mom kept looking at me and looking at Elien with annoyingly significant glances. I shook my head. She mouthed, *Invite him to dinner*. I shook my head again.

"Elien, dear, what are you doing for dinner?" my mom said.

"He has a boyfriend, Mom."

"I'm sure that's perfectly fine, but I just asked him about dinner, Dagobert. Elien, I'm making one of Dagobert's favorite meals: it's a Cajun shrimp pasta with garlic, bacon, and cheese bread twists. Oh, and a light salad."

Emerging from the refrigerator, Elien set carrots, celery, an eggplant, and pancetta on the counter.

"Pasta?" he asked.

"Over there, sweetheart," my mom said.

"Mom, stop. You're enabling him."

When Elien came back, he had dry spaghetti. He grabbed a bottle of red, the loaf of French bread next to my mom, and then he tugged on the strings of her apron and said, "I'll give it right back." And God damn it, the woman giggled as he turned her out of the apron. Elien arranged all of it on the counter, including the apron, and then snapped a picture with my phone. He tapped for a while and held it out.

"Ok?"

I read the message that was waiting to be sent. Along with the photograph of the food and the apron, he had written, *Sorry, had a friend pass away last week, and I'm still dealing with that. I didn't mean to ghost you. I'm missing one ingredient for this romantic dinner: you. Good thing I can swing by the grocery store and pick you up.*

"I think I'm going to throw up," I said.

"He'll like it," Elien said with a laugh. "Please let me send it."

"Dagobert, let him send it," my mom said.

"You don't even know what it says!"

"Please," Elien said.

I groaned.

"Fine," Elien said.

"No, just—ok, press Send before I change my mind."

I heard the little whoosh of the message zipping off into space. Groaning again, I let my head hit the counter.

The phone dinged.

"Told you," Elien said.

He was smirking when I snatched the phone back.

Sorry about your friend. Are you all right? Another ding. *Also, you are such a dork. Are you actually going to ask me to dinner, or do I need to invite myself over?*

Looking up at Elien, I said, "That actually worked?"

"Of course," he said.

"Of course," my mom said.

"Of course," my dad shouted from the living room.

"You don't even know what he did!"

"I know it was cute," my mom said. "Everyone likes something cute."

"You have to actually tell him a day and a time," Elien said, still smirking.

"Do not look so satisfied," I said.

"I'm just happy for you."

"No, you're smug. You look smug."

"Day and time, Dagobert," my mom said.

"Tell Chad what day," my dad shouted. "And a time."

"I'm going to become a monk," I said. "And take a vow of no parents. And nobody will talk to me or bother me."

Elien still had that damn grin on his face when he tapped the screen.

Friday? I wrote. *7?*

A big thumbs up came back. Then, *Are you all right? Really? I'm sorry about your friend.*

I'm ok, I texted back. *Thanks.*

If you need to talk, I'm pretty much always around.

Thanks.

I'll see you Friday!

Great! Thanks for being cool!

Elien grabbed my phone again. "And that's enough. Save something for the wedding night."

My mom laughed so hard she had to sit down.

I grabbed Elien and steered him down the hall.

"Elien," my dad shouted as we passed the living room. "Do you want to watch some golf?"

"Yes," he said, trying to get free.

"No," I said, "he doesn't. Why does everyone in this house like Elien more than me?"

When we got back to my room, I pushed him toward the chair, shut the door, and leaned against it.

"Chad's a very lucky guy," Elien said.

"Will you stop joking?"

His mouth quirked once, and he said, "Who says I'm joking?"

"Can we please try to find David now? A supernatural monster that creates catastrophic, spiraling violence is more important than my love life."

For a moment, Elien looked like he might say more. Then he shrugged, took out his phone, and said, "Let's see what we can find."

I did some online searches and found five people called David Bass in the DuPage-St. Tammany greater area. I searched county property tax records against those five addresses and eliminated three of them; my guess was that the David Bass I was looking for didn't own a two-hundred-thousand-dollar yacht, a hundred-thousand-dollar Tesla, or a two-million-dollar historic home just off the Quartier.

"Nobody has his address," Elien said. "I've tried everyone in the support group except Zahra, and she won't give it to me because she's a doctor and it's confidential."

"What about his phone number?"

"I have his phone number, but he's not responding to my messages, and he doesn't pick up when I call. His voicemail is shut off."

"What's the number?"

Elien read it to me, and I tried a reverse-number lookup.

"Dead end," I said. "What kind of car did he drive? Or did someone pick him up?"

"I don't know."

"You never saw him leaving a support group meeting?"

With a frown, Elien said, "I think he drove himself."

"You think?"

"I didn't catalogue what everybody drove."

"How about a Prius?"

"No, he definitely didn't drive a Prius."

Scanning the tabs of property record searches, I said, "What about an Impala?"

"I don't know."

"A Sonata?"

"Uhh."

"Ok, here's a picture of a 2002 Chevy Impala. And here's a picture of a 2010 Hyundai Sonata. Did his car look like either of those?"

Elien's thin, dark brows drew together. "It was brown?"

Grinning, I said, "So you're definitely not a car guy."

"Sorry."

"No, it's ok. We'll figure it out. We're down to two addresses. One is outside of Bragg, in an unincorporated part of DuPage Parish. Let's see what Google Maps shows. Mobile homes. Ok, and this other address is, ok, back in Moulinbas. Street view says . . . apartment above *Ye Olde Bookes Ande Treasurees*. God, how many extra e's did this person need?"

"What?"

"Nothing," I said. "Moulinbas makes sense, right, because he could have walked to Tamika's?"

"Moulinbas isn't tiny."

"Well, let's map it. Google Maps says . . . twenty-five-minute walk."

"That's pretty far."

"It's definitely walkable."

"But it's pretty far."

"Well, since you're a guest and you salvaged something from the wreckage of my attempt at dating, I'll let you decide."

"You're such a gentleman." Elien frowned and finger combed his blowout hair. "You decide."

"Oh my God, Elien. Just pick one of the two."

"You think Moulinbas."

"I didn't say that."

"Let's try the address in Moulinbas."

"Great. Let's go."

Elien hemmed. "Unless you think we should try the one out in DuPage Parish."

"Let's go."

"I want to know if you—"

"You were much more decisive when it was my love life on the line," I said, kicking him in the shins and ankles. "Get up."

"Jesus, God, ouch, that hurts!"

"Here we go."

"You're a fucking barbarian," Elien said, fighting a smile.

"Whatever it takes," I said.

We drove across town again, and I found a spot across from *Ye Olde Bookes Ande Treasurees*. The bricks had been painted gray, and a maze of Virginia creeper crawled along the wrought iron, the leaves turning scarlet in the autumn weather. Elien and I crossed the street. The second-floor apartment had a private staircase on the side, but a locked gate prevented access. Elien pointed to an intercom, and I buzzed up.

"Yes?" The voice was male and nasally.

Elien looked at me and shook his head.

"Hi," Elien said. "We're looking for David Bass."

"This is he."

Elien gave another shake.

"My name's Elien Martel. I'm trying to find a David Bass I know from a support group."

"I'm sorry, what?"

"Elien Martel. From the support group."

"I don't know any Elien. I'm sorry."

"Ok," Elien said, "thank—"

The speaker went dead.

"—you." With a shrug, Elien said to me, "This is why I thought we should try the address in DuPage Parish."

"Does Richard really put up with this kind of stuff?"

Elien grinned as we made our way back to the car. "All the time."

"That man is a saint."

"And he never kicks me in the legs."

"I'll tell him how well it works."

"Don't you fucking dare."

The drive out of Bragg was pleasant; the October day was drawing to a close, the sun low and fat in the west, the autumn sunlight cutting broad lines through fields of corn, outlining the round bales of bahiagrass, trimming the aisles of the pecan groves. It was the smell of the hayfield, though, that stayed in the car: dusty and sweet. Elien sneezed once.

"Let me guess," he said, running his arm under his nose. "No A/C."

Sticking a hand out the window, I said, "The whole world is our A/C."

"So that's a no," Elien said, but he just had another of those weird smiles.

We reached the mobile home neighborhood twenty minutes later, and if it had a name, I couldn't see it. Most of the homes were trailers with aluminum sidings. They were set up on blocks, which meant they all had stairs and a small deck. The gravel road cut between dirt and crabgrass yards, and dust floated up behind us. It didn't look like a bad place, but it looked like a hard place that people had tried to make better: on one of the homes, a paper banner had letters in crayon that said WELCOME HOME, BILLY; in front of another, a patch of sunflowers gave a shock of color; at the edge of the crabgrass ahead of us, someone had cobbled together a stand out of scrap lumber, and letters in black paint said LEMONADE 25C SMILES FREE.

When we got to David Bass's home, I could see some of the same effort at home improvement: the shutters had crisp white paint, and two potted mums sat on the deck. The lattice closing off the crawlspace looked new, and a raised bed for a vegetable garden was covered by a thick plastic sheet. He had a corner lot, so I drove to the end of the street and turned, wanting to see as much as I could before we approached the trailer.

Then I stopped.

"What's wrong with his door?" Elien asked.

My first thought was that a bear had gone at the screen door on the back of the mobile home. That was the only explanation for the long rents in the screen, for the way the aluminum frame had crumpled along one edge. My mind was already trying to come up with explanations: this was the last street of the trailer park, and it backed up to a stretch of woods that ran all the way to Bayou Pere Rigaud. A bear could have come out of the forest. Sure, I thought. And that same bear just wandered up to David Bass's back door and clawed his way inside.

I put the car in park and left the engine running. "Stay here."

"No way."

"Elien, it's not a conversation. Stay here. Get behind the wheel, and if you see anybody besides me come out of there, you drive away as fast as you can. Come on, slide over."

"Yeah," Elien said, his eyes softening. "Thank you. Of course."

As I got out of the car, Elien reached over, turned off the car, and pocketed the keys.

"What are you doing?" I whispered.

"Going with you."

"You don't have a gun."

"Neither do you."

"You could be in danger."

"So could you."

"Yes, but I'm—"

"What? Butch?"

"What? No, a deputy."

Sliding out of the car, Elien turned his attention to the mobile home. I came around and grabbed his arm.

"I appreciate what you're doing," Elien said. "But I can take care of myself."

I could smell that peppery, prickly heat of him; it filled my lungs like gas waiting for a match.

"I'm going first," I said.

"You might have to let go of my arm."

I gave him a little shake because the other option was growling.

"It'll be ok," he said, and he squeezed my fingers before pulling my hand loose.

The treads of the steps groaned as I went up them. The wind picked up, stirring the chimes that hung from the end of the trailer. Then the breeze snapped the screen door open, and I froze, my knuckles white where I gripped the rail. Sweat broke out across my chest, my back, stinging drops under my arms. After ten seconds, I eased myself up another step, and then the door banged shut. Pennants of torn screen drifted, stirred by the breeze.

When I got my hand on the door, I counted another ten seconds, and then I pulled it open and slipped inside. I smelled death immediately: loose bowels, blood. I was in a small kitchen. A bag of microwaveable wild rice sat on the counter, and the microwave door was open. 0:02 flashed on the timer.

Keeping my steps as quiet as I could, I moved along the trailer, checking rooms as I went: the living room, with a console TV and a plaster Jesus nailed to a six-inch cross; a room filled with banker's boxes; an office with an ancient laptop and a Cheshire cat mural on the resin paneling; a bathroom with a soap dish shaped to look like a rubber ducky. A closet, its door open, dozens of pairs of winter gloves clothespinned to hangers.

In the last room, David Bass lay on a futon. He had been sliced open: three huge gashes that ran diagonally from shoulder to hip. The smell of ruptured bowels made me gag. Elien poked his head past me, winced, and hurried away.

I lingered a moment, trying to figure it out.

David Bass hadn't killed himself. The hashok had murdered him.

ELIEN (13)

I stood in the small office in David's trailer. The Cheshire cat was staring at me.

In the hallway behind me, Dag's footsteps moved closer.

"We need to go."

I nodded.

"Right now, Elien."

I nodded again. And then I disconnected the laptop, wrapped up the power supply's cables, and grabbed both.

"What are you doing?" Dag asked. "Put that back."

I shouldered past him into the hall and made my way to the room with the banker's boxes. With my elbow, I popped the lid off the closest one; it was only half full.

"Hold this," I said, passing the laptop to Dag.

"Absolutely not," he said as he took it. "Elien, David is dead."

"I'm not stupid. I know he's dead."

"We need to leave, and then we need to make an anonymous call to the sheriff's department, and then we need to figure out what the hell is going on."

"What's going on," I said as I rummaged through the documents, "is the hashok killed David."

"We don't know that."

I looked over my shoulder at him, and Dag's eyes cut away.

"Let's take this box too," I said. "It looks like every piece of mail he's gotten in the last month."

"Absolutely not," Dag said again.

I put the lid back on the box and picked it up. "Ok. Just one more thing."

Standing in the doorway, Dag set his jaw. "Elien, we cannot take this stuff. This is going to be a crime scene."

"Do you think the hashok left fingerprints? And they're going to run them through a database and then find his driver's license and get his home address?"

"We're leaving fingerprints, do you understand? We're taking things. If we get caught, we won't just get in trouble for disturbing a crime scene. They'll have an unsolvable murder, and they'll have two people with a weird connection to the victim. Even if they don't want to believe we did this, it'll look so strange they won't have a choice."

"So far," I said, I've only touched the laptop and the cords and this box. I haven't left fingerprints anywhere else."

Dag was taking deep breaths.

"Have you?" I asked.

"The door. We'll wipe it down when we leave."

"So let's take this stuff and go. After I check one more thing."

"Why?"

"Because, Dag, the hashok murdered him. It wasn't willing to wait for the cycle of violence to catch up with him. It needed him out of the way. And I want to know why. If we're going to stop this thing, we need to understand it."

For a moment, those dark eyes were very steady on me.

"Please," I said.

"This is a bad idea," he said.

"Then it's my bad idea. You can go. I know this is crossing over into your professional life; I don't want to make you choose."

With a snort, Dag shook his head and stepped back from the doorway. "It invaded my personal life the minute Mason pulled a gun on you. Now we're just watching the shit fly. Let's go before someone sees us."

"One more thing," I said, turning back to where David lay.

"What?"

"His hands."

When I got to the bedroom at the end of the mobile home, I set the banker's box on the ground. I inched closer to David. His skin was waxy; blood soaked the carpet around him, and the room smelled like shit. I leaned over as close as I dared, and then I used the hem of my t-shirt to tug the winter gloves off one by one. His hands looked shockingly small without them, the skin pale and smooth. Using the gloves, I rotated his hands palm up. Neither showed any sign of a wound or mark.

"Feet," Dag whispered.

I lucked out because David was wearing house slippers without socks; I knocked them off using the back of my hand and studied his feet. Then I shook my head and crept back toward the hallway.

"Anything?" Dag asked.

"He didn't own a toenail clipper, apparently. Nothing that looked like a thorn in his foot or hand. No scars."

Dag grunted. "I guess that makes sense; the hashok wouldn't kill him if he was an evil henchman."

"Let's find a way to talk about this that doesn't sound like we're participants at Medieval Times."

We left through the back door, hurried down the creaking steps, and got in the Escort as fast as we could. Dag drove back to the state road at a leisurely pace; little puffs of gravel chased us, the smell of the dust mixing with the Big Mac aroma from the back seat. When we were on the highway, Dag shot up to sixty, and the end-of-day autumn warmth whipped through the car.

"Could you drop me off?" I asked. "Otherwise I have to ask Muriel for a ride, and she'd just absolutely love that."

"Yeah," Dag said. "Do I cut off up here?"

I nodded.

"Who's Muriel?" he asked.

"She's a nurse practitioner at Richard's office."

"Like, she sees patients too, that kind of thing?"

"Right. She's licensed to work under a psychiatrist, so she can do a lot of the same work, she just can't go out and have her own practice. Does that make sense?"

Dag nodded. "Why does she drive you around?"

"Well, most of the time Richard does. But she lives out our direction, past us actually, closer to Pere Rigaud, and when Richard isn't going into Bragg or when he's got to change his normal schedule, she'll help out."

"Why don't you drive?"

I smiled and leaned my head back. "I was in a terrible car accident. I have a fear of driving."

"Oh, God. I'm so sorry."

"No, that's bullshit."

I couldn't see it, but I could sense Dag rolling his eyes.

"Ok," he finally said. "So what's the real reason?"

"I like it. It's empowering, you know. Making people do what you want them to do? It's kind of like a blowjob. People think giving a blowjob is submissive, but it doesn't have to be. I'm the one giving pleasure. I'm the one with my teeth on his cock."

"Fine," Dag said. "Don't tell me."

"I never learned how to drive."

Dag glanced at me, and then his attention went back to the road as we turned.

"My parents weren't exactly pushing us to learn, and I didn't move out for college, and I don't know. I just never felt like I needed to."

"Oh."

"It's embarrassing."

"No, it's not."

"It is."

"No, not at all. I think that's a lot more common now, actually." Dag ran his hand over the short bristles of graying hair. "I could teach you. If you wanted to learn, I mean."

Closing my eyes, I groaned. "Oh my God."

"What?"

I squeezed my eyes shut even tighter. "Are you even real? Are you a real person?"

"What? What's going on?"

"Nothing. I just feel like shit now."

The Escort rumbled on for another thirty seconds before Dag said, "Oh."

We were passing through a portion of the same forest that ran alongside the mobile home community where David had lived, the same forest that stretched east and north along the Okhlili until it hit the bayou. Black oaks and sugar maples. A few cypresses. With the windows down, I could smell the cool, damp earth between the trees and motor oil and a mixture of sweat and talcum powder.

"The truth," I said. "The honest-to-God truth, I swear, is that Zahra put me on some really strong anti-psych meds when I first started seeing her. I was driving, lost control, and hit a mailbox and tore up a guy's yard. They took my license. I'm not on the anti-psych meds anymore, just so you know, although maybe I need them. I think I can apply for my license again in a couple of months."

He was still focused on the road.

"I'm sorry," I said. "Please don't be mad at me. I do stupid stuff, which you already know, and now I feel really fucking awful."

"It's ok," Dag said, and he gave me a little smile. "I guess I sounded pretty stupid."

"No, you didn't."

"Kind of my curse. Same thing with that guy who took my debit card. I'm just gullible."

"No, that's not true. I'm an asshole. I'm really sorry."

"You were just joking," Dag said. "I can take a joke."

I fell back against the seat for the rest of the drive. I tried to think of what Richard would say, but all I got was a white hiss at the back of my brain and the desire to really fuck something up. Myself, first of all. I just wanted to fuck myself up badly.

When we drove up to the house, dusk was coming down like a curtain, and the automatic lights were already on. Staring at the modern farmhouse aesthetic, the three-car garage, the St. Augustine grass, the Pottery Barn rocking chairs, I had a hard time remembering that monsters were real, and that one of them had nearly killed me just a hundred yards from where I was.

"Please come inside," I said.

"I should get home."

"Please, Dag. Richard's gone, and I don't want to be alone, and I feel awful for lying to you, and I'm sick about Ray and Mason and Tamika and David." I blew out a breath. "I'm trying really hard not to, you know, throw a fit like I normally would, so I'm just going to tell you I really want to fuck myself up, and it would mean a lot to me if you would overlook all the shitty things I've done to you and hang out until Richard gets home."

"Ok," he said. He turned off the car, but he didn't reach for the door. "One condition."

"I will apologize on my hands and knees."

"Nope. Let's hear one thing that you like about Eli."

"I go by Elien now."

"I know," he said. "But your name is Eli."

"What if there's nothing I like about Eli?"

"I guess I'm going home."

"Can I have a few minutes?"

"Sure."

"Can we go inside?"

"Is that a trick?"

"No tricks," I said, my mouth dry. "Can we please go inside?"

Dag nodded. His eyes were very brown and very soft.

He carried the laptop; I took the banker's box. I let us in through the front door, and we set up a workstation in the breakfast nook.

"Are you hungry?" I asked.

"Pretty much always."

"You're missing your mom's bacon cheese knots for this," I said. "I can't compete with that. She's going to kill me after she worked so hard on dinner."

"Honestly? I think they're just happy I'm out of the house."

I opened the refrigerator and took out a chicken, a lemon, and a bundle of herbs. Then I grabbed potatoes and onions from the pantry. "One thing I like about Eli," I said, and I knew I was barely loud enough to be heard over the clatter I was making with the food, "is that he is a pretty good cook. Or he was, anyway, before he got so weird about food."

Dag leaned against the counter; he was breathing normally, but for some reason, it sounded like the only noise in the universe. I imagined I could feel each breath ghosting over my skin. The hairs on the back of my neck stood up.

"Go ahead and sit down," I said. "Do you want a drink? This'll take about an hour."

"A drink sounds nice."

"Bar's over there."

"What do you want?"

"God, I don't know. Those rum and Cokes nearly destroyed me."

For a while, Dag was at the bar. He examined the bottles and said, "You've got good taste."

"Richard does. I couldn't drink while I was still on my meds."

Dag hesitated, his hand stopping in the middle of reaching for a bottle of Bywater.

"I guess I shouldn't have said that," I said.

"Are you supposed to be off your medicine?"

"No," I said, stripping the packaging from the chicken. "But I was sick of feeling dead all the time. This is better."

"Eli—"

"Please don't make this a thing tonight." I got a knife and began halving the lemon and onions. "I've got enough people in my life taking care of me, and I'm so fucking sick of it I could scream."

When Dag came back, he had a tumbler of Bywater; I could smell the bourbon. He slid past me to the fridge, and bottles clinked. He set a glass next to me.

"Vodka tonic," he said.

"That's so civilized."

"Why don't we see how one goes?"

"That's very smart."

He sipped his bourbon.

I brought the knife down hard through another onion. "Sometimes I get fucking sick of doing things the smart way."

"That kind of stuff, you've got to cut it out if I'm going to stay."

"Ok," I said, bringing the knife down hard again. "Ok."

He took a seat at the breakfast table, opened the box, and began sorting the papers. "He kept everything," Dag said. "Electric bills, water bills, rent payments for the lot in the mobile home community. Medical. DuPage Behavioral. Have you heard of them?"

"Once or twice," I said. "That's Richard's practice."

"Wait, what?"

"Yeah. I mean, it's not his exclusively. Him, Zahra, Rodney, Joe, Irene, Muriel. Um, they have some regular nurses, too, I mean, not NPs like Muriel. And they've got administrative assistants, people who handle the appointments, the billing. But the five doctors and Muriel."

"That seems lopsided. Wouldn't it be cheaper to have one doctor and several nurse practitioners?"

"Cheaper? Definitely?" I stripped rosemary; the bruised needles left their scent on my fingertips. "But DuPage Behavioral isn't about cheaper. They're like . . . a luxury provider. I don't know if that makes sense. They focus on behavioral health, but that means they mostly handle substance abuse and what they call 'distressed executives.' In other words, rich white guys who throw temper tantrums or sexually assault employees, and their companies can't get rid of them, so they send them to Richard. And then you've got people like me. PTSD that affects everyday living."

"Is that how you met Richard?"

"No. Other way, actually. I met him, and when we started dating, he suggested I see Zahra."

"Is that, you know, ethical?"

"It was my choice, and I like Zahra."

"Did you know David was a patient there too?"

I shook my head as I stuffed the chicken with lemon, onion, and herbs. "But it makes sense, kind of. The support group is Zahra's baby. It's a volunteer project, but I'm not surprised she refers her patients to it. That's how I started going to it."

"How many other people in the group came from DuPage Behavioral?"

I crushed a clove of garlic with the flat of the knife. "I don't know."

Dag opened David's laptop, powered it up, and said, "No password."

"Are you kidding? That thing looks like it's from the Stone Age. Big surprise."

"It's definitely, um, not fast."

I glanced over and saw the Windows 7 screen loading. "If it's a cycle, where does it start?"

"What?" Dag asked, his attention mostly on the laptop as he dragged a finger across the trackpad.

"You said it's a cycle of violence. Where does it start? It should have a single starting point and then move out from there, right? It gets bigger and bigger."

"I guess." Dag glanced over at me. "What are you talking about?"

"If I tell you something, will you promise not to think I'm crazy? Even though I told you I used to be on anti-psych meds. Even though I told you I stopped taking all my meds."

"We're investigating a monster that can turn into a blue firefly and a million other weird things. Yes, I'll hold off on the judgment."

"I think maybe I saw a blue light in Gard's eyes the night he, you know."

"You think?"

"I don't know. I have these dreams still. And lately, in the dreams, I see blue. The clock was blue, even though it was really green. Blue in Gard's eyes, even though in life they'd been brown. I don't know if it's just my brain trying to make sense of everything or—"

"Or if you're actually remembering something?"

Working butter under the chicken skin, I nodded without looking up.

"It could be both, actually," Dag said. "Now can I ask you something, no judgment?"

"Yes, I think you have earned lifetime immunity for any questions you want to ask."

"You said Gard wasn't well. Did he see a therapist? A psychiatrist?"

I grabbed garlic and rosemary and worked it under the skin. "You're asking if he was a patient at DuPage Behavioral."

"Right now, I'm just asking if he was seeing a therapist or a psychiatrist."

"Yes. He was."

"Who?"

"I don't know."

"Oh. Too bad."

"I'll check." I washed my hands, put the chicken in the oven to roast, and headed for the garage. "Be right back."

After my parents and Gard had died, when I had to handle cleaning out the house and selling it and all the logistical nightmares that follow a tragedy, I'd reached a breaking point. I managed to unload the house, and I managed to collect the insurance and handle the pressing emergencies. I got rid of their stuff. And all the paperwork that I figured I should go through and shred or save, I boxed up and put in storage. When I moved in with Richard, he let me move it into the garage. I flipped on the lights, glad that even the garage was climate controlled, and worked my way through the boxes until I found the insurance paperwork. I stared at the page in my hand, and then I carried it back into the kitchen.

Dag was clicking through files on the computer.

I laid the paper down in front of him.

He glanced at it, and then his eyes flicked up to me. "Is Rodney Gutierrez . . ."

"Yes. He's a partner at DuPage Behavioral."

"Ok," Dag said. "Well, you're not going to like this. Look at these pictures; David had them in a folder on the computer's desktop."

On the screen, Dag scrolled through a series of pictures. They were all taken at close to the same angle: a view of the medical complex where DuPage Behavioral had their offices. Each photograph showed people I knew either entering the building or leaving. Tamika, Kenny, Ray, Willie, Stephanie, Danielle, Leola. Almost the entire support group.

"That's really, really weird," I said. What was David doing?"

"He was hunting it. The hashok. He was doing what we're doing."

I thought about that, not sure if I agreed. "Where's Mason?"

"I don't know."

"That's the whole support group except Mason. Where's Mason?"

"I don't know."

"Do you know who his doctor was?" I asked.

"No. He was really private."

"Who would know? His parents?"

"His parents aren't going to talk to me. They think I killed him."

"His girlfriend?" I asked.

"I don't know. They broke up, but I don't know how long ago. Mason was lying to me about that. And she and I never really got along."

"Do you have her number?"

"Yes."

"So call her."

"It's going to be the same thing," Dag said, ducking his head. "She's going to blame me for what happened to him; I don't want to get into it."

"Ok, give me the number."

"She won't talk to you. She doesn't even know you."

"Dag, I'm trying really hard not to be a bitch right now. Just give me the number."

He read it off his phone, and I placed the call on speakerphone.

"Hello?"

"Is this Mary Ann Pounds?"

"Yes. Who's this?"

"My name is Alex Jones. I'm with the Department of Health. I'm finishing up the coroner's report on Mr. Mason Comeaux, and I just needed some information I'm hoping you can help me with."

"I'm sorry, I wasn't even really dating—"

"I know, ma'am, and I'm sorry to trouble you. It's just part of the job."

"Isn't it late for this kind of thing?"

"Tell me about it," I said. "A herd of cows walked into a helicopter, and we've been cleaning it up all day. I'm trying to finish this before I head out."

"No, I mean—wait, into a helicopter?"

"I really just need your help with one question, Ms. Pounds."

"But I thought this was all finished. We had Mason's funeral and everything. I don't understand."

"This is an amended form 1199C, so it's still working its way through the system."

That was as far as I was willing to push; anything else would send her into automatic refusal, I guessed.

"Ok," she said. "I mean, if I know the answer."

"Did Mr. Comeaux have any unusual injuries? Anything that happened around the same time as the shooting or shortly thereafter?"

She was silent for a moment. "It was months ago."

"Anything with his hands or feet?"

"Excuse me?"

"It's a matter of possible bacterial infection. Similar to tetanus."

"He cut his hand, yes. On the lawnmower blade. He told me he'd been trying to fix it. I don't remember—I think it was after the shooting, but honestly, I'm not sure. He was in such bad shape, and it seems strange now. He was barely leaving the house. He definitely wasn't doing yardwork."

"Perfect," I said. "We'll check into that. We can't get the insurance company to confirm that Mr. Comeaux was seeing a mental health professional. Do you happen to know if he was?"

"Yes. Sometimes twice a week. I don't know at the end because we'd separated, but he was seeing a psychiatrist regularly."

"Do you happen to know the name?"

"No, I'm sorry."

"You're sure?"

She made an apologetic noise.

"All right," I said. "Thank you for your time."

"Oh, Mr. Jones, wait. It was York. Like the peppermint patty."

I must have found a way of ending the call because I disconnected and stared at Dag.

"That's Richard," I finally managed to say.

"I remember when he cut his hand," Dag said, his face dark. I was surprised to realize I was seeing Dag angry, really angry, for the first time. "He told me he'd grabbed the fishing line right before a catfish took off. That fucking monster did something to him. It messed with his head."

I just nodded.

Grimacing, Dag pointed to the laptop's screen. It was a picture of Zahra. A recent picture. David had zoomed in and taken a picture of her from a distance, her expression unreadable as she watched the group. More pictures of Zahra. More.

"He obviously thought she has something to do with it," Dag said. "The pictures go on and on like this. He'd been doing research. He'd learned enough to suspect her, although I wonder how much he had figured out about the hashok."

"She's ranching her own fucking food," I said. "She's picking up clients from DuPage Behavioral. She made the support group into a feeding trough."

"Let's not jump to any conclusions." Then Dag frowned. "But if she was doing that, and if she knew you looked like Noah—"

"Who's Noah?"

"The guy who shot Mason. If she knew you looked like him, and she knew how it would affect Mason, it would explain why she kept you and Mason in the same group. The responsible thing to do, once she noticed that Mason had some sort of issue with you, would have been to separate you."

My phone buzzed, and I jumped. Richard's name showed on the screen.

"Are you all right?" he asked when I answered.

"Yes."

"I heard about Tamika. I'm so sorry. How are you?"

"Fine. Ok."

"Where are you?"

"Having dinner with a friend."

Richard didn't answer right away; his silence said everything. He didn't think I had friends.

"I was going to stay in the city tonight," he said. "We've got a panel first thing in the morning, and Zahra booked a room. I'm driving home right now, though."

"No," I said. "Stay."

"I can't stand the thought of you by yourself right now."

"Richard, I'm fine. I'm sad, but I'm fine. Stay. You don't need to do that drive twice. I'll see you tomorrow, though, right?"

It took a little bit longer to get him to agree, but then the call ended.

"Zahra's staying in New Orleans tonight," I said to Dag.

"Eli, let's think this through rationally."

"Sure," I said. "We'll think it through rationally. We'll eat some delicious roast chicken and potatoes. And then we're going to search that bitch's house and find some evidence."

DAG (14)

I parked the Escort two blocks down from Zahra's house. She lived in a tony section of La Grange, which was the tony section of Bragg: McMansions on quarter-acre lots, all of them painted by exterior lights, like the whole neighborhood was staged instead of a real place real people lived. It had been easy to get her address off a white-page lookup online; it hadn't been quite as easy to convince Elien to let me take the lead.

"You're going to stay here," I said when I turned off the car.

He leveled a look at me.

"I'm just reminding you."

"Consider me reminded."

"I will come back and get you if it looks like the house is empty."

He gave me a mock salute. The green in his hazel eyes glinted in the ambient light.

"Can you please be good for five minutes?" I asked.

"One time I went a solid three and a half," he said.

"Let's try to break that record."

I slipped out of the Escort, jogged back the two blocks, and cut up along the side of Zahra's house. It was a monstrosity with a sweeping slate roof, gray brick, and mullioned windows. The front flower beds held columbine and foxglove; at the back of the house, jessamine climbed a trellis. I kept going, making a circuit of the house, checking the windows, and then I jogged back to the car.

Elien was standing on the curb, leaning against the car door, every long, lean inch of him on display. The night air had ruffled his hair more than usual.

"Lights on timers," I said. "Nobody's home."

"Did you ring the doorbell?"

"I did not."

"I would have rung the doorbell, just to see if anyone came to the door."

"She's got one of those video doorbell things," I said. "It would have sent my picture to her phone."

"Oh," Elien said.

"I'm not totally bad at my job."

"That's not what I meant," Elien said, frowning. "Why do you do that?"

"What?"

"Say bad things about yourself."

"Come on," I said. "Before the neighborhood watch calls in this piece of shit."

His frown got deeper; I headed back to Zahra's house.

We went around back again. French doors opened onto the patio, and Elien approached them and touched the handle. Then he stopped.

"What about an alarm?"

I pointed up, where two of the second-story windows were open. "Doesn't look like she's worried."

"I guess if you're the monster, you don't have to worry."

"Let's not jump to conclusions."

Elien rattled the handle. "Should I break a window?"

Nudging him aside, I drew out the neoprene case from my back pocket. I had a few smaller tools in there, including a nice, thin length of stainless steel that I worked between the doors until the latch slipped free. The door popped open, and from inside came a breath of something foul.

"Last chance," I whispered.

Elien shook his head. I passed him a pair of disposable gloves and pulled on my own.

I pulled open the door and stepped inside. A few lamps laid down pools of light amidst the expensive furniture: a chesterfield with brass nailhead trim; a chaise with its wood painted white and houndstooth upholstery; built-in shelves that featured books and trinkets: a marble piece decorated with dyed feathers, a folio volume open to an antique world map, a textile square dominated by scarlet and cobalt.

The stink grew stronger as I moved into the kitchen.

"What is that?" Elien asked.

When I checked the trash, I pointed to a foam tray, the kind that was used to package chicken at the supermarket.

"God, it's awful," Elien said.

"Guess she hasn't been home for a few days."

I checked the refrigerator, in case she was keeping some sort of monster equivalent of a snack: preserved intestines or severed limbs, or maybe something really horrific like gluten-free bread. I just found eggs and a block of Muenster that was getting a little hairy, milk that had gone over, a few apples at the back of the crisper that were still firm.

"Do you need a snack?" Elien asked.

"Maybe after."

We worked our way through the downstairs and, aside from more reminders that Zahra made a lot of money, we didn't find anything.

"No paintings," I said.

"She's Muslim," Elien said. "I don't know how devout, but she is."

"So?"

"So no images. At least, no images of people."

"Huh."

"See? Sometimes I know things."

"I think you're very smart."

"You think I'm a brat."

"You can be a brat and be smart," I said. "And don't try to pick a fight."

Elien laughed as he followed me upstairs.

The search upstairs didn't reveal anything either: the bedroom, the master bath, the guest room, the office. Elien spent a while going through Zahra's papers; when I'd finished with the other rooms, I came back, and he said, "Nothing."

"Ok," I said.

"No, it's not ok. This is bullshit. We know she's behind this. We know she's feeding on people who are patients at DuPage Behavioral. We know she created her own . . . her own fucking herd to feed on. So where's the proof?"

"Well, what kind of proof would she leave behind?"

"What do you mean?"

"I mean, if she's really our monster, let's say. We know she's got at least this other shape, that big, pale, long-faced thing that attacked us in the woods. And we know she can turn into that will o' the wisp thing. She gets inside people's heads. She can even . . . possess them, I guess, for lack of a better word. She feeds on them, but she feeds on suffering. So what's she going to leave behind as evidence?"

Elien shrugged. "There's got to be something."

"Well, we didn't find it."

"There's something. There's got to be something."

"Ok."

"I know there's something."

"Ok. But where is it?"

Before Elien could answer, a thump came from downstairs.

"What was—" Elien began.

I hushed him.

A moment later, something scuffed on the stairs.

Grabbing Elien by the arm, I shoved him toward the door. He didn't protest; his face was pale, and in the instant before I flipped off the lights, I saw his eyes wide with fear. I kept shoving, forcing him toward the bedroom, where Zahra had left the windows open. From the office to the bedroom was probably fifteen feet, but we had to go past the stairs. The muscles in Elien's arm were like steel cables; his breathing was shallow and fast.

We had crossed five feet of the landing when a long, pale face showed itself on the stairs.

With a shout, I shoved Elien ahead of me. The hashok surged up the steps. If the gunshot wounds Elien had inflicted on it last time had done any lasting damage, it wasn't obvious—the monster moved so quickly that it was hard to get more than an impression of it. That impression was the same one that I had gotten in the dark woods: the elongated frame, unwholesomely white flesh, the head and face that were stretched until the features weren't human. Claws slashed through the darkness, tugging on my jeans. Then, stumbling, I shot through the bedroom doorway, and Elien slammed the door shut.

It rattled in its frame as the hashok collided with it. The jamb splintered.

"I can't hold it," Elien shouted

The hashok smashed into the door again, and this time, it popped loose. Elien skidded a few inches before he managed to slam the door shut.

I cast about for something and settled on the chest of drawers. Setting my shoulder against it, I threw my weight into the side. The damn thing was solid wood.

"Move," I shouted.

Elien stumbled back.

I threw myself into the chest of drawers again, and this time, it toppled onto its side with a crash. Drawers slid open; t-shirts and socks spilled out onto the floor. When the hashok connected with the door again, the chest of drawers rocked unsteadily, but it held the door shut.

With a shuddering breath, I grabbed Elien again, spun him toward the window, and shoved.

He took two steps and hesitated.

"Not without you," he whispered.

I came after him, herding him toward the window. The cool October air washed over me; I kicked out the screen, helped Elien up on the ledge, and pointed to the trellis.

The hashok shrieked and slammed into the door again.

"Fast as you can," I whispered.

He nodded, lowered himself, and his eyes widened for a moment. I grabbed his wrists, and he nodded a silent thanks. Then he must have found his footing because he nodded, twisted his hands free, and began to climb down.

I followed.

Twice more I heard the hashok connect with the door. When I was halfway down the trellis, though, I realized the sounds had stopped. The smell of bruised jessamine was so thick it made me gag. Wooden slats splintered under my grip, digging into my palm. I heard a thump as Elien's feet hit the ground.

"Run," I whispered.

"Not without you."

I dropped the last five feet, and we sprinted around the side of the house. Elien grabbed my hand, tugging me along. I flinched as we charged out onto the front lawn. The hashok must have known we were trying to escape. It would be waiting. It would launch itself at us, and the best thing I could hope for was to release Elien's hand and let him keep running. I might be able to slow the damn thing down for a few minutes.

But the only thing that met us was a quiet street, and the steady glow of the streetlights, and the echoes of our steps clapping back from the silent houses around us.

ELIEN (15)

"Pull over," I said. We'd been driving for at least five minutes; the houses of La Grange blurred around me. Every few moments, one of them would snap into focus—a red-brick Colonial looking painfully out of place, paint peeling from the top of the porch columns—and then the world would dissolve again, and I'd be back in my old bedroom, a hand over my mouth, the taste of grass, the smell of fried catfish.

Dag kept driving.

"Pull over, pull over," I said, slapping his arm.

"Eli, that thing could be right behind us."

"Pull over right fucking now!"

Braking hard, Dag nosed up against the curb. The Escort's grumbly, rumbly engine made the seats vibrate. The Big Mac smell from the back seat was overwhelming, and I rolled down the window. The air was cool against my feverish face, and I heaved once, but nothing came up.

Dag's hand came to rest at the small of my back, and then it bumped up along my spine, then back down, then up again. I focused on the touch, followed it back to the present.

"Oh my God," I said, squeezing my eyes shut so I wouldn't cry.

"It's ok," Dag said. "We're ok."

I tried to hold it together, but I started shaking again.

"Look," Dag said, "we're safe, we're in the car, we're driving away."

"No, we're not ok," I said. "It was there. It's her, right? It's got to be her. We were in her house. She came back, and she found us, and she tried to kill us again. And she's not going to stop, Dag. That's what that the psychic told me. She's going to keep coming, and she's going to kill me, and there's nothing I can do about it."

"Hold on," Dag said. "We're not exactly helpless. We've learned a lot about this thing just in the last couple of days."

"We know its name, Dag." I turned to face him. "We know it likes to cause pain and suffering. That's all we fucking know. We don't know how to stop it. We don't know how to kill it. We don't even know how to prove it's real—we just searched her house, and we couldn't find anything. She has a perfect life, an ordinary life, and under the surface, she's a monster, and we could never prove it in a million years."

For a long moment, Dag studied me, shadows lying thick across his face.

"Means, motive, and opportunity," he said.

"What?"

"That's where you start with a murder."

"These aren't ordinary murders, Dag. You can't prove an escalating cycle of violence. You can't prove that an evil monster possessed your best friend and made him try to kill me. You can't prove that a blue firefly took over a dead man's body."

"Eli—"

"Stop fucking calling me that. That's not my name anymore. Can't you fucking get that? Jesus Christ, no wonder you're such a fucking poor excuse for a deputy."

He sat back in his seat; he cupped his knees with his hands.

"I'm sorry," I said. "I'm really sorry."

"Let's call it a night," he said, shifting the car into gear. "We can pick up tomorrow."

"No, Dag, please. I'm sorry."

"I know," he said, and we pulled away from the curb.

"Means, motive, and opportunity," I said. "Talk to me about that."

Bending, he groped with one hand under the seat, searching for something.

"Ok," I said, "ok, I'll talk about means, motive, and opportunity. Means. She can turn into a monster. She can turn into a firefly. She can possess people, but she can also . . . suggest that they do something terrible. Ray, Mason, Tamika. With David and with us, though, she attacked as a monster. That means she can't always possess people. Not right away. She needs an opening. An opportunity. Maybe it takes time."

Pulling a cassette adapter from under the seat, he tried to untangle the cable one handed.

"Here," I said, "let me help—"

"I'll do it," he said.

"I want to—"

"Just stop, Elien."

"Right, ok, sorry. Motive. The motive is—"

"Stop it with that too, ok?"

"It was your idea. You had a good idea, and we should follow it up."

"I'd like some quiet, please."

"Opportunity," I said.

He hit the brakes. We were still in a residential part of La Grange, and the taillights painted the houses around us red. Aside from us, the road was empty. Dag's chest rose and fell rapidly.

"Once, Elien. Just once, it'd be nice if you weren't so fucking self-centered. Is that so fucking much to ask?"

I sat very still. My hands buzzed like I'd grabbed a swarm of bees. At the very end of the street, a light came on, and I thought for a moment that Dag had woken them up, that everyone had heard him. But, of course, he'd been very quiet when he'd said those words. The way he said and did everything.

"Well?" he asked.

"No," I said.

"Then I'd like some quiet on the drive home."

For thirty seconds, Dag messed with the tangled cable of the cassette adapter. Then he swore and threw it on the floor. Taking his foot off the brake, he let us roll forward again. In a few more minutes, we'd reached the end of the street, and we turned, and I couldn't see that single light in the house behind us anymore.

That was all of it, for a while: the thrum of the tires, the sheared-off ends of Dag's breathing, the traffic lights shedding green-yellow-red auras across the asphalt. I could feel my fingers again, and I pulled out my phone. It was easier to think about the hashok and how I could stop it than to think about Dag, about how his eyes looked darker than ever, how he kept blinking, and his breathing never seemed to get back to normal.

I googled the Louisiana Mental Health Professionals Network. I wanted to find the schedule for this week's conference. I had the vague idea that I could contact the people who had organized the evening panels and see if I could track down Zahra. If she hadn't attended any of the panels, that would explain how she had managed to get back to Bragg and attack us. If she'd been at a panel tonight, then she had an alibi, and I needed to start thinking more creatively.

But two minutes of clicking and scrolling and searching yielded nothing. I stared at my phone, not quite able to believe what I was seeing.

The Louisiana Mental Health Professionals Network had their next annual conference in April. Nothing on their website said anything about an event in October. I tried to search more broadly, googling mental health conferences, October, New Orleans, and combinations and variations of those phrases.

Nothing.

When we stopped at the next traffic light, I said, "I know you're upset with me, but can I please ask a favor?"

"What?"

"Zahra lied to me. She said that she and Richard were staying in New Orleans tonight because of a conference."

"It's barely an hour drive. Why would they stay overnight?"

"Sometimes dinners go late, and sometimes they have panels first thing the next morning. Besides, it's mostly an excuse to drink and have fun, whatever that looks like for psychiatrists." Ahead of us, the traffic light was still red; the humid air glowed hazily around it. "But she lied. There's no conference this week. She and Richard both lied to me."

"Do you think Richard is involved with this?"

"I don't know. I just—I want to go see."

"See what?"

"I don't know."

"This is a bad idea," Dag said. The light changed, and Dag goosed the car forward. "Let's just get you home—"

"Please," I said. "I know I said something inexcusable. I know you don't have any reason to do this for me. I know I'm a petty, bitchy, selfish, spoiled asshole, and I don't deserve your help."

He drove another hundred yards; a strip mall on our right had a sign advertising ALL YOU CAN EAT SEAFOOD and CODY'S HALLOWEEN SURPLUS. From a bar at the end of the strip, a crowd of guys stumbled out into the parking lot, shoving each other, laughing, one guy hooting as two more squared off. A real fight, or pretend? Hard to tell. Along the side of the road, an inflatable skeleton wavered and folded as the Escort whooshed past it.

"Just drop me off, then," I said. "Here's fine."

"This isn't a good part of town."

"Stop the car, please. I just need to catch an Uber."

Dag made a strangled noise, and then he jerked the wheel and cut into a sharp U-turn.

"You don't have to—"

"For the love of Christ, just say thank you."

"Thank you," I said softly.

DAG (16)

We drove east, cut south around Slidell, and crossed the lake on I-10. Traffic was light, and the lake was higher than usual, lapping just below the highway; for long moments, it would be just the two of us skating out across dark waters, and then headlights would spring up in the opposite direction, and the world would be normal again. At night, New Orleans was an amber crescent of sodium glare ahead of us, growing taller and brighter with every minute, hung here and there with coronets of halogen blues and whites. After the lake came Bayou Sauvage: switchgrass and wiregrass grew along the highway's shoulder, their blades tremulous in the Escort's headlights.

"Where are they staying?"

"The InterContinental."

"You're sure?"

Elien trailed fingertips across his forehead like he was trying to concentrate. "No. But that's where Richard likes to go. Where he told me he likes to go, anyway."

Parking was normally a nightmare in the Warehouse District. I drove Poydras east, and then I worked my way down Magazine and up Camp, then west on Poydras. We passed the Zatarain's ad, a huge mural painted on the side of the Queen & Crescent Hotel, a couple of times. It was late, but the city never slept, and people were walking on the sidewalks, laughing, talking, enjoying the cool October air. A man was walking backwards with an enormous foam cup, sipping on a curly straw, talking to his friends. He went down, and I swear I saw him break his wrist, but he just laughed, and his friends laughed, and somehow they got him upright and rescued what was left of his margarita. They were still laughing as we drove on.

"Just let the valet park it," Elien said. "I'll pay for it."

We circled back toward the hotel, coming up north past Lafayette Square this time, where a pair of guys were having a serious make-out session on a bench near the street. One of the guys was black, and the other guy was white, and they were having a really great time by the look of things.

When we got to the InterContinental, I hopped out and took a parking slip from a white guy with locs. A cloud of weed hung around him. He eyed the Escort and then looked at us.

"It's not going to explode or anything," I said.

"Let's not make promises," Elien said.

"He's joking," I said. "Are you bonded and insured?"

The valet was still staring at us.

"I counted the change in the ashtray," I said. "Just so you know."

"Ok," Elien said, taking my arm and hustling me toward the door. "Before you tell him to be careful with your baby."

"It's not my baby," I said, and then over my shoulder, "but it is my only car, so if you could please be careful—"

Elien steered me into the lobby before I could finish. I glanced around and tried not to look like I was glancing around: marble floors, chandeliers, furniture done in varying patterns of black and gold, abstract sculptures that, on second glance, I realized were meant to represent jazz musicians. Mirrors. Televisions. Seating areas were partitioned with transparent curtains, but tonight the lobby was empty. Two restaurants opened off the lobby, and I could smell shrimp and lime. My stomach rumbled.

"How is that even possible?" Elien muttered. "You ate most of a chicken."

My face heated.

"I'm just teasing," he whispered. He was still holding my arm, and he squeezed lightly now. "Are you mad at me?"

"No."

"Would you tell me if you were mad at me?"

"I think I've been pretty good at telling you when I'm mad."

"But you're upset."

Slowly, I worked his fingers loose from my arm. "Enough, Elien. Let's do what we came here to do."

The hurt on his face only lasted an instant. Then he nodded. "How good are you with computers?"

"I know how to turn them on." I frowned. "Some of them."

"Jesus. Ok, well, I guess I'm the genius hacker of this duo. How good are you at acting?"

"I played the Big Bad Wolf in third grade."

Elien groaned. "I can't do both parts of this plan."

"What do you want me to do?"

"We need to get Zahra's room number. And Richard's, I guess. One of us needs to look on the computer while the other one creates a distraction."

"You don't really think Richard is involved in this whole thing with the hashok, do you?"

His hazel eyes were clear as he said simply, "He lied to me."

"I'll create the distraction," I said.

"Pretend to slip," Elien said. "Then you say something like, 'Oh my God, I think I broke my leg.'"

I hemmed.

"Let me hear," Elien said.

"Oh my God, I think I broke my leg."

Elien groaned again. "A little more emotion, please."

"Oh my God, I think I broke my leg."

"Ok, but not like you're at your third-cousin-twice-removed's bat mitzvah and you're trying to convince your mom to let you go home."

"Um. That is a very specific scenario."

"Let's hear it one more time."

"Oh my God, I think I broke my leg."

"You know what?" Elien said. "Just sit here. I think I can do both parts."

"No," I said. "I can create a distraction. I'm a fucking sorry excuse for a deputy, but I can do this."

"Please, Dag, earlier, I didn't mean that—"

"Get ready," I said, nudging him away.

I headed for the closest restaurant, which was called Pete's. The lighting was low, with candles at each table, and the smell of shrimp and lime was stronger, mixed now with the fragrance of garlic and hot oil. Most of the tables were empty, and I spotted only two waiters: one at the back, talking to a pair of older women, and one who was passing me toward the kitchen.

"I'll be right with you," she said.

"Just looking for a friend," I said.

As soon as she had passed through the kitchen's swinging doors, I snagged a candle from the closest table. I turned to go. Then I stopped.

I had only seen Richard once, when he'd picked up Elien after Ray's suicide. But I recognized him at the corner table in the back, and although I didn't recognize the guy he was with, I knew the type: a tight t-shirt, tight jeans, the hint of a jockstrap's blue waistband when he leaned forward, laughing at something Richard had said, touching Richard's arm. Richard's other hand was between the guy's legs. Hard to misunderstand that kind of signal; the way Richard was working that guy, he'd have nothing but pulp down there by morning.

Then I remembered what I was doing, and I cupped a hand around the candle and carried it out to the lobby. I made my way behind one of the seating areas, set the candle flame to the hem of one of the gossamer curtains. When it caught, I blew out the candle, tossed it in a trash can, and walked away.

Then little tongues of fire. Little puffs of smoke.

And nobody noticed.

The flames were licking their way up the curtain, and the lobby was still empty except for me on one side and Elien on the other and a guy behind the reception desk. From a distance, it looked like his name tag said Enrique.

Still nothing.

I decided to help things along, and I shouted, "Fire!"

Enrique got hopping. He grabbed a walkie, shouted something into it, and then he came sprinting around the lobby with a red fire extinguisher in his hands. Elien slipped behind the reception desk.

"Fire," I said again, and this time I pointed helpfully. The flames had climbed almost all the way up the curtain now.

"Holy shit," Enrique was shouting over and over again. He aimed the extinguisher's nozzle, pulled the lever, and powder sprayed out. The extinguisher suffocated the flames quickly, and Enrique stepped around and around like he was doing the box step. He kept looking at me and looking at the smoldering remains of the curtain. Out of the corner of my eye, I could see Elien still behind the reception desk.

Enrique looked like he might be losing focus, so I pointed at a smoking wisp of fabric and said, "Fire."

"Holy shit," Enrique said and blasted it again.

When I risked a glance, Elien was leaning against the wall near the elevator, watching us like we were putting on a show.

Which, I guess, we kind of were.

I didn't want to step on Enrique's lines, so I let him get out a few more "Holy shits."

Then he looked at me and said, "Did you see that?"

I nodded and said, "That was some shit."

And that got Enrique going again with his holy shit mantra.

Running footsteps announced hotel security: a paunchy little guy with a hairpiece and a tall, thin, ascetic-looking man whose name was probably Crookshanks or Jeeves or something like that. I told Enrique I was freaked the fuck out and made my way to the elevator.

"Usually," Elien said, pressing the up button, "I like a little more variety in my dialogue."

I shrugged.

"That's my only note, though. Otherwise, it was perfection."

When the elevator dinged and the polished bronze doors opened, we stepped inside. The doors shut, and Elien jabbed the button marked 15.

"I'm going to tell you one good thing about you for every floor," Elien said. "That's step one in my plan to make you not hate me forever. One, you're tough and brave. You faced down the hashok in the woods without even blinking."

"Stop."

"Two, you're sweet—"

"Please stop."

"I'm going to have to talk really fast to catch up if you keep interrupting me."

"Elien, I saw Richard. He was in the restaurant. He was with a guy."

Leaning against the elevator's rail, Elien wiped his hands on his pants and said, "Oh."

"I'm sorry, but I thought you should know. They were obviously, um, more than friends."

Instrumental music played over hidden speakers. Chopin, maybe. Not whale songs. I would have killed for a beluga right then.

"Well," Elien said, and then he stopped. He tried again. "Well, it's an open relationship."

"I know."

"I mean, I was going to fuck you the other night, but you weren't interested."

"I remember."

"And it's open, you know, both ways."

I nodded.

"It's fine," Elien said. He was staring so hard at the elevator doors that I thought they might melt. "It's totally fine."

I put my hands in my pockets.

"I guess some guys would be embarrassed," Elien said, laughing now, the backs of his hands against his cheeks where a blush burned.

Now, I pulled my hands out of my pockets and gave him a hug. He pushed back at first, hands on my chest, shoving. Then he made a noise that was kind of a sigh and kind of a grunt and collapsed against me. Tightening my hold, I held him there, his face hot and wet through my shirt.

"It's ok," I said.

"It's not ok," he mumbled into my chest. "Why am I so fucked up? Why is everything in my life so fucked up?"

"Let's check on Zahra," I said. "And then let's get you home."

"I can't go back there," he said, sniffling into my sleeve. "I'm never going back there."

I didn't say anything, but I stroked that massive blowout of windswept hair until we hit the fifteenth floor.

"All right," Elien said, pushing away from me and wiping his face. "Here we go. Time to find out if my shrink is really also a monster."

"That sounds like the beginning of a Yelp review," I said.

With a soft laugh, Elien stepped out of the elevator, and I followed.

1517 was at the end of the hall. Elien knocked once, waited, and knocked again.

When he looked at me, I shrugged.

He knocked once more.

No one answered.

"Do we go?" I asked.

Shaking his head, he pulled out a keycard and dipped it into the lock. The light flashed green. Behind us, the elevator dinged again.

"Now or never," I said.

Elien pushed into the room, and the smell of death met us. Every light was blazing. First was the bathroom on our right, with mirrored doors and a collection of toiletries and cosmetics spread out on the counter. Then the bedroom. Zahra lay with her head at the foot of the bed; like David Bass, she had been gutted in three broad slashes.

"Excuse me," a voice said behind us, and I glanced over my shoulder to see the two guys from security standing in the doorway. I realized now that Enrique had pointed me out, and they had followed me up here because the fire was, in hindsight, pretty fucking suspicious. "Just what do you—holy shit. Holy shit. Get on the ground right now. Bill, call the cops. Call somebody!"

"Elien," I said.

"Zahra isn't the hashok," he whispered to himself. "How can it not be her?"

III

At night, when a person is passing along a trail or going through the woods, and meets the Hashok Okwa Hui'ga he must immediately turn away and not look at it, otherwise he will certainly become lost and not arrive at his destination that night, but instead, travel in a circle.

- "Myths of the Louisiana Choctaw," David I. Bushnell, Jr.

ELIEN (1)

The worst part wasn't the hours I spent in the interview room, answering the same questions over and over again, explaining that I hadn't killed Zahra. The worst part wasn't the array of misdemeanor charges and having to wait until Richard could bail me out. The worst part wasn't even facing Richard again, smelling the cheap cologne that was still on him from the other guy. The worst part was Dag's face right before they separated us, and knowing that I'd screwed up his life again, maybe worse than ever.

Richard drove us home from the New Orleans police station; it was late morning by then, and both of us were exhausted. Richard's mouth was a grim line. Sunlight flashing off the lake illuminated the bags under his eyes. His carefully combed hair was mussed, and I could see how very thin it had gotten on top. He looked old. I watched him. I watched the fields of corn flick past us. Pheasants pecked among the chaff. I could still smell the hotel room, Zahra's body torn open. Like the smell in Ray's apartment. Like the smell in David's trailer.

When we pulled into the garage, Richard touched the remote, and the door clattered down behind us. We sat there for a while, and Richard scratched the thick hair on the back of his arms.

"Well," I said, "I guess that open relationship wasn't just for my benefit."

"I really don't think that's what we should be worried about right now."

"I should have known," I said. "I should have fucking known. I told you I didn't want an open relationship. I told you I didn't need one. And you insisted. You said it would be better for me. You said it was important that I feel free. And I never fucking took advantage of it, which was such a fucking mistake, because you were lying to me, picking up street trash, fucking whoever you wanted."

"Your behavior recently has been worse than erratic, Elien. I'm worried about you. Frankly, the way you acted last night makes me think that you haven't been making any progress at all with Zahra, and—"

"Well, she's dead, Richard. Somebody butchered her in that hotel room. So it's not like I can ask for a refund because she didn't fix me."

"This would be a good time for you to practice your breathing—"

"You lied to me. You both lied to me. A conference? Jesus, that is the oldest one in the book, and I still fell for it."

"All right," Richard said. "I suppose we should talk about that. Yes. I lied. That was not good behavior. But you've been frightening me lately. I needed space. We both agreed that an open relationship—"

"No." I started to laugh. "You are so full of shit. Don't do that. You know I didn't want that."

"You certainly didn't seem to mind when you were humping that deputy on my fucking couch."

The garage wall swam in my vision; I blinked to clear my eyes.

"All right," I said and got out of the car.

Against one wall, Richard had a pegboard with tools and sporting equipment. Leaning up against it was a baseball bat. High end, of course, because everything Richard bought was high end. Not aluminum. Not wood. Reinforced carbon fiber polymer. I swung it once, and it whistled through the air. I felt like I could smash my way through a tank.

"Elien, put that down."

I swung it again. I liked the resistance as it cut through the air. "God, I just can't believe how stupid I am."

"Put it down." Richard was standing behind the car door, watching me. "If I think you're going to start hurting yourself again, I will call the police."

"Richard, sweetheart, get a clue: I never fucking stopped hurting myself. I just figured out better ways to do it."

Then I headed into the house. I used the bat to knock down some of the paintings, and then I went to work on the cabinets. Richard followed me, not speaking, his arms folded across his chest. After I'd shattered the glass fronts to the cabinets, I reached into one and grabbed one of the wineglasses on the shelf inside. A chunk of glass sliced open the side of my arm, but I didn't feel it. I got a bottle of red. I got the corkscrew.

"You're bleeding," Richard said. He had his doctor's bag on the table, and he was rummaging through it. "Will you please stop for a moment so I can bandage that cut?"

My hands were shaking, and it took me a couple of tries to get the corkscrew seated. By the time I had, Richard was coming up behind me.

"I'm fine," I said.

"I'd like to look at your arm."

"I said I'm fine."

Then I felt the prick of the needle.

"What the fuck—" I began.

But then I wasn't saying anything because I wasn't inside myself anymore: I was floating just outside, watching myself fall, watching Richard catch me and get me onto the couch. He pulled the ottoman up next to me and bandaged my arm. I just kept drifting; I was a kite barely tethered to my body.

"I'm going to give you something to help you sleep," Richard said.

Special K, I wanted to say. Keeps the doctor away.

And then he gave me another shot, and I slept.

When I woke, it was late afternoon; the sun brushed the St. Augustine grass like velvet, and the magnolia leaves were glossy mirrors. A resurrection fern was opening on a sugar maple. I was a fern. I could be resurrected. I was pretty sure, with all that fern talk, I was tripping pretty hard.

My first attempt at getting up didn't go so well. On my second try, I managed to stay upright. I crawled upstairs. The door to Richard's study was closed, and a strip of light showed underneath it. I didn't trust my feet, so I kept crawling, my arm aching from the cut, until I got to our bedroom. I found a Herschel backpack and stuffed a few changes of clothes inside. I grabbed the essentials from my bathroom. Then, bracing myself on the wall, I shuffled back to the stairs.

The study door was open, now. The room was dark; it smelled funky, like body odor.

When I got downstairs, Richard was standing in the kitchen. The wine and the wineglass and the corkscrew were on the counter. He was eating yogurt.

"How are you feeling?" he asked.

I shook my head. We'd left David's laptop on the breakfast table last night, so I grabbed it and shoved it in the backpack. Then I took slow steps toward the front door.

"Elien?"

"We're done."

"Elien, come back here."

"Goodbye, Richard."

"I know you're upset about earlier today, but you were out of control. You were hurting yourself."

At the front door, I rubbed my eyes; everything seemed doubled. "You can have my stuff," I said. "Or you can give it away. Or you can burn it, for all I fucking care."

"Get back here right now. You aren't well."

I opened the front door.

"Elien, stop it right now. This is childish."

I had to lean on the jamb to get myself out onto the porch.

"I'll have you locked up for your own protection," Richard was saying. He had such a lovely voice. He ought to have been on the radio. "You don't know what you're doing."

I slammed the door.

In one of the rocking chairs, I waited for my Uber. Richard paced on the other side of the windows, watching me. He didn't come outside. He didn't try to talk to me. He didn't have a hypo with more Special K. I thought maybe he knew that I'd kill him if he ever came near me again.

My Uber driver's name was Britton, and he was balding with a graying ponytail. When he dropped me in front of Dag's house, he said, "Kid, take it from me, you gotta lay off the hard stuff every once in a while."

I limped up the steps and knocked on the front door.

When Dag answered, he was wearing running shorts and a tank top; the tank had a cartoon narwhal and, in rainbow letters, THE GAY UNICORNS OF THE SEA.

"I'm sorry," I said.

Or that's what I tried to say. Mostly, I just sobbed.

Dag's expression shifted from anger to irritation to something I couldn't recognize. Then he pulled me into a hug and helped me inside.

DAG (2)

It took a long time to get Elien to stop crying. Part of the problem was that he didn't even seem to realize he was crying. He kept trying to apologize, and I kept trying to get him to use a tissue, and my dad kept trying to hear the golf announcer.

"Pat him on the back," my dad said during a commercial for some sort of joint-pain medicine. "That's what we used to do when you cried."

Patting Elien on the back didn't help.

During the next break, when they were explaining the magic of the new-and-improved Clapper, Dad said, "Maybe try some warm milk."

"The fact that all of your parenting expertise comes from when I was two years old explains why I'm an emotionally stunted adult," I said.

But I went to get the milk.

When I came back, Dad said, "You're not an emotionally stunted adult. You're my big handsome boy. You're my champ."

Elien didn't want the milk.

"He doesn't want the milk," I told Dad.

"Let him think about it. Sometimes they have to decide they want it on their own."

"No more advice, please," I said.

Dad didn't particularly like that, and he started punching the buttons on the remote. By the time the volume was at sixty-five, I was shouting so Elien could hear me. Finally, with a dirty look at my dad, I took Elien's elbow and towed him into the kitchen. Behind me, the volume dropped substantially.

"Elien," my mom said, "what's wrong?"

He was still crying.

"You know what," my mom said, tapping her lips. "I bet he'd feel better if we did something with his hair."

"He's not a doll," I said.

"I know he's not a doll. But I always feel so much better after I do a little self-care. I have the hair-cutting kit in the closet. We'll just do a little trim, and then we'll do his nails, and if he wants, maybe we'll even do a makeover."

"Absolutely not."

"You'd like that, wouldn't you, Elien? See? He nodded."

"How did I survive being a child? How did I make it to adulthood?"

"I'll get the kit."

"I like his hair the way it is."

"Well, yes, but it's a bit long, don't you think?"

I was standing behind Elien, and I pulled his head against my chest, trying to cover as much of his hair as possible. "No haircuts."

"Fine," Mom said with a sniff. "You could try singing him a song."

"This explains everything," I said. "My parents still think I'm three years old. This explains my entire life."

"If I'm such a terrible mother," Mom said, "why did I go to that fancy karate class graduation a few years ago?"

"That was the police academy!"

"Do not take that tone, Dagobert."

"Dagobert," my dad shouted. "No shouting!"

"Elien, sweetheart," my mom said loudly, her face about three inches from Elien's. "Would you like to stay for dinner?"

"Stay for dinner? He can hardly take a full breath."

"That's no reason to be impolite." My mom brought over a sack of beans and a wire colander. "Elien," she bellowed into his face again. "Can you sort these beans for me?"

"He's not deaf," I said, "and he—"

But Elien gave one final sniffle and nodded. Wiping his face with one hand, he leaned forward and examined the beans.

"Terrible mother," my mom muttered as she moved back to the counter.

"I didn't say that."

"Maybe you could think a little," Dad shouted from the front room, "before you say such horrible things about your dying parents."

After scrubbing my face and trying to figure out what was happening, I dropped into the chair next to Elien. We picked through the beans in silence.

When the beans were done, Mom put Elien in charge of slicing the onion, the celery, and the bell peppers. When the vegetables were done, he was in charge of making the cornbread. When the cornbread was in the oven, he was in charge of the wine. The pressure cooker rumbled on the stovetop; hot butter sizzled in a skillet as Mom worked on the succotash. Elien's eyes were still a little puffy, but he hadn't cried in almost an hour, and he sipped his wine and stared off into the distance. After a moment, he glanced over at me, and a tiny smile curved his lips.

"Thank you," he whispered.

I shrugged, and before I did something even more stupid, I made myself a Sugarfield and sat next to Elien, and we drank together.

At dinner, I could see panic mounting in Elien's face as each dish was announced.

"Red beans and rice," Mom said, setting a plate in front of him. "Succotash—those are lima beans, sweetheart. And your famous cornbread."

"He never said it was famous," I said.

"Dagobert gets a little jealous because he likes to make the cornbread," Mom said.

"I do not get jealous."

"One time," Dad said, "he threw Mrs. Dertoneau's cornbread out the window because he was so mad that he didn't get to make his own."

"I knocked it off the counter. On accident. I didn't throw it out the window."

"Mrs. Dertoneau saw the whole thing," Mom whispered to Elien.

"Elien doesn't eat this kind of food," I said, nudging his full plate toward Mom. "It'll make him sick."

"Oh," Mom said.

That was it. Oh. But her eyes got all full and her lip got all trembly.

And Elien fucking Martel caved faster than any man in history.

"No, no, no," he said, pulling the plate back. "I can eat it."

"No," Mom said, tugging on his plate. "I can make something else."

"No," Elien said, glancing at me in desperation, trying to get the plate back. "No, honestly. I think Dag just misunderstood. The other day I was—no, Mrs. LeBlanc, really, it looks delicious—"

"I won't hear of it," Mom said. "We'll make you something you'll like. I know food like this isn't fancy enough for guests."

"Elien did say something about how it wasn't fancy enough," I said.

"Liar!" Elien somehow managed to get the plate free, and he curled his arms around it. "Mrs. LeBlanc, this looks fantastic."

"Well," Mom said doubtfully. "I don't want you to get sick. And I bought the most beautiful bread pudding for dessert."

"Oh, I don't know about dessert," Elien began.

"Yeah, he's being polite, Mom. This food is going to make him so sick he won't be able to eat the dessert."

Elien's eyes were huge when he glared at me. "That's. Not. True. I'm very excited to eat this food."

"And dessert," I said.

"And. Dessert." He managed to say the words through gritted teeth.

"Well," Dad said, "I don't know what all the fuss is, but can we please say grace before I starve to death?"

So we said grace, with Dad's hand in my right and Elien's in my left. We ate. And, to my shock, Elien ate every bite: all the rice and beans, all the succotash, all the cornbread, and two servings of bread pudding. He drank a lot of wine. Mom and Dad told stories, which mostly involved me when I was a child, and which further confirmed my suspicions that both of my parents had gotten mentally stuck sometime around 1999. Elien laughed quietly at first. Then he laughed a little bit louder. Then he started asking questions.

"What about a picture of him when he was wearing your pantyhose?" Elien asked my mom through fits of giggles. "I want to see your photo album from that year."

"Ok," I said, "I think Elien and I are going to hang out in my room."

"No, no, I want to see some pictures from when you were in that school play you told me about."

"Door closed, Dagobert," my dad said.

"We're going to talk, Dad. That's it. Talk." Grabbing Elien's collar, I yanked him out of the seat. "Come on."

"No," Elien said, "we'll do the dishes."

"Oh," Mom said. "And I can tell you about Dagobert's first date."

"Goodnight," I said, still dragging Elien down the hall.

When we were in my room with the door shut, everything suddenly switched: Elien twisted around, grabbing my arm, and he dragged me toward the bed. We fell onto the mattress together, and I grunted as pain flashed through my chest and arm. For a moment we were tangled together, and then I rolled onto my back, our shoulders touching. From the kitchen came the sound of running water and the clink of dishes. From Elien came soft, quiet breathing. I liked the way his breathing sounded. I could close my eyes and imagine it was the only sound in the universe.

"I broke up with Richard," Elien said.

"I saw the backpack."

"I should have done it a long time ago."

Rolling my head to the side, I watched him. He wiped his eyes once. "Do you want to talk about it?" I asked.

"No, thanks."

"Do you need a place to stay?"

"No. I'll get a hotel."

"You can stay."

"No."

"Elien, I'll sleep on the couch. Just stay. You probably shouldn't be on your own tonight."

When he turned to look at me, his eyes were bleary. "I drank too much wine."

"That's ok."

"I'm going to say yes."

"Then say yes."

"Yes," he whispered.

"I'm going to tell my parents. They'll probably spontaneously combust from excitement."

"Dag," he asked when I was at the door.

"Yeah?"

"Will you come back?"

I laughed and said, "Yeah."

In the kitchen, Mom and Dad were drinking coffee. Dad was reading the paper. Mom was playing Bejeweled on her phone.

"Elien's going to stay the night if that's ok."

"Door closed," Dad said firmly.

"Oh, Dagobert," Mom said, one hand over her heart.

"As a friend," I said. "I'm going to sleep on the couch."

Dad folded the paper and stared at me. "Why?"

"Your father is right, Dagobert. He's a perfectly lovely young man."

"And he's into you," Dad said. "Like, really, really into you. He practically melted when you touched his shoulder at dinner."

"And you were so cute when he spilled wine, dabbing at his shirt. I think he had an erection."

I covered my face with my hands and backed down the hallway.

"Go get him," Dad stage whispered.

"Rock his world," Mom said.

"This is why superheroes always have parents who died in a tragic accident," I called back to them.

Shutting the door behind me, I prepared for Elien's smirk. But he wasn't smirking. He was asleep, his lean legs falling off the bed, drooling a little onto my quilt. I slid my arms under him and moved him up to the pillow. Then I got my iPod, popped in my earbuds, and put on some *Humpback Whales of Monterey Bay.* I stretched out next to Elien, enjoying the warmth of him next to me, liking the vanilla and bourbon I could smell on his breath after his second serving of bread pudding. My eyes closed. I drifted.

When I woke up, the room was in shadows, and Elien's hand was soft on my cheek, turning my face toward him. The green in his hazel eyes glowed like jade. After a moment, he pulled out one of my earbuds and slid it into his own, and then his hand was back on my cheek again. The whales sang to me. I was floating deep out in the ocean. His fingers smelled like red wine.

"I want to kiss you," I whispered.

He blinked and said, "God, I thought you'd never say that."

So I kissed him. And then I kissed him again, my hand moving to the back of his head, into that mess of blowout hair, pulling his mouth harder against mine. Rolling onto him, I tangled the earbuds, and then I pulled them free and slid the iPod to the floor. I kissed him again. His hands fiddled with my waistband, and my jeans popped open. He slid the zipper down.

"We should go slow," I whispered.

"I don't want to go slow. Do you want to go slow?"

"I don't want to hurt you."

"I don't want to go slow. I've been waiting for you my whole life."

It could have sounded cheesy anywhere else, but we were in our own universe, and it was simple and true. My heart was brass, ringing out under those words.

He undid the zipper, and he helped me slide my jeans and boxers down to my knees, and then he took me in his hand.

"Shit," I whispered, shuddering as I thrust into his grip. I had to clench my teeth, and not being able to make noise made it hotter somehow. "Oh shit, Elien, shit, it's been a long time, shit, shit, stop."

He pulled away; I was shaking on top of him. Elien used the cooldown to wriggle out of his shirt, and he pulled my hands to his nipples, and I flicked them and twisted and pulled and pinched. He made these little noises under his breath that were even hotter than his hand had been. I could see him going wild and not able to let it out, and it made me wild too. He rolled his hips, grinding up into me, and his pupils were huge.

"Fuck me," he whispered. "I need you to fuck me."

Nodding, I slid off him, and we both stripped, and I came back to the bed with a condom and lube. I knelt between his legs, ran my hands down his thighs, enjoying the way he shivered.

"Dag." He bit his lip. "I'm probably going to cry after. I might freak out. I just need you to . . . to hold me. And let me be upset, ok?"

"What? Why?"

"It's just—I don't know. All these associations."

And I remembered: his first time, some asshole he'd picked up that night, and then staggering out into the house to find his family dead.

"Oh Christ," I said. "I didn't even think."

"No, Dag. Please. I want this. I want you."

"But I don't want—"

"Please."

I slid my hands down to the vee of his legs. I ran my thumbs on the insides of his thighs. I kissed his knee. He was shaking. He was wet.

"Please," he whispered.

"What if we flip?"

"What?"

"Is it better for you that way?"

Those hazel eyes were blank.

My hands stilled. "No one's ever asked you that?"

He gave a tiny shake of his head, and then he squeezed his eyes shut, and tears leaked out the corners. I thumbed them away, kissed him, and took him in my mouth. He was soft at first, but after a few minutes he responded, a murmur building in his throat until he seized my head with his hands, fingers scraping over the short stubble of my hair.

When I pulled off, he was gasping. I dropped next to him, elbowed him in the ribs, and said, "Time for you to do some work."

Shock transmuted into a grin, and he took his place. He was slow. He was unsure. He kept asking, and he was gentle, and neither of us lasted long. I came first, untouched, biting my arm.

"Holy God," Elien said in a strangled whisper, and then he groaned and bucked wildly into me as he came.

For a while we lay together, our breathing syncopated, and I ran a sticky hand down his spine.

"Never," he said. And then he giggled. "Never in my entire life."

"I don't know what you're talking about," I said, "but I feel like I should be insulted."

He propped his chin on my chest and stared at me. "I've never had anything like that in my entire life. Ever. You are amazing."

"You are amazing," I said with a grin. "I just kind of hung around and enjoyed the performance."

He giggled into my side for a long time after that.

Then we had to clean up, and we were like kids sneaking down the hallway past my parents' bedroom, both of us trying not to laugh and both of us being too loud. Then he wanted more bread pudding, and we ate it in bed, sharing a spoon. And at some point, we fell asleep, and I completely forgot about the couch.

ELIEN (3)

When I woke up, it took me a moment to remember: the whale books, the poster of the 2008 Braxton Bragg Memorial High School basketball team, the rippling blue waves of the LED light on the wall. Dag's arm was across my chest, and when I inched toward the edge of the mattress, he flexed, drawing me against him.

"Morning," I whispered.

He kissed my neck.

"I've got to pee."

With a groan, he released me, and I sprinted to the bathroom. When I got back, Dag immediately latched onto me and dragged me into the curve of his body.

"Your mom and dad saw me in my underwear," I whispered.

He kissed my neck again.

"They were smiling so hard I thought they were going to have matching strokes."

Dag's hand skated over my chest, and his fingers slid under the elastic of my underwear.

"Really?" I said.

He kissed lower, where my neck joined my shoulder. His stubble rasped against the sensitive skin there, and goose bumps pebbled my chest. His fingers moved in slow, steady strokes.

"Again?" I said.

"Too early for talking," he mumbled.

It might have been too early for talking, but it wasn't too early for other stuff. Dag rolled me onto my back and rode me like a champ, both of us struggling to be quiet, the creak of the springs getting faster and faster. This was another first for me, and it was as overwhelming as last night: somehow, Dag seemed even more vulnerable like this, his knees spread as he rocked up and down, his head thrown back. He wasn't touching himself again, and I wondered if that was on purpose. I reached between his legs.

"Oh shit," he gasped, his eyes shooting open. "Not yet."

So I let him go, and after a moment, he guided my hands to his hips, and he let me direct him, setting the pace, his body doing all the work and me totally in control. His teeth made white crescents where he bit into his lip. In spite of his best efforts, low moans escaped him.

"Dag," I whispered.

He shook his head once, violently, like a dog.

"Dag, I'm close."

"Give me something," he whispered, his eyes wide and blind. "Shit, give me a pillow or something."

I handed him a pillow, and he bit savagely into it, and I figured that was my cue. I grabbed his dick; after two quick pulls, he was shooting all over me, screaming around his mouthful of pillow. The sight of him like that, wrecked and still pistoning on top of me, sent me over the edge; my fingers dug into the hard muscles of his chest as I brought him down onto me hard, hard, hard and blasted off.

After, he dropped the pillow, grinning sheepishly. He kissed me, tasting like cotton, and he nuzzled into my neck, still straddling me, and he fell asleep. It wasn't exactly uncomfortable, but it wasn't what I'd expected. I ran one hand along his back, following the curve of his shoulder blade, the side of his chest, the bandages on his ribs. I found blood where my nails had bitten crescents into sensitive skin. Then I dozed off too.

When I woke, he had slid off me, one arm still across my chest, and the sheet covered both of us.

"Morning," Dag said.

"Morning," I said.

"Sorry about that." He blushed, and his eyes fell. "I'm, uh, really attracted to you, which you probably figured out."

"It's nice to hear it, though," I said.

"Oh." His eyes came up. "I'm really attracted to you."

I smiled; something rippled in my chest like the water-light on the wall.

"I probably seem super needy," Dag said, "coming onto you like that. Twice."

"Not needy," I said.

"You're this gorgeous guy, and I know you're out of my league, and even though I'm older you're way more experienced because I've had, like, one boyfriend and he stole all my money and the sex probably wasn't even that good."

"Oh boy," I said, propping myself on one elbow. "This is spiraling fast."

"I just, you know, wanted to tell you, um, if you want me to do something different, you can tell me, or I could work out more, and I—"

"Whoa, whoa, whoa." Tugging down the sheet, I ran my hand over the hard lines of his chest, flattening my palm over the ridged muscles of his belly. "I'm here with you. I like you. You are hot, ok? You've got a body like you could fucking break me in half. And the hair is really doing something for me." Releasing a shaky breath, I met his eyes. "But I like you, who you are, I mean, even more. Nobody's ever cared what I wanted. Nobody's ever . . . been vulnerable for me like that. Trusted me."

Dag's eyes were wet. He touched my mouth. Then he kissed me. "I was worried you were going to freak out this morning."

"Well, you were right. I was. Being on the receiving end of the full cowboy, though, went a long way toward changing my mind. That and having a human teddy bear pin me to the bed."

Dag's blush got even darker.

Laughing, I ran my hand over his buzzed, graying hair. "Come on. We have to face your parents sometime."

"Nope," he said. "I'm just going to die in here."

"Up," I said, swatting his butt. "Or I'll tell them you were a gentle and considerate lover."

"Oh my God," he groaned, burying his face in the pillow. "They'd be so freaking proud. They'd never stop talking about it. I'd have to kill myself."

Dag tried to be a good host, but I let him clean up first. He was fast in the shower, though, and when he came back, he smelled like soap and that faint, woodsy smell I had noticed on him before. I took longer, mostly because I had never, in my entire adult life, had to face a new partner's parents over breakfast after the two best sexual experiences of my existence.

After dressing in fresh clothes, I found Dag and his parents in the kitchen. A huge breakfast casserole sat in the middle of the table, along with a baker's box full of beignets. Dag had a piece of casserole almost as big as his plate, and he was working his way through the beignets pretty steadily.

Dag's parents were still smiling.

"Good morning," I said.

"Good morning," Gloria cooed.

Dag groaned, powdered sugar puffing out from the beignet he was working on.

"I'm sure you boys worked up quite an appetite," she said, serving me a piece of casserole almost as big as the one Dag had. "Would you like some orange juice, Elien? Coffee?"

"Stop fussing over them," Hubert said.

"Thank you," Dag muttered.

"The boys pleasured each other last night," Hubert said. "That's all."

Dag expelled another cloud of powdered sugar.

"It's perfectly normal and natural for them to bring each other to the heights of physical ecstasy. No need to cluck on and on about it."

"Oh my God," Dag whispered.

"It's a beautiful thing," Gloria said, hands over her heart. "That's all."

"Please kill me," Dag said.

I just grinned and grabbed a beignet.

When we were finally back in Dag's bedroom, I sat on the bed, and Dag shut the door and said, "I'm going to become a monk."

"That would be a waste," I said.

"The kind that have to cut off all communication with their families."

"I think you're talking about a cult."

"That's right. I'm going to join a cult." He wiped his mouth on the tee he was wearing; powdered sugar already covered most of the gray jersey. "Do you know any good ones?"

"I guess we need to talk about what happened, you know. With Zahra."

His face hardened. "That was a mistake, Elien. Let's not go down that road again."

"We were wrong about Zahra. We jumped to a conclusion. But we weren't entirely wrong. Something is killing people in that support group. The hashok is feeding off the people who are suffering, and anyone who might stand in its way—David, who was trying to stop it, and Zahra, because she wanted to help the people in group. It's all connected to this support group. And it's all connected to DuPage Behavioral. David was following the same trail we were, and he came to the same conclusion."

"Elien—"

"All the victims have had a connection to the support group."

"Elien, hold on—"

"And all the victims have had a connection to DuPage Behavioral. We're close, ok, and if we—"

"Elien, just stop talking for a minute."

His words rang out in the small room. The quiet activity in the rest of the house—Dag's parents talking quietly in the kitchen, the murmur of the TV—stopped completely. Everything was holding its breath.

"They're forcing me out of the sheriff's department."

"What?"

"They're firing me. They won't call it that. And it's not exactly . . . I mean, it's more complicated. But they've got these psych evals, and then there's the fact that I just happened to show up at a murder scene and I can't explain it, and . . . technically, I'm still on paid leave, but I'm done. As soon as they can make it happen, I'll be out of there."

I thought about this, took a deep breath, and said, "Ok."

"It's not ok."

"Dag, I'm sorry about your job. I am. But that doesn't mean we should stop. We're so close."

"What are you talking about? We don't have anything, Elien. Every time we think we have a lead, somebody dies, and we're not any closer. And we're putting our lives in danger."

In the living room, the TV came on again; somebody was talking about birdies, and then the vacuum roared to life, whiting out the announcer's voice.

"What do you want to do?" I asked.

"We're in danger," Dag said. "I asked my parents. They said they'll loan me some money. We'll get out of here for a while. We'll go somewhere else, just the two of us. And when things settle down, we can come back. Or not. We can do whatever we want, Elien."

"I can't imagine how hard it is to lose your job—"

"Fuck my job. I was shit at my job. I don't care about my job. I'm worried about you. I'm worried about us, if that doesn't freak you out to hear it."

"It doesn't freak me out." I took another breath, releasing it as slowly as I could, blinking to clear my eyes. "Will you come over here?"

He grumbled something.

"Dag, please."

After a moment, he stomped over to stand in front of me.

I took his hands and looked up at him. "You were not shit at your job. You are smart. You are brave. You are intuitive. You want to protect people. Losing that job, losing what you worked so hard for, I know it hurts. I'm sorry."

"I tried to be good at it," he said in a small voice.

"I know. And you were good at it. You saved my life. More than once, actually. And you're working hard right now to save other people. The hashok is going to keep killing, whether you're a deputy or not, whether we stay here or not. I'm not going to leave. I've been running from what happened . . . from what happened with Gard and my parents for a long time now. If the hashok had anything to do with it, if there's even a chance, then I want to face that thing and kill it."

"We don't know how to kill it," Dag said.

"But we'll figure it out. We've got that book. And we've got David's computer. We're going to find out who the hashok is, and we're going to find a way to stop it." I squeezed his hands. "I keep saying we. I mean I'm going to do it."

He twisted one of his hands free, and then he ran it along the side of my face, riffling my hair, a gesture that was oddly rough and comforting at the same time. "Don't be such a dummy. I'm going to help you."

"Yeah?"

"Of course. You couldn't do it by yourself anyway. There are too many big words in that book."

I tried to punch him in the gut, but he wrestled me to the bed, covering me with kisses.

DAG (4)

"Do you want something to drink?" I asked. We were standing in the middle of my bedroom; I had just come back with popcorn.

"Nope," Elien said.

"Do you want headphones? I have an extra pair."

"I'm all good."

"Do you want some sweats? You know, something more comfortable."

"I'm comfortable, thanks."

I ate a piece of popcorn. Then, because there were only a few things in the world better than popcorn, I kissed Elien.

He smirked.

I ate another piece of popcorn and kissed him again.

"I don't know when the last time was that I had popcorn," he said with a sigh.

I held out the bowl.

"No, thanks." He rubbed his tummy. "I'm gross enough already, and staying in Carb City hasn't helped."

"I don't think you're gross," I said, setting down the bowl of popcorn and tugging on his shirt.

"Ok," he said, rolling his eyes.

I kissed him again. "Let me show you."

"Buttery," he said, licking his lips.

I herded him toward the bed.

With a smirk, he slipped around me and pushed me onto the bed.

When I squirmed toward the edge of the mattress, he said, "Stay."

"I'm just going to kiss you a few more times."

"Dagobert LeBlanc, stay!"

"Just five kisses. Because I think you're very handsome and sexy."

Shoving the bowl toward him, I said, "Here's your popcorn, there's the book. Get to work."

"Three kisses."

Elien shook his head, still smirking.

"One?" I asked.

"Do some reading," Elien said. "Then we'll talk."

"Ok," I said. "You come do some work too."

"Oh no. I don't know what kind of sorcery you used on me, but I'm not getting anywhere near that bed while we're trying to work."

"That's a little silly," I said, flipping open *New Orleans and La Louisiane: Chorography, Ethnology, and the Native Episteme.* "We're both adults."

"Uh huh."

"We can control ourselves."

"Uh huh," he said again. "Like this morning?"

My face heated.

"Oh God, do you have any idea how cute that is? All that gray stubble on your head, and you blush like a little kid."

"It's cuter up close," I said. "Come over here and I'll show you."

"Nice try."

Shrugging, I flipped pages again.

"I will be working over here," Elien said, setting up David's laptop at the desk.

I stretched out on the bed, searching *New Orleans and La Louisiane: Chorography, Ethnology, and the Native Episteme* for the chapter on the hashok. "Ok," I said, motioning for him to pass me my popcorn. "But that chair isn't very comfortable."

"I'll live."

"You can have the bed and I'll sit on the floor."

"Read," Elien said.

So I read. And Elien began clicking and typing, searching David's computer for documents or other files we might have missed. The morning dragged by. The book didn't say anything about how to kill the hashok, and after my third time of reading the chapter, I'd given up on finding any new clues. I googled hashok and got an abbreviated version of the same information I'd found in the book, printed in an ethnology bulletin from the turn of the century. I thought about that for a while with my eyes closed.

"Wake up," Elien called.

"I am awake. I just had my eyes closed. I was thinking"

"Do you always snore when you think?"

So I opened my eyes, just to make him happy, and went back to searching the internet. I tried combinations. Hashok, monster, possession, vampire, will o' the wisp, PTSD. I got a lot of hits and nothing that was relevant.

Elien was doing a lot of shifting around on the seat.

"It's that chair," I said.

"I'm all right."

"You're going to hurt your back."

"The chair's fine."

"Just bad hemorrhoids, huh?"

He threw a pencil.

"I feel like you don't want to talk right now," I said.

"If I didn't think your parents would enjoy it too much, I'd flip you over and spank your ass right now."

"My parents wouldn't be the only ones who enjoyed it. Come over here and—"

The next pencil got me in the chest.

"Shot through the heart," I said, clasping my hands over my chest and slumping sideways.

"Read," Elien snapped, but when he didn't think I was looking, he was doing an awful lot of smiling.

I googled the author of *New Orleans and La Louisiane: Chorography, Ethnology, and the Native Episteme*, whose name was William Lupton Whaley, and I found several more articles by him. I was just digging into the first one when Elien's stomach rumbled.

When I looked up, he blushed and said, "I'm fine."

"You sound hungry."

"I normally don't eat much breakfast or lunch. I think my stomach forgot."

"I'll order pizza."

"No, Dag, I think I'll just wait until dinner."

"Oh," I said.

He watched me.

"Because I'm still going to order the pizza," I said.

Groaning, Elien dropped his head onto the laptop.

"You don't have to have any," I said.

"You're so generous."

When the pizza came, I paid the guy with cash, ignored my mom and dad, who were hissing questions at me, and carried the box back to my bedroom. I sat down on the bed, opened it up, and fanned the lid a few times.

"You're the devil," Elien said, his jaw rigid as he stared at the laptop.

"What?"

"You know exactly what."

I grabbed a big slice of pizza and dangled it over my face, biting off the individual strands of cheese one by one. Then some sauce spattered my face.

"Ow," I shouted.

"You deserved that."

"I deserved to be blinded by some boiling hot pizza sauce because I was enjoying a piece of pizza."

"You know exactly why you deserved it."

After that, I ate two slices of pizza in silence. Well, without talking. I ate them very loudly.

Finally, Elien shut the laptop. "Fine."

"Fine, what?"

"Fine, I'll have a slice of pizza."

"Oh, no. I don't think you want any."

He squinted at me; it was supposed to be a dirty look.

"I'm really, really, hungry, Dag. And I don't know why I didn't realize it earlier, but I am so grateful you ordered pizza. You're so wise."

"And generous," I said.

"And generous. Now, may I please have a slice of pizza?"

"Sure," I said. When he stood up, I added, "Better bring that laptop."

"What?"

"Rules of the house: if you want to eat pizza, you have to eat it in bed."

Elien ran a hand through his hair, which was looking decidedly less windswept and still achingly adorable. "Let me get this right: the rule of the house is that I have to eat pizza in bed."

Around a mouthful of pizza, I said, "Mmmhmm."

"I can live with that rule."

So we ate pizza in bed. And Elien told me about growing up and going to Catholic school in Harahan, and I told him about Braxton Bragg Memorial High School. Elien told me about Gard building his first computer, and I told him about Mason and me tipping over a Port-a-Potty and getting community service. Elien told me about his mom giving him a bowl cut the night before first communion, and when I didn't believe him, he showed me the pictures. I laughed until he tackled me, and then we wrestled around for a while until he gave up. We lay together on the bed.

"It's no fair," he said. "You're strong."

"Don't be a sore loser," I said, propping some pillows behind us. "You get a fifteen-minute break, and then it's back to work."

"Fifteen minutes?" he said, rolling into me and kissing me.

Twenty-five minutes later, I said, "We should really get back to work."

Thirty minutes later, Elien came up for air from a serious, slightly-pizza-flavored make-out session, and he said, "Holy God."

"You can call me Dag too."

Slapping my belly, he said, "God, you're awful when you're confident."

I brushed his crazy haystack hair.

"I never got to do stuff like this," he said.

"Make out?"

"Not really. But the rest of it too. Be silly. Just spend time like this."

"Researching monsters?"

He slapped my belly again. "You know what I mean. I was just hooking up before . . . before everything that happened with Gard and my parents, and after, I ended up with Richard. He liked to cuddle and kiss sometimes, but not like this."

"It's nice," I said, still touching his hair. "Right?"

"Definitely nice."

"You're really beautiful," I said.

"You don't have to do that. Be nice to me like that."

"You are. You're beautiful."

"Ok." He shifted, sat up, and said, "Is there any pizza left, or—"

Hooking an arm around his waist, I held him in place. My face was buried in his side, but my words were still clear. "When we're all done with this monster business, I'm going to pin you down and spend a full twenty-four hours kissing every part of you and telling you how beautiful you are. And I know you've got some sort of screw loose in your head, and you don't want to talk about this stuff, so just kind of rub my head if you heard me and you know you're in for a crazy awesome twenty-four hours pretty soon."

He held himself stiffly, but after a moment, he scrubbed one hand over my short hair.

"Good boy," I said when I let him go. "Now get your laptop, come back here, and let's snuggle while we work."

To my surprise, he did. He fit pretty nicely against me, and I rested my chin on his shoulder while I read. Elien's eyes were red for a while, and he kept blinking. I let him do what he needed to do while I searched for more articles.

After a couple more hours, I said, "Status report?"

"I've got nothing," he said. "I mean, he obviously used this computer a lot, and it's full of files. I was even able to get into his online accounts, email, that kind of stuff, because he had a password manager and it's still active. But besides those pictures, there's nothing relevant."

"Well," I said, "I figured out how to kill the hashok."

"What? How?"

"Burn it."

"Are you sure?"

"Whaley sounds pretty sure."

"Who's Whaley?"

I told him and said, "I guess he was a pretty serious ethnographer or whatever they call them, but he kind of went off the deep end before he died. He was convinced monsters were real. Told everyone he was being hunted. He lost his academic position, and it sounds like he hit rock bottom pretty fast. He sold all his papers to a tiny private college because he needed money."

"Jesus. What happened then?"

"He died. Want to guess how?"

Elien shook his head.

"Animal attack," I said. "Sound familiar?"

"That's crazy."

"Not really. Look what happened to David when he got too close. Look what happened when you and I started poking around."

"I thought he figured out how to kill it," Elien said.

"Well, I guess that was in theory more than in practice."

"And what's the theory?"

"Fire."

"Ok."

"He talks about the grass of the field burning, the chaff consumed by the cleansing flame."

"Sounds Biblical," Elien said. "Our monster isn't Biblical."

"Maybe he just liked a nice turn of phrase."

"Ok, let's assume he's right. How do we find the hashok?"

"Well, let's think about this," I said. "Process of elimination. We know it's someone who's connected to DuPage Behavioral, right?"

"We don't know that, but it's a pretty safe bet. All of the victims have had connections there."

"And it's not Zahra, because she's dead. And it's not Richard."

Shaking his head, Elien said, "I know you're trying to spare me—"

"I'm not, actually. Richard was in the hotel restaurant with that guy, remember? Even if he had somehow managed to get to Zahra's house, attack us, and make his way back, he's got that guy as his alibi for the whole night. I asked after they took us in to the station, and one of them finally told me. Richard was with that guy all night."

"Oh."

"Sorry. It sucks to hear that."

"No, it's just kind of confirmation."

"So," I said, "who else from DuPage Behavioral has a connection to these victims? Can we find out which doctors they were seeing? Do you think that's the pattern?"

"No," Elien said slowly, "remember? All the doctors in the practice see people with PTSD. Their money makers are addiction and 'distressed executives,' but they all take patients with PTSD."

"Do they all have access to each other's records? If the records were computerized, anybody in the practice could have tracked victims easily."

"Maybe," Elien said. "I don't know how secure those records are."

"Somebody could have broken into Zahra's office," I said, "and examined the physical files."

Frowning, Elien opened his mouth, but his phone buzzed, and he glanced at it.

"You can take it," I said.

"No, it's Richard."

"You should take it."

He shook his head. "It's just a text. Muriel's there, and she's telling him I asked for a ride, which is crazy because—" He faltered and then looked at me. "Oh Christ."

"What?"

"She has access to all the records because she does administrative work on top of seeing patients." His words tumbled out. "She lives out by me too, Dag. She lives past us, upstream on the Okhlili. Right on the edge of the bayou. She drove me to the support group a ton of times. She would have recognized everyone; she could have pulled their files easily. She had her own private herd."

"And now she's cleaning house," I said. "Making sure no one can point back to her."

"Oh shit," Elien said, scrambling off the bed. "She's there right now. She's going to kill Richard."

ELIEN (5)

When we got to the house, the front door was open. Muriel's Subaru was nosed up to the garage.

Dag caught my arm as I was unbuckling myself. "Will you please stay here?"

"No."

"Will you at least let me go first since I have the gun?"

After a moment, I nodded.

We got out of the Escort. The St. Augustine grass was as neatly trimmed as ever; the magnolia trees and the black oaks and the sugar maples stood still. When I took a deep breath to steady my nerves, I could smell pine sap and freshly cut grass; Richard must have had the lawn-care guys out again. In the house, nothing moved. The windows held our reflection, and behind the reflection, I could make out the dark shapes of furniture.

Then the door slammed shut.

I jumped, and Dag shot around the car to put himself in front of me. One of his hands was on my chest; the other held a pistol. He wasn't breathing fast or trembling or anything. After a moment, he said, "Fuck."

I didn't sound quite as controlled when I muttered, "Holy fucking hell."

"Please stay here."

"I can't."

"I know," he said, "but a guy can hope, right?"

He took slow, careful steps toward the house. I came after him, leaving a yard between us; I knew he might have to move fast, and I didn't want to tangle him up. He'd given me a fixed-blade hunting knife before we left his house, and the fucker was about as long as my hand. If anything got close to me, I was going to stab the fuck out of it. My muscles were spasming, and my movements were jerky as I planned and lived halfway inside that future moment. I briefly considered that I was out of my goddamn mind.

When Dag got to the front door, he did a silent three count on one hand and then kicked it open, charging into the front room. I came after him, slamming the door behind me, and I checked the corners the way he had told me on the drive up. Dag was still moving, passing the stairs and cutting across the living room and into the kitchen. He was still silent, but someone was screaming, and it took me a moment to realize that the sound was inside my head. I went after him, and it was like I was inside a stranger's house: I cracked my shin against the coffee table, checked up against the couch, caught a cord with my sneaker and pulled a lamp down behind me.

I was coming around living room, just getting a glimpse into the open-plan kitchen, when Dag flew through the air. He crashed into the windows, and glass shattered, but he didn't go through them. The frames just buckled and splintered, and he fell to the ground. I couldn't tell if he was breathing.

When I looked up, the hashok was there. This was the first really good look I'd had at it: a human form stripped of anything that might have identified it, nose and ears barely more than nubs, its skin ashen and its eyes black all the way across. Its frame and head were elongated, giving it a stretched-out look, but it had an easy, relaxed stance that reminded me of a basketball player—lots of muscle, and ready to move.

"Shit," I whispered. "Shit, shit, shit."

Holding out the knife, I grabbed my phone and called 911. I kept my eyes on the hashok, but it was still in the kitchen, still watching me. The dispatcher came on, and I shouted the address and officer down. I didn't know if that was the right phrasing, but I figured it'd light a fire under their collective asses. Then I tossed the phone on the couch.

The hashok sprinted, and I made an involuntary stab at the air, but it wasn't moving toward me. It shot toward the back of the house, smashed through the door, and blurred across the grass. Then it was gone.

I wasn't ready to be tricked again. The damn thing had tried this last time. It liked to try to pick its victims off one at a time. It liked to try to sneak up behind you.

Crouching by Dag, I checked him as quickly as I could. He was breathing, although something sounded wrong, a kind of whistling, and his eyes were half open. I whispered his name. "I need you with me, please. That thing is going to come back, and it's going to try to get us again."

He moaned. He was bleeding in a dozen places, and when I rolled him over, I had to steady myself with one hand on the wall: part of the window frame had splintered and gone straight into his back. His lung, part of my brain informed me. That's the whistling. He's got a punctured lung.

When he coughed, bloody froth spouted from his mouth.

"Oh my God," I whispered. "Oh my God."

For a moment, I slipped back into memory: the weight of my hookup pinning me to the mattress, the smell of fried catfish, the taste of grass, the helplessness as he thrust into me, my brain playing out the horrible things happening just outside my door.

Then, shuddering, I grabbed Dag under the arms and dragged him away from the windows. He screamed. I didn't know if this was doing more damage, but I knew if I left him by the windows, the hashok would get him. We'd barely made it to the edge of the kitchen when my prediction came true: the hashok smashed through the glass where Dag had been lying. It let out a yowl of disappointment; it had obviously expected us to still be there, with me tending to Dag's injuries. I released Dag, held up the knife, and flipped the bird.

The hashok rocked side to side, its liquid black eyes watching.

"Fuck off," I said to it. "I know how to get rid of you. This is your one warning: fuck off right now, and never come back, and I won't hunt you down and burn you to ash."

The hashok yowled again. For a moment, I thought it was going to charge. Then a soft sound behind me drew my attention, and I shot a glance over my shoulder. There was nothing. When I looked back, the hashok was gone, and splinters of glass trembled in the frame where it had run out of the house again.

Playing with us, I thought. It's playing with us the way a cat plays with a mouse.

Seizing Dag under the arms, I dragged him back a few more feet. There wasn't anywhere safe in the house, but if I could get into the pantry, at least I'd only have to defend one door, and maybe we could wait it out until help arrived. Unless the hashok just smashed through the wall or the door. Unless it decided it didn't need the element of surprise anymore. I dragged Dag a few more feet, and he screamed again.

I had to stop for a break. I had zero upper-body strength, and Dag was all fucking muscle, which was nice for sex and nice for having a tough boyfriend, but it was a real bitch right now. My back and arms ached. Sweat stung my eyes. Another sound, maybe nothing, made me check over my shoulder, but I still didn't see anything. My brain was having a hard time making sense of everything. Part of me recognized this place: the same furniture, the same paintings, even the same bottle of wine, complete with corkscrew, that I had gotten out before I left. This had been my home for over a year. But part of me felt like I was in a funhouse, all the angles crooked, all the hallways mazes, all the glass a mirror.

Grabbing Dag again, I shuffled back toward the pantry. It had been a few minutes now. Where was the hashok? Where was Richard? Was he bleeding out upstairs? Was he already dead? Had the hashok gutted him the way it had killed Zahra and David? Or had it toyed with him, torturing him, Muriel finally exacting payback for all the petty grievances of working under Richard?

If he was alive, I thought, I had to help him. Maybe I could get Dag safely into the pantry, barricade the door somehow, and search upstairs. If there was even a chance, I owed Richard that much.

Shards of glass chimed as a rush of air swept through the house. I guessed that it was from the hashok, but I couldn't see it. Maybe it was sprinting past the house. Maybe it was looking for the best way to approach. The door to the pantry was less than five feet away. Slipping my arms under Dag's, I groaned and hauled him for another yard. When I looked up, the hashok was standing ten feet away, watching.

It stayed there, rocking side to side.

"Come on," I shouted, stabbing the air with the knife. "Come the fuck on!"

That noise behind me again.

Then something pricked me on my neck, and my brain said, jugular vein. The world incandesced, and then a filament in my brain burned out, and everything went dark.

"Welcome home, Elien."

Richard's whisper followed me as I fell.

DAG (6)

The world floated in a haze. I had only a blurry recollection of the hashok charging me, grabbing me, and hurling me across the house. When I struck the windows, the world had fragmented. I vaguely remembered sharp bursts of pain, movement, Elien's labored breathing. My sense of self was coming back together now in bits and pieces. The pain in my head. The shortness of breath. Sharp zaps of lightning ran through my back every time I breathed. I'd hit my head a few times in my life, but I'd never been this disoriented before. The sound of air moving in my lungs was wrong; I could tell that much. I wasn't getting enough oxygen, a small part of my brain informed me, but then the world disintegrated again, and I had to close my eyes.

When I opened my eyes the next time, I could see more clearly. The first thing I noticed was Elien lying on the ground next to me. His eyes were closed, his face smushed against the tile, and a tiny bead of blood marked the side of his neck. One hand was outstretched and open; the hunting knife I had given him lay a few inches away, where it had fallen from his grip. The next thing I noticed was the red: a flood of it covered the tile. At first I thought it was Elien's blood. Then I thought it was mine. Then I caught the bouquet of expensive red wine, and I spotted the broken glass, the corkscrew. Elien must have knocked everything off the counter when he fell.

A loafer moved into my field of vision, kicking the hunting knife across the tile. Then the loafers came toward me and stopped. An angry shriek broke the stillness. I would have flinched, but I was still so deep in the haze of pain that the noise barely registered.

"Calm down, Muriel," Richard said. "They're both still alive. We'll have plenty of time to enjoy them."

Another shriek answered.

"I don't understand why you prefer that form," Richard said, and the loafers moved away, splashing through the wine as he rounded the counter and moved out of the kitchen. For the moment, I was alone with Elien again. "It only makes you bloodthirsty."

The air seemed to warp; it reminded me of a sail filling with wind, the whole world becoming concave for an instant. Then everything was normal again, and a woman's voice answered, "You're being self-indulgent. Let's kill them and be done with it."

"Self-indulgent? You've spent the last two weeks chasing them, pretending to hunt them, getting just close enough to kill and then letting them escape."

"It adds savor. They're so bland otherwise. We don't have time for that anymore, though. Let's be done with them."

"Don't be hasty. I've spent over a year nibbling the crumbs of his suffering. I'd like to enjoy a full course now."

"He called the police. They're coming. You've got ten minutes, maybe. We need to kill them and be gone."

"No," Richard snapped. "I won't throw away all those months of listening to him whine and moan."

My eyes fell on the knife. It had slid under the cabinets, and it was no more than five feet from where I lay. Bracing myself for the pain, I dragged myself across the tile.

I stopped almost immediately as the wound in my back flared to life. For a moment, all I could do was lie there, frozen by it, panting, my eyes stinging with tears. The pain ebbed slowly, and I looked at the knife again. Gritting my teeth, I dragged myself forward a few more inches.

It was worse this time, but somehow I made it a full foot. Then I had to stop. I was on fire, every inch of me, sweat pouring down my face and dampening my shirt. The tile was cool against my cheek, and I focused on that as the pain twisted my gut. When I could breathe without fear of puking, I crawled forward again.

The pain made me stop. Black pinpricks marked the edges of my vision. The knife was still three feet away, and I had to close my eyes and fight a sob.

"I don't know why," Muriel said, "but you sound like you think you're in charge."

"I am in charge," Richard said. "This was my plan. I was the one that found Zahra. I was the one who put the thorn in her hand. It's unfortunate that we had to get rid of her."

"She was becoming difficult," Muriel said. "Unreliable. What else could you do?"

"If it were up to you, we'd still be fool lights drifting in the bayou. We'd eat a few times a year at most. Do you remember? In a bad year, we might eat only once."

"It was never that bad," Muriel said. "You're exaggerating."

"It wasn't like this."

"No. And I'm not saying it was. But I'm saying you can pretend to be the boss at work, but don't forget that your game is just a game. I like an easy meal as much as the next, but you're not lord and master. You should remember that."

"The boy will be delicious, Muriel. So much guilt and self-loathing and grief, all of it tangled up so he doesn't know where to start. What I've tasted has been very . . . satisfying. He'll be exquisite."

I pictured Elien's hair, windswept. I pictured the shock on Elien's face the first time we were in bed together. I pictured Elien sorting beans, and Elien with an earbud. Elien, the real Elien.

Holding my breath, I scrabbled forward. My hand closed around the knife. Then I had to stop, trying to listen over the pounding of blood in my ears, trying to keep from puking as the pain turned in my gut.

"—have it your way, then," Muriel said. "You always do."

I wouldn't have time to get back to my original spot. And I would only get one chance at a surprise. I tucked the knife into my waistband, covered it with my shirt, and slumped on the tile. The air warped again, and I heard Muriel shriek. She came around the counter in the elongated form of the hashok.

Her slender claws gripped my ankles, cutting through the jeans and into my flesh as she dragged me across the tile. I screamed. The claws biting into my flesh hurt, but worse was the pain in my back as I was dragged across the kitchen. Then the pain seemed to hit some sort of threshold, and my mind switched off for a moment.

When I came back, my vision was full of pinpricks again. I heard the soft, padding steps of the loafers. Then a slap. Then another.

"Elien, dear." Slap. "Wake up." Slap. "Time to finish what we started."

My sight cleared. I blinked up into Muriel's oily, hashok eyes. She had no lips, and her mouth was a slash exposing razor teeth, but she grinned when she saw me looking at her. She batted at me once, the tips of her claws slicing my thigh. I screamed in spite of myself, jerking upright. Her grin got bigger as she pinned me to the tile, her nails driving easily into the fleshy part of my shoulder. Arteries, a panicked voice was saying. Did she get an artery? I couldn't see the wounds in my thigh, but I kept thinking femoral artery, femoral artery. I could feel the wet heat soaking my jeans, spreading under me.

"Stay still, Deputy LeBlanc," Richard said. "You're not going anywhere, and Muriel has the ugly habit of playing with her food. Better not encourage her."

Behind me, Elien groaned and mumbled something.

Another slap, this one louder and harder.

Elien cried out.

"That's right, dear," Richard said. "Welcome back."

ELIEN (7)

For a while, I was floating, and then little islands of reality poked up through the fog: the grit of the tile under my cheek, the smell of wine, the stinging in my neck. As my vision cleared, I tried to make sense of what I was seeing. Shards of glass from the broken bottle. The corkscrew. Directly in my line of sight, the hashok—Muriel—stood over Dag. Dag was breathing harshly; he was covered in blood.

Then a hand covered my mouth, and a weight settled on top of me.

"Is this how it was?" Richard asked in my ear.

His hand smelled like fried catfish; his weight bore down on me. Richard, who liked an extra big slice of cake. Richard, who joked about getting more exercise. Richard, who probably weighed fifty pounds more than me. And he was strong, too, his fingers biting into my jaw, his other arm around my neck, a loose hold that he could tighten if he needed to.

"I asked you a question," he said, pulling hard with his arm and cutting off my air. "I've enjoyed a taste here or there, of course. But I've been wondering for so long. Is this what it was like with him on top of you? Is this what it was like, when you couldn't move, when you couldn't do anything but lie there, while I sent your brother from room to room with a gun in his hand? When I saw him the first time, I knew he'd be perfect, but you—you were a bonus."

He held me until stars spun in my vision, and then he loosened his grip. I sucked in air through my nose, every breath with that fried catfish smell. Tears stung my eyes. I hadn't known, I wanted to say. I hadn't known. I hadn't known what Gard was doing, I hadn't known what was happening. I hadn't known anything. It didn't matter, though. Since the minute I'd walked out of my bedroom and found them, since the minute I'd learned what had happened while some bozo I'd picked up at the club fucked me, it had been my fault. I'd heard a weird noise, hadn't I? I'd heard that noise, and I hadn't gone to check, hadn't gone to see what was happening. I'd been too fucking selfish. Literally.

"That's right," Richard said, mouthing along my neck between words. "God, you're delicious. All that self-hate. All that guilt." He bit directly over where he'd injected me, and his teeth broke skin, the mark of his mouth cold and burning. His tongue laved blood from my neck. "You heard a noise," he whispered. "You could have gone and looked. You could have checked. Maybe you couldn't have saved all of them, but you might have saved one."

He rocked into me slightly. His tongue ran over the wound, the cold blaze burning brighter. Venom, I thought from a distance. Maybe it would burn all the way through me. Maybe I could die like this, not feeling anything except polar fire.

"Go ahead," he said, and for a moment, I thought he was giving me permission. Then Muriel bent and slashed her claws along Dag's leg.

He screamed.

I couldn't help it: I bucked, trying to throw off Richard, kicking wildly, hands sliding through the puddled wine. With that same irresistible strength, he yanked my head back and bore down until fireworks exploded across my vision and I went limp.

Static hissed in my ears.

Then the static faded. My vision cleared.

"Good," he said. "You're back. Was it like that? Is it the same?"

I could hear my own breathing—I was trying to suck air through my nose, but I couldn't seem to get enough. Catfish. Fried catfish. The weight on top of me. The hand over my mouth. The pressure at my neck. The pressure building in my head. His weight as he rocked against me. He wasn't fucking me, not yet, but he was hard. I thought that would come later. Some clear-thinking part of me understood that would come at the end, when they made me watch Dag die.

Richard bit hard where my neck joined my shoulder. This time, the cold fire was worse, spreading through my shoulder and chest. I shouted, struggling again, and this time he let me squirm and thrash. His tongue lapped at the blood.

"Again," Richard said.

Muriel dragged her claws down Dag's arm, and he howled and tried to move, but I saw now that she had pinned him to the tile, her other set of claws transfixing his shoulder. Suddenly he jerked and went still.

This time, I almost got Richard off me. I bucked and rolled. My hands splashed across the tile. My fingertips brushed something and sent it rolling. I got an elbow in Richard's side, and he growled as he yanked back again, and my vision imploded.

The next time I came back, I heard sirens.

Richard was breathing rapidly. I knew the sound. I knew the jingle of his belt buckle. Then one hand was at my jeans, fiddling, and I tried to get free again, but he had me pinned.

If Dag was dead because of me.

"That's right," Richard said, desire making his voice rough. His teeth punctured my other shoulder this time; the venom, if that's what it was, made my chest feel like it was locking up. "You're going to watch him die. Helpless. Held down. Fucked. And you can't do anything about it. You couldn't do anything about it then, either. If you'd been stronger." He yanked my jeans down. "If you'd been smarter." He yanked my underwear down. "If you hadn't been so fucking selfish."

They were my own words. I'd been hearing them since that night.

Richard pressed against me; he was naked and hard.

And then I heard Dag talking about college: *Should have, would have, could have. Nothing good at the end of that road.*

My hand swept out across the tile, closed over the handle of the corkscrew, and I brought it up and back. I felt it connect and sink into something soft that gave with a slight pop.

Richard screamed.

I kept pushing. He was flopped off me, trying to get away, but I rolled with him, driving the corkscrew with all the strength I had. We tumbled around until I was on top of him, shoving the corkscrew into the socket of his ruined eye, punching it into his brain. His hands raked at me, long claws that weren't quite human, and I realized he was trying to shift his shape—or perhaps had simply lost control. I was beyond pain, beyond everything. Bone crunched, and then the handle of the corkscrew caught up against his forehead and wouldn't go any deeper.

I scrambled back and watched him, his back arching, his half-transformed claws scratching the tile. He flopped in the wine like a fish. And then I realized he couldn't do anything else. He couldn't die, but he couldn't change, couldn't control his body anymore. He'd stay like that until I ripped the corkscrew loose.

Or until I burned the motherfucker to ash.

A shriek made me turn, and too late I remembered Muriel. She ripped her claws out of Dag, freeing him from the floor, and reared back. Then she charged toward me.

DAG (8)

One moment I was lying on the ground, pinned there by the hashok's claws, being tortured—sliced to pieces, listening to Elien scream. The next moment, I was free. The hashok shrieked, rearing back, its claw coming free from my shoulder. My first instinct was to curl up into a ball, but I forced myself to lie there. Play possum. The hashok was still screeching. Whatever had just happened, it had pissed off Muriel fiercely. I could hear Elien struggling behind me, and I realized that somehow, impossibly, Elien had gotten free.

Muriel leaped over me.

I reacted without thinking, reaching up and catching her by one pale, elongated leg. She crashed into the tile; the house shook from the impact. She kicked at me, and she swiped back, trying to get loose. But Muriel and Richard had been dealing with prey too long. It had made them sloppy, and sloppy had made them careless. She must have expected that I'd pull back, trying to avoid her claws, and maybe let her loose. Instead, I dragged her closer, climbing up her body, knocking the claws away.

Shock was on my side; the dark, oily eyes were full of it, as though she couldn't believe anyone—anything—would dare to fight back. She was so shocked that she let me knock her claws aside, let me move closer. She probably couldn't believe what she was seeing.

Then the moment of advantage ended, and she surged back toward me. Her lipless mouth gaped open; rows of razor-sharp teeth moved toward my face. Her breath stank of rotten meat and fetid waters that had stood still too long.

During all that torture, she'd never cut up my chest, never sliced open my shirt. I yanked out the hidden hunting knife and lunged to meet her. Surprise again. At the last instant before we connected, a hint of doubt showed on that monstrous face, the possibility that she had made a mistake. Then the fixed blade of the knife was shearing through the soft palate at the back of her mouth, and I drove it up into her brain.

She dropped back, her long, pale limbs kicking and jerking like she'd grabbed an electric line. I stared at her as she did that helpless dance across the tile. Spasms twisted Richard around in the same way. Elien had driven a corkscrew into his eye. He had lost most of his hair, and his face was lipless and too long; Elien had caught him in the middle of a transformation.

Elien stood with his back to the refrigerator, a chef's knife in one hand, the blade trembling. Blood soaked the front of him, and I could see bite marks, puffy and inflamed, across his neck and shoulders, exposed where his shirt was pulled askew. Then his eyes cut to me.

"They're not—" My words came in short bursts; it was hard to breathe. "Why aren't they. Doing anything?"

"Fire kills them," Elien said. "Isn't that what you told me? They can't die this way, but their brains are broken. Short circuited. Something like that."

Nodding, I circled around the two thrashing monsters and grabbed another knife from the block. The only sound were their limbs slapping the wet tiles, the rustle of Richard's clothing, the weak grunts they released. Then I picked out the sirens in the distance.

"Come on," I said.

"What are the police going to do?"

"I don't know. We have to get out of here." I took a step, and then dizziness rolled over me, and I had to grab the counter. I still couldn't seem to get a full breath; when I opened my eyes, I could see that my fingertips were blue.

"We're ending this," Elien said. "Today. I'm not letting them hurt anyone else."

I nodded. After a moment, I opened my eyes and said, "What's in the garage?"

It only took him a moment. "I'll check."

I leaned against the counter, listening to the monsters mewl and scrabble, while the sirens came closer. After a minute, Elien jogged back with a five-gallon can of gasoline in one hand and a can of paint thinner in the other.

"Gasoline on the stairs," I said, "and then all over the place upstairs. Curtains, bedding, that kind of stuff. Give me the paint thinner."

Picking a path around the hashoks, Elien handed me the can.

"Dag, are you—"

"Gotta be fast."

He nodded and sprinted to the stairs; the gasoline fumes wafted back to me. I opened the can of paint thinner and began dumping it on Muriel and Richard. It was easy with Muriel. It was less easy with Richard. He still looked human, kind of. The thought of him pinning Elien to the floor made it easier.

When they were both drenched, I staggered to the windows, soaking the curtains and blinds, and then I started on the furniture. I saved a little to make a trail from Muriel and Richard to the front door, which I opened, and then I sagged against the jamb, panting. The night air came in sweet with the smell of grass and trees and the wet clay banks of the Okhlili.

Elien took the stairs down two at a time, and he shook the empty gas can in demonstration.

"Rags," I said. "And matches."

He took off again.

"Toss the can over here."

He shot it back at me without looking.

"And the stove, Elien."

That made him stop.

"See if you can get one of the burners to leak gas without the starter igniting."

"Oh. Shit."

Then he was running again. When he came back, he had a kitchen towel and a box of matches. I listened for the hiss of gas but didn't hear anything.

"I tried," Elien said. "But the sirens are getting close."

"Wipe the paint thinner down," I said.

"How do I hold it so I won't get more prints on it?"

"Your prints don't matter. You live here."

"I lived here," he corrected as he scrubbed the towel across the paint thinner.

"Throw them back inside. Anywhere, doesn't matter."

He did.

"Now do me a favor," I said, "since I'm having hard time breathing. If I bend over, I'm not sure I'll get back up." I offered him the box of matches. "Burn this fucker down."

Elien's smile was hard and huge as he struck the first match, and then he hooked an arm around me, and we stumbled backward down the drive. Through the window, we watched the fire. The flames caught quickly, racing along the trail of paint thinner, dancing up the curtains, following an invisible path of accelerant into the kitchen. Then there was a flash of flame as the concentrated paint thinner that I'd dumped on Richard and Muriel caught. Until now, the hashoks had been silent. Now, they screamed. It was high, almost at the edge of hearing, and it was like a needle passing through my ears and into my brain.

"There were two men," I said to Elien. The sirens sang out; I could see the lights through the black oak and sugar maple that screened us from the road.

He nodded.

"They killed Richard and hurt us. They didn't tell us what they wanted or why they picked us."

He nodded.

"They were setting the fire, getting ready to destroy the evidence. I managed to get a knife into one of them, and we ran outside. The other guy set the fire and ran."

Biting his lip, Elien nodded again. Then he said, "Will they believe that?"

"No, it's total bullshit, and they'll know it. But they'll need some way of explaining what happened here, and when they find those bodies, and neither of them is human, I think they'll want all the help they can get."

"You think they'll just . . . they'll just pretend it didn't happen?"

I didn't answer; I was having a hard time standing on my own, and I realized distantly that Elien was supporting most of my weight.

"You're stronger than you look," I mumbled.

"Shit, Dag, you do not look good. Let's get you down."

He helped me lie on my side. I was staring out at the road as the first DuPage Parish Sheriff's car sped down the drive, lights whirling, siren blaring. A vinyl pumpkin decal clung to the side of the car. I started to laugh.

"Are you ok?" Elien asked, touching the side of my face.

I kissed his hand and said, "Happy Halloween."

ELIEN (9)

Dag was in Bragg Memorial Hospital almost a week, and I was there too: half the time, as a patient myself, and the other half sitting in his room and picking at my bandages. We watched game shows, and Dag beat me at *Jeopardy!* every afternoon. At lunch and at dinner, I'd go out and get decent food for us, Dag issuing lengthy requests that included po'boys, beignets, a crawfish boil, and once, smoked alligator. I reminded him that there was no call for him to be a stereotype. He reminded me that he'd gotten stabbed through the lung. I brought him all the smoked alligator he wanted; a guy sold it out of a stand in the Quartier, making a killing off tourists who couldn't wait to try the local delicacy.

The first night I was released, I slept in the chair at the hospital. The next morning, Dag was so furious that he actually yelled at me.

"You got hurt," he shouted. "You need to sleep in a real bed."

"You probably shouldn't shout," I said. "Hole in your lung, remember?"

"You are either going to a hotel or going to my parents' house right now, and you're going to get some good sleep, and you're going to get some real food, and you're going to get better."

I raised an eyebrow.

After a moment, he winced and pressed on his chest, and he shrank back against the pillows.

"Sorry," he said.

"Just so we're clear," I said, "I don't like people yelling at me."

"I know. I'm sorry."

"For some reason, you're the exception."

His eyebrows drew together.

"It's just so cute," I said.

"Oh God."

"It's like a puppy barking. You know how their little legs get all stiff and they think they're so fierce."

Groaning, Dag pulled one of the pillows over his face.

But after that, I slept at his parents' house, in his bed, smelling that woodsy aftershave on his pillow and floating in the rippling blue light. I would lie there, thinking about a man who loved whales and oceans, who was gentle and giving and wild when he made love, and who cried after his first domestic callout. I slept deep and dreamless every night.

The days at the hospital had their own challenges. Dag's parents liked to visit, and his mom was always passing me folded-up magazine pages and giving exaggerated winks. The first time it happened, I thought Gloria might be having a stroke. She stopped me when I went to open the page, winking again, and I realized I was supposed to wait until they'd left. The world's most doting and supportive parents liked to spend time with Dag, though, and their visits could stretch out for three or four hours. At first, I expected it to be awkward, but they were so . . . doting and supportive that I couldn't help but find the whole thing endearing. It also helped that they had decided to be doting and supportive of me.

"You look very sharp today," Gloria told me.

I hooked a finger under the collar of Dag's *Blackfish* t-shirt, which had been washed so many times it was gray instead of black, and said, "This?"

"I think you might be the most beautiful man in the world," Gloria said. "Don't you think, Hubert?"

Hubert was reading the *Times-Picayune*, but he looked up and said, "Oh yes, perfect ten. Right, Dag?"

"I do not discuss boys with my dad. Or with my mom."

"What about your son?" I asked.

"What?"

"Well, he's your son, so shouldn't he be the most beautiful man in the world?"

Gloria laughed like I was a little simple. "Elien, he's the most handsome man in the world. After his father."

"Now, Gloria," Hubert said, but he shook the paper a little, fighting a smile.

"We'll have to have a night," Gloria said in a stage whisper, "just the two of us, and you can give me some new tricks for how to drive a man wild."

"Please call a nurse," Dag said. "Or a doctor. Anyone with a puke bucket."

"Hubert has this little spot," Gloria said.

"Where is the emergency call button?" Dag said, dragging on the cables around the bed.

"And I think you could try it with Dagobert."

"Nope," Dag said, "a regular doctor's not going to do it anymore. Somebody call a surgeon. A brain surgeon. Frontal lobotomy."

"But, of course," Gloria said, "the gays are lightyears ahead in sex, so I bet you'll have all sorts of ideas for us."

"I think we're doing just fine," Hubert said, shaking out the paper again. "If you'll recall just last night I made you—"

"An execution squad," Dag yelped. "Somebody please call an execution squad.

Every day, when Dag's parents left, I opened the page Gloria had given me.

"I don't want to know," Dag said.

"You're a little curious."

"Nope." He shook his head. He crossed his arms. "Throw it away. Or better yet, burn it, just to make sure the evil is really gone."

"Today's offering," I began.

"Don't you dare."

"This is part seven in a ten-part series."

"Please stop."

"Is there a doctor in the house?" I quoted from the title. "Helping your man be a sexual commando from the hospital bed."

"You are a monster."

"Part seven has a subtitle."

"I will do whatever you want," Dag said. "I will have your babies."

"Pass," I said. "Part seven: don't let that cafeteria food go to waste."

Dag pretended to vomit over the bed rail.

"There's a whole section on Jell-O," I said.

At night, after we'd eaten whatever food I'd brought in—at Dag's request—and with the TV playing a sitcom quietly, we'd just sit. We didn't really need to talk. I'd done a lot of talking over the last couple of years, and I didn't feel the need to do any more. Dag seemed ok with that. Most of the time, he just wanted to hold my hand, and sometimes he'd hold it really tight, and sometimes he'd kiss my knuckles, and sometimes he'd turn my hand over and run his fingers up the inside of my arm.

"What are you going to do now?" Dag asked.

"Probably head to your parents' house in a little bit."

"No," he said with a smile. "Big picture."

"Oh." I thought for a moment. "I don't know."

"What do you want to do?"

"I don't know. I hadn't really thought about it."

His fingers dragged up and down my arm.

"I guess," I said, "my life kind of stopped after everything with Gard and my parents. For a while, I was just treading water. Then I met Richard. After that, everything happened fast: we were dating, we were serious, I was moving in. I think I needed a lifeline. I mean, obviously he had his own reasons too. I'm twenty-two, and I feel like I haven't had a life of my own."

Dag made a small noise; his fingers kept moving.

"I did the club scene after high school," I said. "You know, until my family died. And I was with Richard. But I never really dated. I never lived on my own. I was never an independent, functioning adult."

"I think you're pretty independent," Dag said. "And you're definitely functioning."

"I guess we'll see what my new therapist has to say about that."

"Is that what you want?"

"Oh, I definitely need a new therapist."

"No, I mean . . ." Dag seemed to fumble for words. "To be independent? On your own?"

"Yeah. Kind of figure out who I am."

Dag's hand stopped. He looked at me, those very soft, very brown eyes holding steady. "I know who you are."

"You've known me for a couple of weeks."

"I know you. I know you're brave. You're smarter than you give yourself credit for. You're tough. You see things through. You don't give up when you hit roadblocks. You're funny, and you're really hard on yourself. You're maybe the most compassionate person I've ever met, and when you're scared or hurt, you're brittle and you lash out."

"You don't know I'm compassionate."

"Yes," he said, "I do."

My eyes stung. "Dag, I think I should go. I'll be back tomorrow."

"Ok," he said, but he didn't release my hand. "I love you."

In the silence, the studio audience brayed laughter. I tried to work my hand free, but Dag held on.

"Thank you," I said. "I appreciate that. It means a lot to me, but I'm not ready to be in a relationship again, and I care about you so much, but I'm not ready to—"

Laughing quietly, Dag kissed the back of my hand again. "It's ok, Elien. Take a breath. I'm just telling you: I love you. You don't have to say it back. You don't have to say anything. I'm not demanding you be my boyfriend or move in."

I thought about twisting free and heading for the door. I thought about putting my hands over my ears and channeling my inner five-year-old.

Instead, I said, "This is really fast."

"It's love, Elien. It's not a checklist."

"I'm not a nice person, Dag. I've treated you like shit. Plenty of times, actually."

"Elien." He tugged on my hand until I looked at him. "I love you. You can't talk me out of it. You can't convince me I'm wrong. They're my feelings, and I get to decide what to do with them. I'm not asking you for anything."

"Then why are you saying it?" I asked. I pulled my hand free. "Why can't we just have what we have and enjoy it?"

"Because I want you to know."

I was having a hard time breathing. I stood up too fast, and the molded-plastic chair snapped back against the wall.

"I'm not going to say I'm sorry for telling you," Dag said. "I'm not going to take it back because it's scary."

"I need to go."

"I wish you'd stay so we could talk about this."

I shook my head and left. That night, I stayed at a motel. And the next day, I didn't go back to the hospital.

DAG (10)

I was waiting outside Elien's motel room when he came back from the convenience mart, a plastic sack in each hand. Two weeks had passed since that night in the hospital. He looked much better. He looked great, in fact: hair wild and windswept, hazel eyes bright, the lean lines of his body barely discernible under a gray sweatshirt and joggers. He was smiling until he saw me.

The Overnight Motel was a single row of rooms, an exterior light hanging by each door, the harsh illumination spotlighting rubberized doormats and flowerboxes with dead leaves. The November night was cool and quiet. A few cars rolled past the motel, but the parking lot itself was silent aside from the buzzing fluorescent VACANCY sign. When Elien got closer, I could smell weed on him.

"Do you really think it's a good idea to smoke a joint while you're taking medication?" I asked.

He passed me without looking over, juggled the bags, and produced a key with a big plastic tag.

I waited.

"I guess you want to come inside," he said.

"I'd like that."

Another car rolled past, headlights picking out the foil wrapper of a Klondike bar, and then he pushed into the room. I followed him inside.

It wasn't as bad as I'd expected: a russet-colored coverlet on the bed, a high-def TV, a small refrigerator and a microwave. The door to the bathroom was open, and his clothes were hanging from the shower curtain rod. It smelled a little funky—weed, yes, but also like a second-hand store. I caught just a hint of that peppery, licoricey heat that I associated with pure Elien.

"It's weird, you showing up like this," he said as he unpacked the bags. From one, he drew out a stack of microwaveable dinners; from the other, a bottle of white wine. He put all of it in the refrigerator. "You understand that, right?"

"I was worried about you."

"They didn't give you my message at the hospital?"

"Oh, right, the one that said, 'I'm ok, but I can't see you anymore.' That message?"

Elien shut the refrigerator and met my eyes for the first time. "I only left one."

"Ouch," I said.

He shook his head.

"Want to get anything else out of your system?" I asked.

Dropping onto the bed, Elien looked away.

"Want to tell me how I'm a shitty deputy again?" I asked. "That one really hurt last time."

"What do you want, Dag?"

"That's it?"

"That's it."

"No, come on, Elien. You can do better than that. You want to hurt me. You know how to do it. So let's have it."

He closed his eyes. He looked tired. When he opened them again, he said, "Do you want something or not?"

"I wanted to tell you what I heard from the sheriff's department."

Nodding, he said, "Hold on." He fished the stub of a joint out of one of the drawers, lit it, and drew hard. "Ok."

"You're not supposed to—"

"I'm not on meds, Dag. Just tell me what you need to tell me."

"Is that smart, going off them like that?"

"Yes. My therapist knows. We agreed that we could try it." He blew out a thin stream of smoke. "Now, tell me whatever you want to tell me."

"Well, this is kind of anticlimactic, but I'm pretty sure Richard and Muriel were taking the life savings of the people they killed. Mason emptied his bank accounts shortly before he died, and a deposit for about the same amount showed up in one of Richard's accounts a few days later. That was probably part of the compulsion. Apparently evil vampire monsters blow through a lot of cash."

"Gee," Elien said. "Alert the IRS."

"Oh, and breaking news: they decided a bear killed Richard."

Coughing and laughing, Elien fanned smoke from in front of his face. "Holy fuck. No way."

"Yep."

"And you stabbed that bear."

"Yep."

"And who burned down the house?"

"The bear's accomplice," I said.

Elien laughed even harder, wiping his eyes, trying to take another drag and not able to do it. I laughed too.

When we'd both calmed down, Elien said, "It feels unreal. I'm awake some nights, and I can't even believe it happened."

"It was real. Nobody would tell me what the medical examiner put in the report, but everybody was freaked. I heard there was a break-in at the ME's lab."

"Somebody made the hashok's body disappear."

I nodded. "And apparently Richard had an advanced form of cancer that explained the strange disfigurement to his bones."

"Big news," Elien said and drew hard on the joint again. "I guess you'll get the full story when you're back at work."

"Uh, no, actually," I said.

He looked at me again, the hazel eyes a little hazy now. "Did they fire you, or did you quit?"

"Technically, I guess I quit. They made me a pretty nice offer. I decided to take it."

Butting out the joint, Elien blew out another streamer of smoke. Then he said, "I'm really sorry."

"I'm not."

"I know. But you were good at that job. You don't agree with me, but you were. And you're the kind of person who needs to be in that job: you don't want the power, you don't want to be in charge, and you care about people. Even people who don't deserve it." He pinched the bridge of his nose and made a weird hiccupping noise. "I hear how that sounds, and I want you to know I'm trying really hard not to feel so fucking guilty and shitty about myself all the time, but it's not magic. I killed that son of a bitch. He messed with Gard, and he murdered my family, and he tried to murder me. But I killed him. And I know it wasn't my fault, what happened with Gard. But fuck, I just feel so fucking awful all the time."

I sat on the bed next to him. The first time I tried to pull him against me, he fought back, driving the heel of his hand into my chest. The second time, he let me. He didn't cry or sob. His face was hot through my shirt. My hand followed the ripple of his spine. By degrees, he relaxed into me, his breath warm and soft against my neck.

"I think I'm going to be a marine biologist," I said.

"God, that'd be perfect for you." He pulled away, his eyes puffy, and studied me. "I hope it works out. You deserve it."

"It means going to school."

"Yeah, I bet. Lots of school."

"I'm going to try to stay here. Tulane has a good undergraduate bio program, and I can live at home."

"Your parents will be happy about that." He took a breath. "Do you have to go?"

"Not unless you're kicking me out."

"Are you hungry?"

"Pretty much always."

Grinning, he ran his thumb along my cheek and then stood. He got two of the microwave dinners out and held them up. "Salisbury steak or sweet and sour chicken?"

"Which one do you like?"

"I like them exactly the same, which is about a one out of ten."

"Sweet and sour chicken."

He popped it in the microwave. "Do you want wine?"

"Are you having some?"

"I don't know. I already forgot to kick you out. I'm not sure I should mess with my judgment any more."

I smiled. "I'll have some wine."

Elien opened the bottle and poured some into ultra-thin plastic cups, and I took mine and sipped it. It tasted like it was about one step above vinegar. He drank some too, leaning against the wall, smiling.

"You have a nice smile," I said, the fumes from the wine burning my eyes, and I had to blink to clear them. "You're beautiful, but I really, really like your smile."

"God," he whispered. "Are you even real?"

"Come over here," I said, setting down the wine and spreading my legs. "Find out."

He eased his weight onto my lap. He smelled like cheap wine and weed, but underneath, I could smell anise and the slow burn of his own fragrance, and it hooked me in the gut like a hot wire.

"I'm being careful," he whispered. "Because I know your legs are still healing."

I swallowed and played my fingers up his ribs.

He kissed me once, too rapidly, and then he froze. Then he kissed me again.

The microwave dinged; the smell of sweet and sour chicken seeped into the room. Pulling back, Elien ran his tongue over his lips. He tried to laugh, and the sound caught in his throat.

I kissed him again, slower, and when he tried to pull back, I cradled his head and held him.

"Don't let me run away," he whispered when I broke the kiss.

"Yeah?"

"My therapist says I have trouble forming emotional attachments." He squeezed his eyes shut and laughed. "That doesn't make any sense because I'm attached to you. I don't know how I could be more attached to anyone. I think about you all the time. I want to be near you. I want to listen to your stupid whale songs and have dinner with your parents and wake up late on Sundays when you're making pancakes."

"Pancakes have a lot of carbs," I said.

He was crying a little now. "I don't care."

"And whale songs aren't stupid."

"Please don't let me run away. I'm scared I'll lose it all again."

"Let's start with your shoes," I said.

Laughter filtered in from the windows, voices moved along the sidewalk, and Elien nodded. I ran my hand down his leg and popped off the sneakers.

"Ok?" I asked.

"Not freaking out yet."

I kissed him again. My thumb strummed his ribs. "What about this?"

His breath hitched, and he nodded, so I peeled him out of the shirt. I ran my hand over his chest, the slight swell of his belly, back up to his nipples, up higher to his collarbone where the bite marks were still healing. He shivered.

"Ok?" I asked.

"I don't know."

"Let's take a break, then."

So we kissed, and after a while, he found my hand and pressed it against his chest, and I ran it back and forth.

"I don't know why this is so scary," Elien whispered when he pulled away. "We've done this before."

"You know why." My fingers played with the button on his waistband. "Well?"

He nodded and stood. I moved quickly so he wouldn't have time to reconsider, undoing the button and zipper, lowering his jeans and underwear at the same time. I pulled him down onto the bed next to me, kissing again, my hands exploring him. We'd been together, yes. But this was different, and we both knew it.

"Still thinking about going somewhere?" I asked.

Jaw tight, he shook his head. He was hard when I slid my hand down his body. Moaning, he bucked into my touch.

"Are you going to run away?" I asked.

He shook his head again.

I wrapped my fingers around his dick, the grip tight and possessive, and ran my thumb over the head.

"Tell me where you're going," I said.

He gave another jerk of his head.

"Tell me," I said.

"Nowhere."

"That's right," I said, kissing him again.

After I stripped, Elien moved slowly with me, examining me with his hands and his mouth, hesitating at every injury. Finally I was sick of it, and I grabbed his hair and yanked his head up.

"Fuck me," I said.

For the first time in weeks, I got to see a real Elien Martel smirk.

The sex didn't last long; both of us were too keyed up, too desperate, too eager. At the end, Elien went wild, and when he'd finished, he kept whispering, "I'm sorry, I'm sorry," until, laughing, I pulled him down next to me and kissed him.

"Did I hurt you?" he asked.

"I don't know," I said. "Let me figure out if I'm still alive, and then I'll tell you."

He poked me in the ribs, and then he squirmed around until he was under my arm, his head on my chest.

"I love you," he murmured.

"To my face," I said.

The tension turned his muscles to wire, but he lifted his head and looked at me and bit his lip and blurted out, "I love you."

"I love you too."

He grinned, relaxed, slumped down on me again. He walked his fingers across my chest. "A marine biologist?" he asked.

"If I can get the grades."

"And you're going to Tulane?"

"I still have to apply, but I should get in."

The struggle in his face was real; he was trying to say something, and it wouldn't come out. Someone in the room next to us put on "Free Bird," and someone else screamed with excitement.

"They are so fucking loud," Elien grumbled. "Every night."

I just stroked his back, gathering the sweat there, feeling the heat still dissipating from his muscles.

"I have some money," Elien said carefully.

I raised an eyebrow.

"And I need a place to live," Elien said.

I nodded.

"And I don't want to live here anymore. I want to be away from here."

I nodded again.

"I was thinking about New Orleans."

"It's a great city," I said.

"And if you're going to school in New Orleans, it makes more sense for you to live in the city too, instead of commuting across the lake every day."

"That does make sense."

"Would you please help me out here?" Elien asked, slapping my stomach.

Grinning, I said, "Only because I'm so proud of you for earlier."

He rolled his eyes.

"When you told me you loved me," I said.

"Yes, I remember."

"I think we could find somewhere really nice," I said, my hand moving more slowly on his back. "I think we could find somewhere we could be really happy." Then I nudged him toward the edge of the bed. "But until then, can we please get out of this motel right now and go just about anywhere else?"

"You just want to go home so your mom will coo over you some more."

"You're my home, Elien Martel," I said. "Starting right now."

He propped himself on an elbow. "Hey, Dag? Would you—do you mind calling me Eli?"

I shook my head.

"I think I want to be Eli again."

I ran my hand through his hair, smiled, and said, "Hello, Eli."

THE SAME BREATH

Keep reading for a sneak preview of *The Same Breath*, the first book in a new series by Gregory Ashe.

1

Teancum Leon had barely gotten home from the Division of Wildlife Resources when a knock came at the door. Scipio, his black Lab, was in the middle of doing a welcome / please-take-me-out-for-a-walk dance, but the Lab adjusted his priorities and began to bark.

"All right," Tean said, stroking the dog's ears as he bumped him out of the way.

Mrs. Wish, his neighbor from the end of the hall, was wearing her usual ensemble, regardless of day or night: a full-length house dress, something Tean imagined her picking from a color page in the Sears Catalogue, and a chemically pink terrycloth robe over it. Her long white hair was free of its usual bun, and her eyes were wide.

"There's an intruder," she said between gasps for breath.

"Oh my gosh. Did you call 911?"

"Not that kind," she said, and then she grabbed his arm and dragged him out of the apartment. "It's a spider."

"In that case, I've got to take Scipio for a walk," Tean said.

Mrs. Wish drew herself up, glancing back at Tean's door and then looking down the hall toward her own home. "I'll walk him," she said, like a woman offering to step in front of a firing squad. "You deal with that nasty little murderer."

Tean sighed and nodded. While Mrs. Wish hurried back to rescue Scipio, Tean made his way along the hall and pushed open her door. He had to snag the domestic short-hair that tried to slip out of the apartment—he thought this one was Senator Frank B. Bandegee, because he remembered the white patch on her chest—and then he was inside the apartment, pushing the door shut behind him.

Very little ever changed about Mrs. Wish's apartment: the smell of dander, animal and human, mixed with wet cat food and a floral scent. Collectible presidential ashtrays, holding the mounds of potpourri that provided the flowery note, were placed on occasional tables and shelves and ledges around the room. Doilies. A million doilies. A framed, larger-than-life portrait of President Woodrow Wilson, hanging where most people would have placed a television (once Mrs. Wish had sent Tean into the bedroom to examine a . . . deposit that Senator Henry Cabot Lodge had left on the carpet, and he had stumbled onto an autographed photograph of President Gerald Ford in a heart-shaped frame. President Wilson's illicit rival? Tean was dying to know). And, of course, the Irreconcilables, perched on bookshelves and the back of the sofa, crawling through their cat mansion, swishing past Tean with disdainful looks that said they would accept a display of affection, albeit unwillingly. Their numbers varied between twelve and eighteen; Tean no longer tried to keep track.

Setting down Senator Frank B. Bandegee, Tean made a quick tour of the apartment. He made the mistake of getting too close to Senator Poindexter, a vicious Siamese, and earned a nasty swipe at his ankle for his mistake. In what Mrs. Wish optimistically called the guest bedroom, which was a confection of pink, sateen, and spills of creamy lace—canopy bed included—he found the intruder. The closet doors were open, and Mrs. Wish had dragged one of her heavy dining chairs into place so she could reach the shelf at the top where the spider was hiding.

Tean climbed up onto the chair and examined the shelf: several folded blankets, a lacquered wood box, and a manila folder. On the tab of the folder, Mrs. Wish's Palmer script read: *Reagan – Shirtless*. In smaller letters below, she had added, with quotation marks included, *"The California Showboat."* Tean was reaching to open the folder when he heard the front door. He jerked his hand back.

"Oh, Dr. Leon," Mrs. Wish said, wringing her hands from the guest bedroom's doorway. "You really have to be careful."

Tean shifted his attention to the intruder: a small black spider hanging from its web in the closet's upper corner.

"He looks like a nasty customer," Tean said.

"Well," Mrs. Wish said, obviously at a loss for words. "Smash him!"

"I don't think we need to do that."

"Dr. Leon, I know a black widow spider when I see one. They can kill an adult. Think of what their poison could do to the children."

"Venom," Tean said absently. "Not poison. Do you have a pen? Never mind, I've got a Blackwing in my pocket." He drew out the pencil, got the eraser as close to the web as he could, and tapped the wall. The spider scuttled along the web, following the vibrations. Tean withdrew the pencil, watching as the spider searched for its prey.

"Perhaps my bust of the lesser Roosevelt," Mrs. Wish offered.

"I don't think that'll be necessary."

"Be honest, Dr. Leon. How much danger are the Irreconcilables in? I'll book a hotel. I assume you'll be available to help with their carriers. We can transport them in two trips—"

"I don't think that'll be necessary," Tean said hastily.

"If something happened to one of the children, I'd die. I'd just die."

"Well, we're all going to die, Mrs. Wish. And they're technically not children. They're cats."

That seemed to throw off the rhythm of Mrs. Wish's performance. She put her hands on her hips, staring up at him, and said, "I hardly think a crisis is the time to wax philosophical."

"I'm not being philosophical. I'm just pointing out that we're nothing but complex molecular chains that will eventually dissolve and be recycled into something else. A plant, maybe."

Mrs. Wish stared at him.

"Err. Like catnip. Some of the same basic building blocks that make up Mrs. Wish could one day be inside a cloth mouse, giving some lucky cat hours of entertainment. That'd be nice, right?"

For a moment, Mrs. Wish didn't seem to know what to say. She settled for: "I should think not."

Wiping sweat from his forehead, Tean said, "Right. Well, about the spider—"

"I'll get the lesser Roosevelt."

"Hold on, and then you can decide. First of all, it's not *Latrodectus hesperus*—not a black widow, I mean."

"I know what a black widow—"

"You can see for yourself." Tean offered her the chair, but she shook her head. Pointing with the Blackwing, he said, "No hourglass marking on the ventral abdomen."

"Perhaps you're confused about which side the marking should be on."

Tean tapped the wall again, and the spider scurried across its web, exposing its dorsal side, which was also dark and unmarked.

"Well," Mrs. Wish said, tugging on her terrycloth sleeves. "What is it then?"

"I think it's *Steatoda grossa*, what's called a false black widow."

"I still think a good smashing is in order."

"If you like. But just so you know, *Steatoda grossa* preys on a variety of pests, including *Latrodectus hesperus*. Real black widows, I mean."

Mrs. Wish thought about this. "It won't harm the children."

"No, it won't bother you or the cats."

"And it might even stop something from harming them."

"That's right. There's almost always one thing higher on the food chain. Predators who prey on predators, you know? All the way up to the apex."

After a moment, Mrs. Wish nodded and proclaimed, "Then it stays. If you'd please hand me that folder, though, while you're up there." She murmured something vague about "important documents" and "setting my affairs in order" and tucked the Reagan folder inside her robe like she was robbing a bank.

Tean carried the dining chair back to the front room, with Mrs. Wish dogging him.

"Violet will be very sorry to have missed you," Mrs. Wish said. "She'll be here in a couple of hours."

Tean smiled and nodded.

"I'll send her over with a plate of cookies."

"That's really not necessary."

"She's already got age lines, unfortunately," Mrs. Wish said, tracing them on her own forehead to illustrate. "But I imagine if you squint, or perhaps if you close your eyes when you kiss her, they won't bother you too much."

"Uh. Yes. Well—"

"Twenty-seven, poor dear. Practically a spinster. We tell everyone she's twenty-five because it's just too embarrassing otherwise."

Edging toward the doors, Tean nodded.

"I think she's had the one dead tooth fixed," Mrs. Wish was explaining, "so you won't be bothered by that, at least."

"I hear Scipio barking," Tean said, throwing open the door. "I've got to run."

"I don't hear—"

But he was already sprinting down the hall.

When Tean let himself into the apartment, Scipio was waiting for him, pressing a cold nose against his arm, snuffling, trying to scent out all of the Irreconcilables that had dared get too close. Tean thought of Mrs. Wish's granddaughter coming over with a plate of cookies that were the sugary equivalent of hard tack. He grabbed Scipio's harness and asked the Lab, "What do you think about another walk? A really long one, this time?" The dog park, he thought, was far enough away to be safe.

2

"People suck," Tean said, letting Scipio off the leash. The dog park was busy on Friday afternoon, and Scipio ran off to join Bear, a hundred-and-thirty-pound St. Bernard who dwarfed Tean's black Lab but had still become a regular playmate.

"Ok," Hannah said with a sigh. She was still removing the leash from her own dog, Divorcee. She worked with Tean at DWR, and she had called as he was leaving the apartment to ask if he was interested in being set up on a blind date with a guy she knew. When Tean tried to dodge by explaining he was going to the dog park, she had insisted on joining him. It was nice to have company, even if Hannah didn't realize she was helping a fugitive.

October in the Salt Lake Valley was beautiful; the underbrush on the Wasatch Mountains to the east burned red, and the sun setting over the Great Salt Lake to the west painted everything else gold. Autumn in Utah was a precarious pleasure, always ready to slip early into winter and stay there. Days like this one, with the breeze coming off the mountains and the skies perfectly clear, made sure the dog park stayed busy.

"What does that mean?" Tean asked.

"It means you're trying to get out of this date."

"Everyone's trying to set me up today. Why won't anyone let me have forty or fifty years of peace before I die?"

"Go have fun, princess." This was directed to Divorcee; the teacup Yorkie scampered five feet away, stopped, and looked back. "Go on."

"I'm not trying to get out of a date," Tean said.

"Ok."

"I'm just pointing out an incontrovertible fact."

"Here we go."

"People suck," Tean said, varying the tone a little in case she'd missed the point.

Hannah just sighed. "Can we talk about something else?"

"Miguel asked me if you were single today."

"Did you tell him I'm married?" Hannah said.

"Yes."

"Great. End of conversation."

"I saw those reports you put together on—"

"Not work."

"Well, I wanted to ask—"

"Nope. Work stays at work. I don't want to think about work. Sook's funeral is this weekend, and I don't need anything else making me think about work." Hannah studied the leash, which she wrapped around her hand as she asked, "I don't suppose you've heard anything new from the detectives."

"I don't think it's that straightforward." In fact, Tean thought, nothing had been straightforward about the case. Sook Hyeon, one of the DWR's conservation officers, had been killed the week before. She had been in a bad part of town, late at night, and nobody could explain why a nice, smart Mormon girl with a 401k and a master's degree, with a good job and a boyfriend, with overprotective parents who still called to make sure she was home safe at the end of every day—nobody could figure out why that kind of girl had been where she'd been, had died the way she had died.

Hannah nodded, tears in her eyes. "I know. It's just—she was my friend, you know? And it doesn't seem real."

"I'm sure they're doing all they can," Tean said.

Nodding, Hannah wiped her cheeks as the tears came faster.

"I'm so sorry," Tean said. He moved in for a hug, reconsidered, but was already committed. He ended up giving her an awkward, one-armed embrace from the side, and Hannah laughed brokenly and patted his arm.

"I went through her logs and reports," Tean said as he stepped back, "and I made some calls. Nobody could tell me anything out of the ordinary. And I gave all the information to the police."

"You didn't have to do that."

"I know; the detectives would have looked at it on their own eventually."

"No, I mean, you're a good guy for doing it."

"I'd be a better guy if I weren't planning how to ditch this blind date."

Hannah slapped his arm. "Sorry. I told myself I wasn't going to bring Sook up again."

Scipio and Bear had both gotten hold of a rope, and Bear was dragging Scipio around in an uneven version of tug-of-war.

"We could talk about books," Tean said.

"Pass."

"If you ever read a book . . ."

"Let's talk about the very exciting date that I'm setting you up on. Why do you think you won't like Rand?"

"Because his name's Rand. Why can't Utah people name their kids anything normal?"

"You are Utah people. And you have a weird name too. Anyway, he's a nice guy, and he's cute. I showed him your picture, and he said you were hot."

"That doesn't say much for his taste," Tean muttered.

Hannah slugged him.

Across the park, Scipio and Bear were wrestling. Bear's owner was a young guy with a lot of muscles and who apparently owned only tank tops. A couple of times he and Tean had talked. He had a faux-tribal tattoo on his shoulder. Between the tank tops and the tattoo, he was the closest thing to a bad boy Salt Lake City seemed capable of producing.

"That guy's straight," Hannah said.

"Straight's a twentieth-century term. Everybody's on a sexual spectrum now."

"Not on the Wasatch Front they aren't."

"Hence my point," Tean said. "People suck."

"Ok, sweetie, get it all out of your system."

"If you insist—"

"I was talking to Divorcee."

The Yorkie was pausing every eighteen inches to investigate another clump of grass, obviously trying to choose the best spot.

"Oh. Well, I'm going to tell you anyway."

Sighing, Hannah nodded.

"In the ocean—" Tean began.

"So help me, if you bring up the whale thing again, I will kill you, and then I will kill myself."

Divorcee trotted back toward them, steering straight for Tean. She had some sort of obsession with using his shoes as her personal potty pad, and he darted behind Hannah. "I wasn't going to bring up the whale thing."

"Uh huh."

"I wasn't."

"The ocean was just a logical place to start," Hannah said.

"Exactly. Where all life began," Tean said. "As a biologist who specializes in native aquatics, you should know that."

"Oh my gosh," Hannah said. "I might honestly have to kill you."

"Do you know how many people get murdered on first dates? Especially blind dates?"

"How many?"

"A lot," Tean said.

"Just because you saw one Lifetime movie about it doesn't mean it happens a lot."

"He might want to harvest my kidneys."

"Rand doesn't need your kidneys; his kidneys are perfectly healthy. That's the first thing I ask every guy before I set you up with him."

"He could traffic me. I could wind up in sexual slavery."

"Heaven help whoever buys you."

A breeze picked up; crabapples lined one side of the park, and the too-sweet stench of rotting fruit floated on the air. Tean decided to try a different tack. "Do you know how many bear-related fatalities occur every year? In the United States, anyway."

"On average, three," Hannah said.

"You only know that because you work at DWR too," Tean said. "Other people would be suitably shocked."

Hannah paused long enough to tuck her chestnut hair behind her ears and arrange her features in an expression of surprise.

"That's better," Tean said. "And do you know how many homicides occur every year?"

"Five."

"Don't do that."

"Do what?" Hannah asked.

"Four hundred thousand, globally. Every year. In some countries, it's the leading cause of death. People killing each other is the leading cause of death."

"Please tell me this is not what you're going to talk about with Rand."

"And do you know how many bears kill other bears?"

"It's rare," Hannah said.

"Again, insider knowledge; unfair advantage because you're a biologist. Most people wouldn't have any idea. It's so rare that the *Smithsonian* dedicated a whole article to it."

"Divorcee, sweetie, come on."

The Yorkie was investigating the shoes of an old woman perched on a bench.

"Leave her alone," Hannah said. "I'm sorry!"

The old woman waved and laughed.

Divorcee saw her moment of opportunity and struck, spraying the woman's foot.

"Oh my gosh," Hannah shouted, "I'm so sorry!" Then, to Tean, "I've got to handle this. Good luck tonight."

"People suck, that's what I'm trying to explain."

"See you at Sook's service?"

"And if you compare the number of bears—"

"Don't screw it up," Hannah called back as she ran toward the old woman, who was now trying to hop on her unsullied foot while using the back of the bench for balance.

"Animals are better than people," Tean shouted after Hannah.

"You're a wildlife vet," Hannah shouted back. "You know that's not true!"

"At least animals don't—"

"Talk about movies," Hannah shouted over him. "Rand loves movies." She turned to the old woman, apologizing. When she reached for Divorcee, the Yorkie sprinted away from her.

"The whale story is better," Tean informed Divorcee as she pranced up to him. He glanced over to check on Scipio, who was playing tag with Bear now, both dogs sprinting the length of the park. The late afternoon sunlight drew long shadows: the fence, the dogs, the guy with the tank top and tattoo.

Out of the corner of his eye, too late, Tean registered what was happening. Sniffing his shoe, Divorcee got into position and gave him the last drops in the tank.

"Damn it," Tean shouted. "Your dog, Hannah!"

"What were you saying about animals?" she called.

3

"People suck," Jem said, carrying the TV tray with a Stouffer's single-serve lasagna into the living room. He had to kick aside some of the bagged newspapers, and his foot came down on something that was soft and squishy. On his next step, he connected with a loose can of store-brand cola, and it shot out, ricocheted off the entertainment center, and hit a pyramid of root beer bottles. The bottles came tumbling down, brown glass tinkling, but at least none of them broke. "God damn it, Benny, you've got to clean this place up. You're supposed to be an adult, for Christ's sake. This place is a sty."

Benny swiped at the stringy hair hanging in front of his face, glanced up from the mess of papers in front of him as Jem set down the lasagna, and mumbled, "Doesn't matter. Nothing matters anymore. They're gonna kill me. This time I'm serious. They're really going to kill me."

"Nobody's going to kill you. People suck, sure. But nobody's going to kill you."

"Yes, they are. They are."

"Who's they?"

Benny just mumbled to himself and bent closer to examine pages filled with his scrawl.

"Hey, dummy," Jem said, rapping Benny on the head. "I'm talking to you."

"Cut it out," Benny said, swiping at Jem.

Jem was faster, though, and he rapped on Benny's head again. "Meds?" he asked.

"Doctor took me off them."

"No joke? That's great."

Benny scratched out a line on the topmost page and scribbled something in the margin.

"Don't lie to me, Benny. Where's your medicine?"

"I don't like how it makes me feel. I'm not taking it anymore."

"Not your choice."

"I flushed all the pills."

Jem had to walk into the kitchen. The apartment was a shithole in West Valley, built in the 1970s by guys who had never cared about the place looking nice or lasting long. Now, almost fifty years later, the whole complex was a shrine to greedy landlords. Ancient paint bubbled and peeled, evidence of water damage and, probably, mold. The carpet was brownish gray and matted—Jem had been shocked when he had moved Benny's bed to discover a patch of robin's egg blue that must have been the original coloring. The linoleum in the kitchen was peeling, and half of the time when Jem came over, he ended up using crazy glue to stick it back to the floor. In the bathroom, the ceiling bulged and sagged ominously, and once, Jem could have sworn he'd seen a drop of water.

He stood in the kitchen, staring at the pile of dishes in scummy gray water, at the refrigerator with the door that wouldn't close all the way, at the range with the foil-wrapped drip pans, crusted now with a layer of burnt food. At least the place smelled like lasagna, even if it was only temporary. For another minute, Jem stood there, flexing his hands. Then he did what he always did.

First, he went through the cabinets, checking cans.

"Why haven't you eaten any of the vegetables?" he shouted into the living room.

"I don't like French-cut green beans."

"These aren't French cut."

Silence for thirty seconds. Then, "They have too much sodium."

"Why didn't you eat the fruit cocktail?"

"I'm on a diet."

"You've got to eat something that didn't come in plastic wrap," Jem said. "I'll make carrots; I saw some in the freezer." He opened another cabinet. "Benny, where's that spice rack? I'll put some garlic powder in the carrots."

The only answer was papers shuffling.

"Benny?"

Next door, Mrs. Johnson was shrieking about her lying, piece-of-shit husband, and then there was a deep, gonging noise that made Jem picture a cartoon cat getting struck by a cartoon frying pan.

From the opening to the living room, Jem asked, "Benny, spices?"

Benny wouldn't look up.

"Jesus Christ, Benny," Jem said. "Again?"

"I needed cash to buy my girlfriend dinner. Elisa said she'd give me twenty bucks for the spice rack."

"Jesus fucking Christ, Benny. That shit costs me money, ok? All this costs money. I don't buy you fucking groceries so they can sit in your fucking cabinets, and I don't buy you fucking spice racks so you can sell them to fucking Elisa so you can have twenty fucking bucks to buy your fucking imaginary girlfriend a fucking hamburger."

"She's not imaginary," Benny said.

"What's her name?" Jem said, louder than he meant to. "Where'd you meet her? What's she do for work? What's her favorite fucking color, Benny?"

Flinching, Benny tried to maneuver his bulk closer to the pages, tried to make himself smaller, which was hard to do when he was over two hundred pounds.

Opening and closing his hands, Jem said, "Sorry."

Benny crossed something out; his hand was shaking.

Moving to the couch, Jem dropped down, met by the sour stink of body odor. "Benny, I'm sorry. It's just—it's a lot of stuff."

"I don't need you to buy me anything."

"I know."

"I never made up an imaginary girlfriend in my whole life."

"I know."

"I'm fine," Benny said. "I don't need you."

Jem studied the bagged newspapers, the magazine pages cut out and pasted over the windows, the greasy smears in the carpet, the handwritten manifesto spread out in front of Benny. He closed his eyes and said, "I know."

Next door, Mrs. Johnson was sobbing.

"Why did I tell you to be careful around girls?" Jem asked.

"The same reason you're careful around boys."

"Which is what?"

"You don't want your dick to do your thinking for you."

"Right. And what else?"

"It's easy to believe someone likes you because everybody wants to be liked."

"That's right," Jem said. "And people will believe anything if they want it to be true. Even you. Even me."

Benny just shrugged.

"What's her name?" Jem asked again.

"I don't want to tell you."

"For Christ's sake."

"Anyway, I won't be your problem for much longer," Benny said. "They're going to kill me."

"You're not a problem. And nobody's going to kill you, Benny."

"They are. I know too much; it's all right here. They have to get rid of me."

"Benny, I know you don't like how you feel on the meds, but you can't just go off them. We'll go see the doctor again. We'll find something that helps you and doesn't make you feel bad."

Benny shrugged.

"How's your pump?"

"Fine."

"Insulin?"

"Fine."

"Did you test your blood sugar?"

"It's fine, Jem."

"When's the last time you tested it?"

"Dunno."

"Ok, I'll get a strip."

"This morning."

"Benjamin Lindsey Guthall, if you are lying to me, I will beat your ass."

He flashed Jem a wounded look. "I checked it this morning."

After that, there wasn't much Jem could do. He conducted his final walkthrough and spotted the backpack with a pup tent strapped to the top. When he got back to the living room, he said, "Are you going to the Jenkins' place?"

"Maybe."

"No, we don't play that way."

"Yes."

"When?"

"I don't know."

"When, Benny?"

"Tonight."

"For how long? It's Friday, so when are you coming back?"

"I don't know."

"Jesus Christ," Jem said.

"I don't! I know too much, Jem. I've got to lie low for a while. I'll be up there until it's safe to come back."

"Did you tell the Jenkins you were coming?"

"Not yet."

"Fine. I'll call them. Next week, Benny, we're going to see your doctor, and we're going to try different meds."

Benny was reordering the pages in his lap.

"Tell me you heard me."

"Ok, all right, I heard you."

"What's our rule?"

"You've got a million rules."

"What's our rule, Benny?"

"Cell phone on and charged, and I answer when you call."

"Even if you're in a movie."

"Even if I'm in a movie," Benny repeated.

"Even if you're taking a dump."

"You're so gross."

"Get up and give me a hug."

"Jem," Benny whined.

"Get your fat ass up."

After some more groaning, Benny stood, and they hugged.

"Eat that before it's cold," Jem said, pointing at the lasagna, where the red sauce was already congealing.

Benny just nodded and mumbled.

Outside, at the bottom of the stairs, Tommy Johnson, twelve years old, was smoking a fatty blunt. His eyes were glazed when he looked up at Jem.

"That bad?" Jem asked.

Tommy blew a ring of smoke, his head sagging back as he stared at the October sky.

"Let me get a hit," Jem said. Tommy passed it over, and Jem took a few long drags, holding the smoke, his eyes closed, letting the world soften. When he passed it back, he said, "You eat dinner?"

Tommy shook his head like he was in slow motion.

Digging out his last ten, Jem said, "Go get something to eat."

Then Jem headed back into the city, trying to figure out the best place he could get an asshole to buy him a drink.

Acknowledgments

My deepest thanks go out to:

Cheryl Oakley, for keeping track of my tenses, for catching dropped articles, pointing out consistency in dialogue, and giving me so much encouragement with this book!

Dianne Thies, for her careful proofing of this book, for pointing out the number of gloves, telling right from left, and mapping the Zatarain's ad—including direction of travel.

About the Author

Learn more about Gregory Ashe and forthcoming works at
www.gregoryashe.com.